Through the Gates of Death
–And Beyond

ADVENTURES IN THE LOKAS
OF IMMORTALITY

by Nayaswami Savitri Simpson

Copyright © 2018 Savitri Simpson

Swami Kriyananda's song lyrics included in this book are used with permission, Copyright © Hansa Trust 2011.

Cover and book design by Surya Crisman

Back cover photography by Barbara Bingham

Edited and proofread by Bob Stolzman, Dambara Begley, Jagrav Quinn, Sudarshan Simpson, and Punita Greenberg

Many thanks to all who helped bring this book to completion.

Printed in the United States of America

Embrace life! Embrace death!
For they are two sides of the same coin:
The coin of our eternal, immortal Selves.

— Nayaswami Savitri

This book is dedicated to anyone who might have even the slightest curiosity or lingering concern about death, what it is like to die, and what happens to us after death. May the truth about these subjects, given to us by the Great Masters, bring us complete freedom from any fear of death and answer all our questions about life, death, rebirth, and immortality.

TABLE OF CONTENTS

Introduction. i
Preface. ix
Through the Gates of Death. 1
What is a Yuga?. 249

INTRODUCTION

Through the Gates of Death—And Beyond is the third and final book in a series of three novels that I have named "The Treta Yuga Trilogy." Just like the first two books, *Through Many Lives* and *Through the Chakras*, this novel can stand alone, meaning that it is not necessary to read the first two novels in order to understand the third one—although, naturally, I hope that you will read them all.

The continuity of the three novels lies with the main characters' lives, as we watch them grow through their student years, their productive and busy mid-life years, and finally, their later years, as they prepare for and experience death and what follows.

In 2009, Swami Kriyananda, my spiritual teacher for over 40 years, asked me to write my first novel, *Through Many Lives*. He read it just after I completed it and not long before he died in 2013. He was able to offer me many corrections and instructive suggestions, for which I am extremely grateful. He is one of the finest writers whose works I have read.

I wrote the second novel, *Through the Chakras*, in 2015. While writing it, I continued to feel Swami's inner guidance and blessings. His closeness and inner instructions have been with me as I wrote the third novel—to the point that he even managed to emerge as a character in it!

Thank you Swamiji! I am sure that "The Treta Yuga Trilogy" would have been impossible for me to write without your ongoing support.

****

Do not think for one moment that death is an unsolvable mystery. For most people, memories of their deaths, after-death experiences, and subsequent rebirths, are not easily accessible. Nevertheless, the Great Masters know *very well* every nuance of death and dying. They have been through the gates of death and beyond countless times. The difference is that they *remember* it all and are able to reveal the secrets of this hidden realm to us so that we will be prepared, when it is our time to pass through these portals.

The spiritual teachings offered in this book are taken from the written works and lectures of Swami Kriyananda, Paramhansa Yogananda, and Swami Sri Yukteswar. The clear information that they present about death and what comes afterwards, is enthralling and filled with great hope for everyone! Even though this book is a novel, that is, a work of fiction, I did my very best to convey and remain true to their powerful teachings.

The next Ascending Treta Yuga, which is the setting of this novel, will arrive a few thousand years in our future. We are now (as of 2018) 318 years into Ascending Dwapara Yuga, which lasts 2400 years. If you are unfamiliar with the "Yuga Theory of Cycles of Time," please see the Appendix at the end of this novel, entitled "What is a Yuga?"

In Ascending Treta Yuga, human beings will make great progress on many levels—especially spiritually. They will develop the useful ability to communicate telepathically instead of vocally. In this novel, when the dialogue reads, "He said," or "She asked," please understand that the characters are always communicating *mentally* with each other (unless otherwise indicated).

Furthermore, most people who live in this part of Ascending Treta Yuga have learned to move their bodies and/or energy patterns through space, time, and other dimensions.

Instead of including a glossary to define unfamiliar Sanskrit words, as I did in *Through the Chakras*, in this book I did my best to define them as I went along.

As I was writing *Through the Gates of Death—And Beyond*, someone told me that a book with the words death or dying in its titles might not be popular or sell well—unless it is a murder mystery. Trigger words like these can cause the fear of death to arise in peoples' minds and cause potential readers to shy away from the book, because they do not wish to think about their own or anyone else's deaths, *ever*!

So be it, for this book really *is* about death, dying, and what follows. I feel that the title should reflect the contents. Moreover, I am convinced it is healthiest and best for everyone to accept death fearlessly. Thank you for having the courage to read about what is a challenging subject for most people. Remember, knowledge is power!

****

In closing, I offer you a story. In March 1978, Swami Kriyananda gave me the spiritual name, Savitri. I had never heard the name before, so naturally, I asked him what it meant. He replied, "I want you to think of it as meaning loyalty to God."

Then he suggested that I ask Nayaswami Shivani, whom he had trained as an excellent Ananda teacher and storyteller, if she would tell me the amazing tale of Savitri, an East Indian princess. The next time I saw her, I asked her to share the story with me. Her telling was excellent, and I was wonderstruck by this popular legend from the great Indian epic, *The Mahabharata*.

Because it is a story about a brave woman who outwits death, I feel it appropriate to include it here, in my introduction. Many different versions of this story exist, but this is my favorite one. I hope you enjoy it.

The Story of Savitri

...till death do us part (or maybe not).

Once, a very long time ago, there was a great king, who had a beautiful and clever daughter named Savitri. Princess Savitri lived a quiet life and spent most of her time in inner, spiritual pursuits.

One day her father, the king, reminded her that she was old enough to marry, and that he would soon be having a *swayamvaram* for her, to allow her to choose her husband from among all the eligible princes of neighboring kingdoms in India. A swayamvaram was a large, traditional festival, during which great crowds assemble to watch a kind of tournament. Its purpose was to allow a royal princess to observe the eligible princes, as they exhibited feats of skill, talent, and bravery, so that she could choose whom to marry. At the close of the tournament, she would place a flower garland around the neck of her chosen one.

At Savitri's swayamvaram, she closely watched the performances of the brave and gallant young princes, who were all eagerly seeking her hand in marriage. As the tournament concluded, she went to her father and said, with great determination, "Father, these are all fine young men, but I cannot and will not choose my husband from among them, for none of them is worthy to be my husband."

The king was very distressed. He said, "My dear daughter, it is time for you to marry! You must choose someone! What shall we do?"

Savitri answered, "I have a solution, Father. Let me go on a spiritual pilgrimage, visiting the four most sacred spots in our country. Surely, during such a holy pilgrimage, God will guide me to my future husband!"

Her father agreed, and Savitri soon set out on her journey, with a large retinue of the king's men to guide and protect her. The king's trusted Prime Minister led the group.

The journey was long and the Prime Minister was growing worried because although Princess Savitri seemed to be having an inspiring visit to each of the holy shrines, so far she exhibited no inclination towards finding a husband.

One day, at about noon, they passed through a pleasant wooded area, where they stopped to rest and take refreshment. Savitri wandered a little ways into the woods, where she heard the sound of someone chopping wood. She felt drawn to investigate further and soon found herself in the presence of a very handsome, though obviously poor, woodsman. They looked at each other and fell in love at first sight. Savitri reported to the Prime Minister that she wished to return immediately to her father's kingdom, for she had finally located her future husband.

Upon their return, Savitri told her father about Satyaban, the handsome young woodcutter, with whom she had fallen in love. Naturally, the king was upset, for surely his only daughter must marry well! How could he even consider her marrying a simple woodcutter?

Just as he was about to tell Savitri of his disapproval and forbid the marriage, Sage Narada arrived to advise him. Narada said, "Don't be hasty, dear King! Satyaban is not the simple woodcutter he appears to be. He is, indeed, a royal prince and worthy to marry your daughter. Unfortunately, his mother and father, the rulers of a large and prosperous kingdom, have fallen under a curse. This has caused them, and their son Prince Satyaban, to lose their sovereignty and seek refuge in the forest. Satyaban supports them through woodcutting.

In addition, Satyaban has fallen under another curse, and he has only one year left to live."

Savitri's father was shocked to hear this sad tale. He turned to his beloved daughter and said, "Savitri, you have heard what Sage Narada has revealed about Satyaban! You must realize that you cannot marry him! You would become a widow in a year. Surely you do not want this to happen!"

Princess Savitri knelt to honor her father, then stood tall before him and said, "Father, I will have Prince Satyaban for my husband. I will have no other!"

The king knew his daughter well enough to realize that once she made up her mind, there was nothing in heaven or earth that could change it.

Savitri and Satyaban were married. She went to live with him and his parents in the forest. Their life together was simple and they were blissfully happy.

A year passed and Satyaban's death was rapidly approaching. When the day arrived, she asked her husband to allow her to accompany him into the forest as he went about his woodcutting duties. At noon, he began to falter and grow faint. She saw what was happening to him and helped him to sit on the ground nearby. She asked him to lie down and place his head in her lap; she stroked his forehead, as she prayed deeply for him.

Very soon, Lord Yama, the lord of truth and of death appeared. He was a giant shining God-like figure, and in his hands he carried a magical golden noose. This he placed around the neck of the dying person to lead his soul to the afterlife.

As he began to do this to Satyaban, Savitri cried out, "Stop! I will not allow you to take away the soul of my husband."

Lord Yama was astonished, because no one ever can see him when he comes to take a soul away, and much less had anyone ever tried to stop him!

He asked her, "Savitri, how is it that you can see me, when most mortals cannot?"

Savitri said, "I do see you, and I will not let you take away the soul of my husband with your magic golden noose."

"Why not?" Lord Yama was perplexed. "It was his time to die. He must come with me. Please excuse me, Princess Savitri, but I must leave you now."

"Then I shall follow you!" Savitri said with strong determination.

"You cannot!" Lord Yama said.

Savitri said nothing further, but began to follow along behind Lord Yama.

He ignored her, thinking he would find a way to leave her behind soon enough.

The difficult journey took them over steep mountain ranges, across vast wastelands, up into the sky, and down into the darkest, subterranean nether worlds. Lord Yama did his best to lose Savitri, but he always heard the tinkling sound of the tiny silver bells she wore on her ankles as she followed along behind him. She showed no signs of fatigue and had no trouble keeping up.

Finally, Lord Yama stopped and turned to her, saying, "Savitri, you are amazing! I would never have believed that any mortal could follow me as you have done. I do not know by what means you have accomplished this feat, but I greatly admire your loyalty and persistence. Therefore, I am going to give you three boons (magical gifts). The one condition is that you may not ask that the soul of your husband be returned to you. Will you agree to this?"

Savitri agreed. "Thank you, Lord Yama. For my first boon, I ask that my husband's parents' kingdom be restored to them."

"Done!" said Lord Yama. "What is your second wish?"

"I would like for my husband's parents to be able to live long and healthy lives, reigning over their kingdom in peace and prosperity."

"Again, done!" said Lord Yama. "But you have used the first two of your boons to ask for favors for others. For this last wish, I insist that you ask for something for yourself."

"Very well," Savitri said. "I would like to bear and raise a hundred strong sons."

"That's a lot of sons, but very well, if that is your wish, then so be it!" Lord Yama proclaimed. "Now you must leave me and let me take the soul of your husband away."

"But Lord Yama," Savitri said humbly. "You know that in our culture a pious widow can never remarry. Therefore, I cannot bear and raise the sons you have promised me, unless you return to me the soul of my husband."

Lord Yama was astonished at her cleverness! "You tricked me!" he said with great admiration. "That is not easy to do, for I am the god of truth as well as the god of death. Very well, I have given my word and must give you back the soul of your husband."

Prince Satyaban's life was restored to him. He and Savitri returned to his parents' flourishing kingdom. The couple had many sons, and in time they became the king and queen of the realm.

Indian folklore honors Savitri as the epitome of a woman's loyalty to her husband and for her astonishing cleverness in being able to outwit death.

I feel honored to have been blessed with this beautiful and meaningful spiritual name. As to whether or not I will be able to outwit death when the time comes, that remains to be seen.

****

So yes, death, and what comes after death, are the primary themes of this novel. I hope you enjoy reading it as much as I have enjoyed writing it. I wish you blessings, love, and joy, throughout eternity.

May you embrace the reality of your own immortality.

In loving friendship,
Nayaswami Savitri
Ananda Village
318 Ascending Dwapara Yuga

PREFACE

Swami Kriyananda often wrote and spoke on the topic of how to face death. Here are a few of his inspiring words on the subject:

"Everyone should confront and overcome the natural fear of death and dying, for sooner or later all must die!

"Life itself should be a preparation for the 'final examination' of death.

"It would be helpful to face your coming death matter-of-factly, not morbidly. For example, whenever you take a shower, say to yourself, 'This arm that I am washing will be ashes or dust someday. It is not me!'

"Or at night before going to bed, make a mental bonfire of all your possessions, your desires, and your attachments. Cast them one by one into the flames, and then watch as they crackle merrily and disappear. Enjoy yourself as you watch everything you are, have, or ever hope to be, disappear in those mental flames."

Paramhansa Yogananda also offered many wonderful suggestions about living and dying:

"Learn to live in this world as a gracious guest. Your true home is not here! This world is not yours; it is God's. God is the 'Doer,' not you!

"The deed to the house you live in may be written in your name, but whose was it before you acquired it? And whose will it be after you die? Your present lifetime in this world is only a wayside inn, a brief halting place on the long journey to your home in God.

"Think of yourself as a visitor on this earth. Of course, as long as you are here, try to be a good guest. Be on your best behavior. Act responsibly in discharging all of your earthly duties. Take good care of the things God has given you to use. Never forget for a moment, however, that they all belong to God and are not your own."

"Let us always remember that nothing belongs to us—not even our own bodies, personalities, or egos. Nothing, not even death itself, can touch what we truly are inside: the ever-conscious, ever-existing, ever-new bliss of our own Souls."

****

The Great Ones tell us that manifesting calmness and courage in the face of all of life's challenges, up to and including death, will lead us into pure, unending joy and inner freedom.

May we plant these seeds of wisdom in our own and in all receptive hearts and minds, so that each one of us may grow and bloom in perfect freedom, as we were meant to do.

Through the Gates of Death
–And Beyond

ADVENTURES IN THE LOKAS
OF IMMORTALITY

CHAPTER ONE

*Stars, rivers, oceans, spiral nebulae,
sun furnaces, cataclysms,
Cloudbursts, lightning, yawning spaces,
Snow-white winters, flower-decked springs,
leaf-carpeted summers,
Weeping rain, and sorrowful clouds,
All stand ready to help us play the drama of life and death,
Of coming and going, of appearing and disappearing,
And perhaps of reappearing.*

—Paramhansa Yogananda

As Sabellina sat beside the Joyuba River, she asked herself the question: "Why am I sitting here?" The sunny, cool day made the shining river especially enticing, enhanced as it was by her fond childhood memories of this lovely setting.

Nevertheless, Sabellina, or Bellina, as she preferred to be called these days, felt uneasy wasting her precious time lolling about on a river-beach, even one as beautiful as this one.

After all, she was an adult now. She led a busy life and rarely took the time to enjoy herself. *Really!* Who has time to sit by a stream and just *be*? Childish nonsense.

On the other hand, Bellina clearly knew that she definitely had been called here today by her renowned great-grandmother, Sabella Lovingheart. This was unexpected, as she had heard from her only occasionally in recent years! Sabella must have something of real importance on her mind.

"Why *did* she ask me to meet her by the river today?" Bellina wondered impatiently.

Despite her impatience, the memories of her frequent visits here as a twelve-year-old girl brought a smile to her face.

She recalled the many afternoons spent at this same scenic spot, sitting beside her Great-Gramma Sabella. As a small child, Sabellina had a hard time saying Great-Grandmother Sabella, all in one breath, so she sometimes shortened it to "G-G-Bella," or more often, simply "Gigi."

Waiting in a cool, shady spot on the sand, she also remembered the many magical tales that her amazing Gramma Gigi had woven, spun, and even claimed to be *true*!

The date is 2047 years into Ascending Treta Yuga. Bellina was a young woman of 50. Her friends and family had often remarked that her physical resemblance to her great-grandmother was truly astonishing. However, Bellina saw herself as her own person, despite the close facial and bodily resemblance to her great-grandmother.

Bellina firmly believed that one sign of the differences between herself and Gigi was the mysterious genetic trait that had given Bellina her long, shiny black hair, shot through with rainbow highlights. The previously unknown hair color among their family was one that definitely highlighted her good looks.

Though still magnetically attractive, Sabella/Gigi was truly old now, 303 earth-years old to be exact. Moreover, she looked it—and more than most people did in Ascending Treta Yuga. The fact of their age difference also set them apart as very distinct individuals.

Sabella's formerly long golden-brown hair had turned to bright silver. It fell in soft waves down her back, to just below her shoulder blades. Her turquoise eyes were somewhat faded from their original brilliance. Her kind face was wreathed in sparkling smiles, most of the time. Nevertheless, the truth was that Sabella had allowed her smile-lines to etch themselves into permanent face-wrinkles.

Oh yes, the wrinkles could have been removed quickly and easily. No one had to look old in Treta Yuga, if he or she did not wish. However, Sabella thoroughly enjoyed the way she looked and chose not to change her appearance in the slightest way. Over the years, several of her beautiful daughters, granddaughters, and great-granddaughters (including Bellina) had suggested and even offered to treat Sabella to a "Cosmic Luminescent Makeover," the popular anti-aging procedure at that time.

Sabella always declined declaring, "I earned every one of these lovely facial lines. I would not care to look like Thomas's granddaughter instead of his mature, life-linked partner, who is still serving faithfully by his side, after all these decades!"

"We could re-do him too!" they routinely answered.

This suggestion always evoked much laughter, for they all knew very well that Thomas Timetraveler, their family patriarch, was firmly opposed to physical makeovers of any kind. Through his life of time-travel adventures, he had re-lived so many past lifetimes and had occupied so many bodies of numerous ages, shapes, and forms that he cared very little about how he looked to others. He well understood that what was inside a person is of far greater importance than any outward appearance.

Exactly how Thomas *did* look right now was anybody's guess, for Thomas was "away" and had been for several years. It was beginning to appear that his "away-ness" might have become a permanent condition.

When asked where he was, Sabella would reply, "Don't worry. He's fine!"

It was a mystery for all his friends and family to ponder.

Thus, it was that as Bellina waited, she began to worry. It was not like Gigi to be late.

To take her mind off her concerns, she removed her soft slippers and dangled her feet in the river. The coolness of the river was so refreshing that she soon gave into temptation, dropped her simple aqua-colored robe on the granite boulder nearby, and gracefully dove into the river.

Ah-h-h-h-! It was blissful! Bellina had forgotten how a swim in the Joyuba River could instantly lift her consciousness and float her cares and worries far away.

After a time, she noticed Sabella quietly watching her from the bank. "Come on in, Gigi! The water's fine!"

Sabella only shook her head—a little sadly, it seemed to Bellina.

"Good heavens! What is going on?" she wondered to herself. Sabella loved swimming in the Joyuba. Bellina realized that she had never seen her great-grandmother look so sad. Sadness and Sabella's personality simply did not go together, as far as Bellina was concerned.

Quickly swimming back to the small sandy beach, Bellina grabbed her clothes to dry herself. She gave Sabella a big hug and thought these words to her, "Gigi, I love you very much! Please tell me immediately what is wrong?"

"I love you too, my precious Bellina! Let us sit together here, as we did so many times when you were a little girl. I will tell you all about the recent events of my life and the implications that they may have for *your* life's path."

"Uh-oh!" Bellina thought, finally becoming truly alarmed. "Double and triple-giant uh-oh's!"

CHAPTER TWO

Life cannot die!
Only death can meet death!

— Swami Kriyananda, from the *Christ Lives Oratorio* ©

"My dearest Bellina, I sincerely apologize for being late. I know I should have sent a mental message, but there is a reason for my lateness and lack of communication.

"As you know, I am a member of the High Council. This morning, during one of our regular Council meetings, which are usually short, our High Council leader, Lauwknor Laughingwater, surprised me when he asked me to give a short speech, after which he and the other Council members posed many difficult questions.

"From my perspective, the question-and-answer session lasted much too long. As you can imagine, the task took up most of my mental circuits."

"Difficult questions, Gigi? I can't imagine anyone being able to come up with a question you would have trouble answering!"

"You are kind to say that, my dear, but you don't yet know the subject he asked me to talk about."

"True, but I think that you are going to tell me now."

"Yes, I will," Sabella smiled at her impetuous great-granddaughter. "I was asked to speak about life, death, rebirth, and immortality."

"Large subjects, I agree! However, I am sure you were as eloquent as you always are—but what do these subjects have to do with me?" Even as Bellina mentally posed the question, she felt the cold chill of misgivings run through her body. What was it that Sabella was trying to say? Was she going to announce someone's death? Or maybe she was finally going to talk about Thomas and tell her about where he had so abruptly and mysteriously disappeared. On the other hand, perhaps Sabella was hinting about her own death. Or perhaps....

Bellina could speculate no further before her great-grandmother, a natural telepath, addressed her sharply, "Quit trying to figure this out, Bellina! I *am* going to tell you!"

Then Sabella's face softened as she thought, "You remind me so much of myself at your age—impatience personified!"

Sabella continued, "As you may have suspected, dear one, I know exactly where Thomas is now. He *has* left the material plane forever and dwells on the high astral planet Hiranyaloka, serving with the great Master, Swami Sri Yukteswar.

"In that unimaginably lofty *loka*, or location, he has the joy of welcoming souls arriving from lower astral worlds to this astral loka and helping them to become accustomed to their new surroundings. At other times Thomas helps Sri Yukteswar prepare a few, highly advanced souls to move from the astral plane into the causal universe."

"...left this material plane *forever*? But Gigi!" Tears were forming in Bellina's big blue-green eyes. "Why didn't you tell us this before?"

"Because Thomas asked me not to. Please, let me explain. One evening, about six months ago, we sat together for many hours in deep meditation, here beside the river on this exact spot."

Bellina shuddered a little and looked around carefully to be certain they were truly alone.

Sabella laughed, "Dear one, you act as though you expect to see the ghost of your Great-Grandpa Thomas! You should be so lucky! Believe me, if Thomas joined us, you'd know it, and he would not seem the least bit ghost-like!"

"Sorry, Gigi," Bellina looked chagrined. "Please continue."

"I knew for about a year or so that he had something serious on his mind, but I was aware that I couldn't pry it out of him until *he* was ready to reveal it to me.

"At the close of our long and blissful meditation, he suggested a swim, something we always loved to do together. As you know, Thomas was still quite vigorous and in excellent health.

"After our swim, just as we were about to climb out onto the sandy bank, he surprised me by catching my hand and saying, 'Sabella, dearest love of my life, please stay in the water with me a few more minutes.'"

"He drew me back to stand facing him in a waist-deep, sandy-bottomed pool. The calm water was a lovely teal color, cooling to our bodies on that warm evening, and clear enough to let us observe some small green and silver fish, as they investigated our toes.

"The shadows of twilight were falling all around us, leaving only a few lingering shafts of sunlight shining through the tall trees and piercing the surface of the calm water. The soothing river sounds murmured and rustled their cheerful songs. As usual, I was in awe of the magnificent beauty surrounding us.

"As I faced Thomas, waiting to hear what he would say, I was dumbstruck by the look in his eyes and the expression on his face.

"Oh, Bellina, I knew that sweet face intimately and never tired of looking at it; but now, his face looked very different to me. It was suffused with—what words can I use to describe it? Divine light! Bliss! Ultimate joy! Yet there was also a tinge of sadness in those deep, dark blue eyes.

"We stood right here in these living waters, facing each other. He grasped both of my hands in his and looked deeply into my soul. His piercing gaze was not only looking into my eyes, but through them, into the depths of my being.

"His thoughts were clear and calm, as the images and concepts he wished to convey to me floated gently into my mind. 'Sabella, dearest one, life-linked as we have been for most of this lifetime, it is now time for me to leave my physical body and the material plane forever. The mystic summons has come, and I must follow it soon, and move on to my next destination.'"

"Thomas paused to allow what he had just said to sink in to my being. What did I think and feel at that moment? I must admit that I had to struggle to control my emotions. I knew he did not want to feel any sadness or sorrow in me. He was just that way, you know?"

"I remember, Gigi," Bellina said softly, trying to stifle the tears running down her beautiful, young face.

Sabella continued pouring vivid thoughts and images into Bellina's receptive mind. Bellina found that she was mentally connected to her great-grandparents through this profound and personal moment of their lives together. She was astonished that Sabella would share such an important private event with her! And why her?

"Bellina, I will admit that I fought hard to stay calm. Years of meditation helped me greatly in that moment. Nevertheless, I fought the urge to grab him, hold him in my arms, and beg him not to leave us. Thomas knew how I felt, of course. There have never been secrets between us.

"In his kind way, he pulled me into his arms to comfort me, and said, 'Be calm, my sweet Sabella. We can never be apart in essence. You know this! We are one, now and always!'"

"'I'm going with you?' I thought to him, preferring to ignore his choice of the phrase, '...in *essence*.'

"Then I changed my question to a statement of definite intention, 'Thomas, wherever you go, I *am* going with you!'"

Bellina interrupted, "But I see you didn't leave since you are here with me right now! Or did you leave and come back? You are not telling me that you are going to die soon too, are you? And is Great-Grampa Thomas really dead? Tell me the truth! Please!"

"Sweet Bellina, please don't cry or be so sad, or we may have to send you back to the Heart Chakra Pyramid for some remedial work on controlling and transmuting your heart's emotions. Remember all that we learned there about attachments and grief?" Sabella chuckled at the memories of the fine times they had together, as she guided Bellina, at the very young age of 40, through the Valley of the Seven Chakra Pyramids. Truly, it had been unusual for someone that young to participate *successfully* in such an advanced inner and outer journey.

"Sorry! I'll detach and go to my inner temple of peace." Bellina was grateful for the reminder.

Sabella went on, "That's better, dearest. Now didn't you hear me tell you that Thomas is living on the highly advanced planet, Hiranyaloka, serving people there, just as he did here?"

"Yes, I heard you, Gigi, but I thought it might be only a temporary assignment."

"Well, in a way it is! Just as everything is always temporary—until it isn't."

They laughed together, gratefully feeling the remaining emotional tension dissolve away.

"I'm calmer now," Bellina smiled. "Please tell me more."

"I'll answer your questions as best as I can. No, I did not go away with Thomas. He is definitely not dead, as nobody is ever dead, Bellina. Surely, you must know this! All that has occurred is that he has relocated to a distant astral *loka*.

"He told me about where he was going, but emphasized to me that it was not my time or destiny to join him there yet. Perhaps in the future. Moreover, no, I am not going to make my transition away from the earth any time soon, dearest. We do have many more years to enjoy each other's company.

"Now, let me show you in mind-pictures a little more of what happened when Thomas relayed his important news to me.

Sabella agreed and allowed her mind to become so closely linked to Bellina that even mental communications were no longer needed. The two of them were simply there, observing the past as a kind of mind-movie.

CHAPTER THREE

I am going to kick the frame...by the second Kriya Yoga.

— Autobiography of a Yogi

"Thomas, wherever you go, I'm going with you!" Sabella hugged Thomas tightly in her arms.

"Listen to yourself, my love! After all these years, do you not realize our oneness in spirit?"

Sabella relaxed her grip a tiny bit. "Yes, of course, I know we are one in all the best possible ways. Nevertheless, I demand that you tell me what this is all about—slowly and clearly!"

Thomas smiled fondly at his feisty wife. "Sabella, in your extensive study of history, did you ever come across the phrase, 'kick the frame' in reference to a person discarding the physical body consciously and deliberately, rather than going through the often long and arduous experience of what might be called a 'regular death?'"

"Why, yes! It is an obscure idiom, but I remember seeing it. It is a phrase, used occasionally in ancient literature, and it primarily refers to dying consciously.

"This exact phrase is used in *Autobiography of a Yogi*, in the chapter that describes the passing of Swami Pranabananda, one of the most spiritually advanced disciples of Lahiri Mahasaya:

> After the feast, Swami Pranabananda sat on a high platform and gave an inspired sermon on the Infinite. At the end, before the gaze of thousands, he spoke with unusual force, "Be prepared; I am going to <u>kick the frame</u>. Be not selfish nor grieve for me. I shall be reborn shortly. After enjoying a short period of the

Infinite Bliss, I shall return to earth and join Babaji."

He cried again, "I <u>kick the frame</u> by the second Kriya Yoga." ...the disciples touched his body, seated in the lotus posture, but it was no longer the warm flesh. Only a stiffened <u>frame</u> remained; the tenant had fled to the immortal shore.

"The human body is sometimes referred to as one's 'frame,' such as in the term, 'he has a large frame'. We also say 'frame' in reference to emotional moods, such as 'she was in a very bad frame of mind.'

"Such strange wording though—I have never fully understood the word 'frame' and why it needed to be 'kicked.'"

Thomas laughed at Sabella's delightful and irrepressible humor. "Perhaps it's a little like 'kicking the bucket.' Do you remember that old euphemism for dying?"

Sabella said, "Actually, I do remember that rather strange phrase very well and know something of its origin. Language can be so entertaining, even though we rarely speak it aloud in this part of Ascending Treta Yuga. Nevertheless, I believe there is often some interesting history hidden in language.

"There are several theories about the origins of the phrase, 'kick the bucket.' In order to commit suicide a person would stand on a large upturned bucket with his head in a slip noose and kick away the bucket from under his feet. Or in the case of an execution, the bucket would be kicked out from under him by the executioner."

Sabella grew solemn again, "Thomas, are you trying to ease me into understanding that you have decided to 'kick a bucket?'"

Thomas looked closely at his wife's sorrowful face. "Dearest, we have had such a wonderful and fun-filled life together. I would never ask you to assist me in 'kicking my bucket' in that way. Nevertheless, I am going to ask you to be with me as I 'kick the frame' through a specific Kriya Yoga technique, as it was described in that quotation from *Autobiography of a Yogi*."

"Oh, Thomas, NO! Not really, not now! Please, dearest one, please don't do it!"

"I didn't want to spring this on you suddenly, my love. Please forgive me! I didn't know how to break the news of my departure from the physical plane to you in a more graceful or kinder way."

"So you are speaking of a permanent departure, Thomas?" Sabella asked, looking deeply into his eyes.

"Well, let's just say it might be 'lengthy.'"

"And the reason I can't join you is...?" Sabella inquired.

"Try looking into the depths of your own being for that answer, my sweet Sabella."

Sabella closed her eyes to do just that.

The answer came clearly and almost instantaneously. "If it were my time to leave this earth plane along with Thomas, I would know it, feel it, accept it, and rejoice at the very thought of it. I do understand why I cannot join him at this time, in this part of his spiritual journey. I still have a final mission here on earth—a mission that cannot be neglected."

Opening her eyes and smiling into Thomas's bright eyes, she did not need to say or even think anything else to him. Their souls danced together and merged in perfect accord.

Thomas took her hand and led her to the nearby sandy, sun-warmed river-beach. He sat cross-legged, in the lotus posture, and went into deep meditation. Sabella sat facing him and did the same. From her purified heart, she offered him a loving "Farewell," and released him into cosmic freedom.

Time stopped for the couple. Timelessness embraced them with its soft wings of compassion and bliss.

Eventually and from far, far away Sabella could hear a faint echo of Thomas's spirit moving through the vast corridors of endlessness and immortality, into perfect freedom and oneness with all that is.

"Sabella, through the power of Kriya Yoga, I have deliberately and consciously shed my mortal, earthly frame forever. Remember, with all your heart, mind and soul, that I am always with you. Never forget that you and I are one, now and forever—just as all is one, ALL IS ONE, one, one, one, one, one—melting into the Eternal AUM-m-m-m-m-m-m-m-m-m-m-m-m-m-m-m-m-m-m...."

Absolute silence reigned there on the banks of the Joyuba River. For three days, Sabella sat alone, unmoving, dwelling in greatest bliss.

When she finally opened her eyes and returned from her state of superconscious ecstasy, she saw that the sandy spot in front of her, where Thomas had been sitting close before her, was completely smooth, as though his body had never been there at all.

She turned to listen to the river flowing nearby. She was at peace and ready to face whatever came next in her life.

CHAPTER FOUR

Is the river's roar Thy reminder,
Always running through me,
In distant closeness?

— Paramhansa Yogananda

Sabella and Bellina returned to awareness of the present time and place. They first noticed the soft roar and rush of the river. A few birds twittered in the willow branches overhead.

Sabella looked closely at Bellina. She was concerned that the news of Thomas's departure would upset her. Sabella saw only peace in Bellina's lovely face and was touched by the comfort it offered her.

They hugged each other for quite some time, and then sat quietly on the sand leaning against a large, cool boulder, their warm shoulders touching. For a while, they silently enjoyed a deep sense of calmness and closeness with each other.

"Do you miss Thomas very much?" Bellina finally asked.

"No, for he is still with me in many ways. I hear his voice in my mind, and we often laugh together. Our priceless, shared memories are always available to me. I admit that I am still getting used to this change, and I know that it will take time to adjust.

"With all that said, the indescribably glorious blessing of experiencing his conscious exit from the body was so uplifting that no mundane human sorrow could ever steal away that joy. Still, we shall see how it goes, as time goes by.

"I didn't mention that he assured me that soon I would be able to visit him in the place of his new divine assignment. Just the thought of being with him again thrills me!"

Bellina sighed and addressed Sabella mentally, "Gigi, who else in our family knows about this?"

Sabella answered simply, "You are the first I have told."

Bellina was surprised to hear this news. "When do you intend to tell the others, and why did you tell me first?"

"I wanted help telling everyone about Thomas's transition and encouraging them to rejoice together in remembrance of his lifetime and its myriad accomplishments, as much as we will miss his physical presence. Your face came to me in meditation, helping me to understand that you are the one who has sufficient strength to help me.

"There is another reason I told you first. Do you recall that I said that it is not time for me to depart from this plane, because of an assignment from the High Council? Before I accepted the task, I requested an assistant for the project—namely you, my sweet one."

"Me?" Bellina exclaimed in a loud, squeaky voice.

Sabella frowned at her, reminding her that it was always best to communicate mentally, for it made it easier to remain inwardly peaceful and in tune with each other.

"Gigi, other than you, I've never even met any of the High Council members. I am still relatively young and inexperienced. Although I have completed my studies in the Halls of Wisdom, I have not yet chosen my life's profession. I can't begin to imagine how I might be of help to you in your important new mission!"

"Bellina, my dear, you underestimate yourself and your potential. In addition to what we can accomplish together, I am sure the experience will help you to prepare for whatever you choose to do for the rest of your life. Not only that, but your young and fresh perspective should be invaluable to our mission.

"After I tell you about the project, take time to meditate on it, and let me know your decision later.

"I have dedicated my life to meditation, music, and the

upliftment of souls by instructing graduate students in the Halls of Wisdom. Working with my beloved mentor, Issoweet, we developed the learning protocols for the famous Chakras Paradigm/Advanced and Experiential Course of Study (CP/AECS) and established hundreds of Chakra Rejuvenation Clinics and Resorts worldwide and on other planets also. Issoweet was such a remarkable being. I am sorry you are too young to have met her.

"Recently, the High Council requested that I drop all my responsibilities with CP/AECS and place them in the hands of my many competent assistants, in order to coordinate a new learning protocol for the Halls of Wisdom. They assured me that this will be my last assignment for this lifetime."

"What sort of 'new learning protocol' are they asking you to develop?"

"We don't have a formal name or acronym yet, but the project will involve a deeper study of life, death, rebirth, and immortality," Sabella transmitted her thoughts to Bellina in a very serious manner.

Bellina startled her by bursting into riotous laughter, causing the small frogs in the river shallows to cease their twilight croaking. "That," she said doubling over with mirth, "covers just about everything in the known and unknown universes, doesn't it, dearest Gigi? I can see why you need an assistant. Maybe a thousand assistants, both dead and alive would be more like it!"

Not missing a beat, Sabella replied to her still giggling great-granddaughter, "Well, I think that would certainly be *overkill*, don't you?" Sabella laughed at her own sly pun.

"And besides that, I can barely deal with *you*, my dear. How would I deal with 999 others like you, dead or alive?"

Together they laughed, and their light-hearted mirth relaxed them both and allowed them to settle down and talk in a more informal way about the proposed project.

Sabella continued, "Bellina, I don't know the details about what these new courses and protocols will include. Everything is only in idea-form for now. However, I believe I know *why* the High Council feels it important that these subjects should be offered to our Halls of Wisdom graduate students. They are issues that need to be explored with greater clarity and depth, especially during this part of Ascending Treta Yuga.

"Bellina, you are my favorite and brightest descendent, and because of that, you are receiving this invitation from the High Council, as a special favor to me. Please accept it as the great honor it is to both of us."

Bellina began to blush and stammer, "Oh, Gigi, it is so kind of you to compliment me like that. How can I ever live up to such high praise from someone I so deeply respect?"

"That's easy to answer, dearest," Sabella transmitted. "All you need to do is listen carefully to what I ask of you and then do it to the best of your abilities. You will accompany me on all my upcoming travels through many realms and on various planes of existence. I need you to record everything that happens—just in case I don't make it back to report to the High Council, myself."

"Wait just a minute, Gigi! 'Don't make it back to report?' Exactly where would we be going? Will we be risking our lives to complete this assignment?"

"Well, when making a firsthand study of death and dying, one might suspect that there may be a few risks involved." It was Sabella's turn to laugh at the look on Bellina's startled face.

"No, dear one. I am joking with you. We will both be safe and alive at the end of our mission, I promise you that.

"However, I don't want you to feel that you have to make your decision just yet. Sleep on it, meditate on it, consult your parents or friends as you like, and then get back to me as soon as you decide.

"On another subject, I would appreciate having you by my side tomorrow, as I call a family conference for all our closest relatives and descendants, to let them know where Thomas is and what he is doing."

"Oh, Gigi! I would be honored to help you with what, I am sure, will not be an easy task; but please, let's not call it a 'family conference.' Let it be a *celebration* of Thomas's amazing life on earth!"

Now it was Sabella's turn to stifle a few tears as she hugged Bellina, her remarkably sensitive and wise great-granddaughter.

"You are right, Sabellina! So perfectly correct! Thank you for your thoughtfulness. A celebration of your Great-Grandpa Thomas's life is exactly what we need to have—and very soon, too! Let's start planning it right now."

Silver-haired Sabella and raven-haired Sabellina strolled arm in arm from the river-beach to Sabella's nearby pyramid home. Heads inclined towards each other and smiling with joy, they started making their plans.

CHAPTER FIVE

Clothed you now are in garments of radiant light!
See your past actions as scenes in a vast,
unfolding tapestry.
O Free Soul!
Feast not your gaze wistfully on episodes already finished,
But look ahead!
New adventures await you—fresh, joyous victories,
As you advance toward perfect freedom.

— Swami Kriyananda, "Astral Ascension Ceremony"

Sabella felt that the ceremony celebrating Thomas Timetraveler's honored life was a successful event that greatly blessed all who attended—including his immediate family, colleagues, friends, students, and many admirers.

Dressed in the gloriously colorful, formal robes of her position on the High Counsel, Sabella performed an Astral Ascension Ceremony for her life-linked mate, with dignity and grace. Bellina assisted her in leading the special celebration of Thomas's life before the massive crowd that had come together on this day.

Bellina's sweet, calm vibrations and her fresh, shining young face helped everyone there to lift their hearts from a place of sorrow for the loss of Thomas's presence among them, to a place of rejoicing together in his ascension to a much higher, bliss-filled loka.

Dressed in a simple white robe, Bellina spoke briefly reminding them that being overly sad about his departure was only a descent into ego-centeredness. She expressed simply and kindly that Thomas's strong, expansive nature was selfless at its core. To honor him now, everyone (including herself) must lift their consciousness from self-absorption in grief to pure, unconditional love and gratitude for the time they had spent with him.

The music comprised a large part of the ceremony; much of it was taken from a special concert Sabella had written many years before, soon after she completed her first visit to the Fifth Chakra Pyramid in the Valley of the Golden Pyramids. Her compositions were inspired by the magnificent oratorio, which King Yudhisthira had composed and presented in her honor, at the close of her first visit to his kingdom.

A symphony orchestra, a large choir, and soloists performed Sabella's music. Many famous dancers also participated in the ceremony. The energy of the music uplifted all in attendance into higher spheres of consciousness, just as Sabella and Bellina had hoped.

Sabella closed the ceremony by offering the time-honored Astral Ascension Ceremony, during which she paused occasionally to comment on the beautiful and meaningful words:

> Dearest Thomas,
>
> You, who have gone before us, have entered a realm which our souls remember: A place of freedom, light, and laughter. Take with you on your journey our blessings, and our love.

[Sabella's comments: "Many of you have asked me where Thomas is right now, if I am in contact with him, and if he is coming back soon. Yes, Thomas has visited me twice, since he departed for the high astral planet of Hiranyaloka a little over a month ago. No, he will not be returning to earth in his physical form."]

> We shall miss you! Our desire is not to hold you back, but only to tell you: Friend, we are yours; our love and support are ever yours, and our prayers for your highest happiness. We shall meet again! Once more, we shall laugh together, rejoice together, and share in the joy of seeking Him!

[Sabella's comment: "We all miss his physical presence deeply, but he is with us in many other ways. We can feel his presence more tangibly, if we wish. All we need do is take the time and make the effort needed to tune in to his presence in our meditations.']

> Claim your soul's freedom! Bless all who ever harmed you, or ever wished you harm. Give them your love and your prayer for their freedom in God.

[Sabella's comment: "Thomas asked me to tell you that his greatest wish for me and for all of us at this time is to follow this simple directive, 'Claim your soul's freedom!' This is what he has done. This you may do also, for it is already yours! This sacred ceremony instructs us exactly how to accomplish this.]

> Friend, cast from your heart all outward attachments! Realize that earthly goals, however shining, are but dreams: God is the only Reality.

At this point Sabella astonished those present by emitting a blindingly bright stream of fire from her right index finger to light the *homa*, a small ceremonial fire, in the bronze bowl before her. Those who knew her well understood that this was one of the *siddhis* or yogic powers she received at the close of her visit to the Fire Chakra Pyramid. She had never demonstrated this power in public, but this seemed to her to be a fitting occasion.

In her mind, she could hear Thomas chuckle, "Ever the dramatist, my love? Don't worry, it is fine with me—I don't mind at all! I'm enjoying every moment of this magnificent ceremony!"

Sabella sang the following words aloud, in her beautiful clear voice:

> Burn your earthly desires in the fire of wisdom! Burn earthly limitations in the blaze of inner freedom! Burn earthly disappointments in the flames of spreading peace! Burn earthly joys in the bonfire of divine bliss! See your physical form as a discarded garment: Clothed you now are in garments of radiant light!

Just as Sabella sang the last phrase, a holographic image of Thomas appeared to the inner vision of each member of the congregation. He was arrayed in garments of radiant light, smiling in heavenly bliss, eyes unfathomably wise, deep, and beautiful, with his hands folded, palms together at the heart chakra.

A gasp went up from the audience. It was so real, and yet it was obviously a vision. Sabella's voice was strong and clear in their minds as she concluded her part of the ceremony:

> O Free Soul! See your past actions as scenes in a vast, unfolding tapestry. Feast not your gaze wistfully on episodes already finished, but look ahead! New adventures await you—fresh, joyous victories as you advance toward perfect freedom!

Bellina now spoke the final words of the Astral Ascension Ceremony. Tears streamed down her face as she softly said:

> And what of us, dearest Thomas, who love you and would be remembered by you? Behold us as threads of light in the tapestry of your life—threads, which, through the magnet of soul-friendship, will appear ever and again, woven with increasing beauty as our hearts expand together in God's love.

Asking all to rise, Bellina and Sabella said a prayer together, asking everyone to repeat after them:

> Divine Mother! Receive this, Thy child, Thomas. Purify him in Thy perfect light and love. Grant him eternal freedom in Thee! AUM, Amen!

Bellina led everyone in sending love and blessings to Thomas. They rubbed the palms of their hands together briskly and then lifted their hands upwards, palms facing forward, eyes closed and uplifted to the spiritual eye, while loudly chanting AUM three times. Many reported later that they felt Thomas blessing them at the same time.

Any tears of loss were removed instantly by the great waves

of divine bliss that encompassed them all.

The dignified, silver-haired Sabella turned to gather her radiant great-granddaughter in her arms, and whispered to her mentally, "Well, done, dear one. Very well done!"

Bellina was transfixed with awe. Who, indeed, were these great souls she claimed as her great-grandparents? They seemed fathomless and free! After all that had transpired, she now felt much closer to them both.

CHAPTER SIX

*The Self is not born, nor does it perish.
Self-existent, it continues its existence forever.
It is birthless, eternal, changeless, and ever the same.
The soul cannot even be pondered by the reasoning mind.
Realize this truth, and rise above all sorrow.*

— *Bhagavad Gita*

The ceremony was over and all the guests and family members left. When they were once again alone, Bellina's face was serious as she told Sabella of her decision to accept her place by her side, assisting in her newly assigned mission.

Sabella expressed her delight at Bellina's somewhat formal acceptance. "We'll have great fun together, my dear, and I'm sure we'll learn many new and wonderful things. Just wait and see!"

A few days later, Sabella and Bellina met in the small pyramid-shaped chapel in the High Council Halls. Sabella related that it was here, many years ago, that she and Issoweet, her beloved mentor and friend, had begun their intensive study of the chakras and embarked on many adventures together.

Sabella began by instructing Bellina to set aside the next two weeks to prepare herself for their upcoming study project.

"What do you mean by 'prepare?' Do I need to pack? If so, I absolutely must know something about where we are going and how long our journey will be!"

Sabella smiled at her energetic great-granddaughter and thought to herself, "Ah, youth! How impulsive the young ones can be. How carelessly they scatter about their natural, bountiful energy, which they have in such great abundance, but don't yet know how to focus effectively."

"Your great-granddaughter reminds me of someone I once knew, as she was about to launch into the greatest adventure of her life in the Valley of the Seven Golden Pyramids." A sweet, familiar voice had wafted like a summer breeze into Sabella's mind, unannounced and unexpected.

"Issoweet!" Sabella cried. "Where are you?"

"I'm right here, dearest Sabella," Issoweet transmitted. "Where are you?"

They laughed happily together and said simultaneously, "No matter where you go, there you are!" This was an old joke they often shared during their long-ago days traveling together."

"What I meant to say is that I have not heard from you in many years. After you transitioned to...to wherever it is you are 'residing' these days, you were uncommunicative. Did you get busy and simply forget me? Do you still love me? Do you miss me, as I miss you?"

Sabella's mentor sighed as she told her dearest student, "Sabella, I love you always, you *know* that! And even after all these years, you *still* have the impulsive habit of asking too many questions, one after another, giving me no time to answer even one of them, before you ask another!"

"True!" Sabella said, chagrined. "But I've missed you so much that I want to know everything *immediately!* Why have you been so silent?"

"There you go again, my dearest Sabella. A little patience, please and I shall explain. I apologize for disappearing from your life in such a mysterious way," Issoweet said.

"Did you die?" Sabella wanted to know.

"Well, not exactly. I just relocated to a different loka, as requested by my twin brother, Simeon."

"Simeon! I should have guessed that he was involved in some way in your sudden disappearance."

"Be careful, Sabella!" Issoweet warned. "Simeon might be listening in on our conversation right now. I told him that I would be contacting you today."

"Simeon!" Sabella mentally shouted. "If you are listening in, reveal yourself to me!"

"Since when do you give orders to me, child?" Simeon's unmistakable voice rang in her ears.

She fell to her knees in awe and overwhelming joy! It had been decades since she had heard from Issoweet, but Simeon had been absent from her life for well over a century.

He had been her childhood mentor and beloved spiritual father, protector, and teacher from shortly after her birth until well into her adulthood. He taught Thomas and her to travel through time and revisit numerous past lives. Eventually Simeon had helped Thomas and Sabella to realize that they were destined to become life-linked mates, and he had performed a delightful wedding ceremony for them.

Later in her life, and just before Simeon disappeared, he introduced Sabella to his twin sister, Issoweet. Having been separated at birth, Issoweet and Simeon found each other late in their lives and intuitively sensed that they were siblings. This perception was supported by the fact that their physical appearance was almost identical. Through a short time-travel session, they validated their relationship as brother and sister.

During the ensuing years of their association, Issoweet was able to win Sabella's love and trust, and in many ways, to take Simeon's place as her mentor. Nevertheless, Simeon had been such a strong father figure for her, that it had been difficult to adjust to his prolonged absence from her life.

"Oh, Simeon! I apologize for my overreaction. I am just glad to see again you after all these years. Are you dead, too?"

"Do we seem dead to you, little one?"

With those words, both Simeon and Issoweet appeared to her clearly in their old familiar forms. They were holding hands and smiling their nearly identical smiles at her. With their long white hair and piercing silver eyes, they still seemed like masculine and feminine versions of each other.

As Sabella's hungry eyes gazed at their dear forms, she felt she could never tire of looking at them. She also sensed that they were sending her wave after wave of powerful healing energy, soothing the places in her heart, which were still raw from losing Thomas—even if the loss was only temporary, as she so fervently believed.

Meanwhile, as all this was happening, Bellina stood transfixed, watching Sabella as she was obviously communicating inwardly with people, whom Bellina could not see. She was respectful enough of her great-grandmother's privacy to remain silent and not intrude on what was happening.

In fact, as she carefully observed the unusual situation unfolding before her, she realized that she was surrounded by a muffling cloud of silence.

She watched Sabella fall to her knees with a wondrous look on her face. Bellina felt moved to do the same, although she did not understand exactly what she was doing, or why. However, there was no mistaking the powerful vibrations of divine energy swirling all around them.

Sabella finally tuned into Bellina, who was quietly kneeling beside her in the little pyramid-chapel, and realized that Bellina must be very curious about what had just transpired.

Sabella humbly asked, "Simeon, Issoweet, will you make yourself visible to my great-granddaughter, Sabellina? I would love to be able to introduce her to you, and I know she would be greatly honored to meet the ones she has heard so much about, throughout all of her young life.

"Yes, of course," came the hoped-for answer.

Instantly, Bellina saw Simeon and Issoweet standing before her, gloriously encircled in golden light. She knew immediately who they were and was glad she was already on her knees, as that made it much easier for her to bow and touch her head to their holy feet. In turn, both of the radiant elders placed their hands of top of her head, to pray for her and bless her.

It was simply too much energy for Bellina to receive all at once. With a small sigh, she slipped down onto the floor of the chapel and lost consciousness.

CHAPTER SEVEN

I assure you, by the rejoicing I have in Jesus Christ, that I die daily!

— Saint Paul, *Holy Bible*, First Corinthians, 15:31

Bellina awoke to find her head resting comfortably in Sabella's soft lap. They were once again at their favorite beach by the river. Sabella was dribbling a little water onto Bellina's forehead from of a tiny, rainbow-hued mussel shell.

"Wha-a-t...? Bellina was, for the moment, lost in confusion. "What happened, Gigi? Did I faint?"

"Just rest a moment, dear one, and collect your energy. Do you remember what you saw in the Pyramid Chapel?"

"Oh yes! I saw Simeon and Issoweet. They were blessing me and then...nothing more, until now, when I felt you dribbling water on my head. Why are you doing that, Gigi, and could you please stop now?"

"Certainly, little one. If you feel grounded enough to complain, then I know you must be fully awake and ready to have me explain what happened to you.

"As you may remember, we were in the chapel on the High Council grounds. I was beginning to tell you what we should do to prepare for our upcoming mission, when Issoweet showed up in my mind's eye and began talking to me. Simeon soon joined us in a happy reunion.

"You must have wondered what was going on, for I was sure that only I could hear and see them. As we mentally conversed, I began to want you to be able to see and hear them, too. They are so dear to me, and they have been away for such a long time, especially Simeon.

"I asked them to appear to you also, which they graciously did. It was a short appearance, because they quickly 'over-amped' you with the power of their blessings and love. We all should have known better, Bellina."

Bellina looked at her great-grandmother's troubled face. She reassured Sabella saying, "Gigi, it was worth it. I am thrilled to have had even a short glimpse of those two great souls, especially having heard your many wonderful stories about them. And the blessings I received! Wow! There are no words to describe how blissful I feel now, in spite of the fact that it did, as you say, 'over-amp' me for a little while."

"Yes, I know, dear one, and I also realize now that those blessings will be an essential part of what you need to strengthen you for what is to come."

"Well, then, Gigi," Bellina said as she suddenly jumped up from her comfortable spot on the shady beach, "Let's get started!"

"So be it, Bellina. As I was starting to say back in the Chapel, I want you to first take two weeks to prepare...."

Bellina interrupted, somewhat rudely, "Why wait two weeks? I'm ready right now!"

Sabella laughed at the bright orange energy sparks she perceived emanating from Bellina's already radiant aura.

With surprising strength, Sabella scooped up her granddaughter and tossed her into the nearby river, immediately joining her in the water. Bellina needed a good cooling off—that was certain!

Later Sabella said, "To answer your recent question, no, you don't need to pack anything for where we are going. Everything you need will be provided. However, it is essential that you first spend two weeks in silence and engage in many hours of longer, deeper meditations. This will prepare you inwardly, and bring that sparkly, fiery energy—that I *still* see all around you, even after our cooling dip in the river—under control!"

"Starting tomorrow, we will meet every day at sunrise in the Pyramid Chapel and meditate together. I will help you deepen your spiritual practices in preparation for our adventures."

"Will I see Simeon and Issoweet again soon?" Bellina said, in a slightly quavering mental voice. Sabella could see that her great-granddaughter was still somewhat shaken from the massive energy surge she had just received.

"Not anytime soon, dearest child. They told me to give you their love and to say to you, 'Farewell Bellina, until we see you again.' They promised to visit us once more, when the time is right and you are spiritually stronger."

"May I make another small request?" Bellina said shyly. "Could we meet to meditate here, instead of at the Pyramid Chapel? It feels better to me."

"Of course! That would be fine. I thoroughly enjoy this splendid 'natural chapel.' Would you like to stay with me in my home for the next two weeks? It's very close to this beach, and spending more time together will make it easier to blend our auras."

Bellina happily accepted the invitation.

The next morning at dawn, Sabella and Bellina sat for meditation close to the river. They were perfectly still, with straight spines and open hearts. The Joyuba River sang its lovely morning songs. They had begun their sadhana by singing a simple chant:

> *Krishna, playing his flute, on the banks of the blue river.*
> *My mind is always floating, on the thoughts of my Lord!*

After chanting together, Sabella led Bellina in a series of especially powerful breathing exercises, which were all new to her.

"Please be sure to let me know," Sabella instructed her earlier, "if you become light-headed or feel strange in any way."

"I will, Gigi. I trust you completely. I am sure you will instruct, guide, and protect me in all the best possible ways."

Each day they meditated a little longer, going deeper and deeper into the Kriya Yoga techniques, which were followed by many hours of perfect silence and stillness.

Sabella always ended their meditations with an inspiring song or chant. They remained in silence as they swam in the Joyuba River and ate a small snack that Sabella had lovingly prepared for them the night before.

When they were not meditating, they remained silent and inward, as Sabella had requested. In the beginning, Bellina had a difficult time maintaining a graceful silence.

However, after a few days, she found herself adapting and began to hunger for the silence. She began to love and appreciate the abundant sense of joy, inspiration, strength, and focus.

"I really can see now that I think and talk too much, most of the time! The silence is so soothing and helpful to my peace of mind!"

Another benefit that Bellina observed was how much less food and sleep she needed. It was obvious that this condition was a direct result of her longer hours of meditation and the energy it provided. This was an amazing revelation! She previously had thought that it was primarily food and rest that gave her the energy she needed, when she felt depleted.

Being with Sabella all the time, in itself, provided an unexpected joy—a continuous inner upliftment of her spirits.

From time to time, as Bellina meditated, she felt the same tingling sensation at the top of her head that she had perceived when Simeon and Issoweet offered her their powerful spiritual blessings. Gone were her trepidations about how overwhelmed she felt in that moment. Now she could hold on to the great hope that intense blessings she had received from them would happen again someday soon!

Happy days sped by. Bellina did not bother to keep track of the passing time, being so absorbed in the Eternal Now. Thus, it came as a bit of a surprise when she arrived at their usual meditation place at the prescribed time to find that

Sabella was not preparing for their long meditation in her customary way.

Bellina felt engulfed by a great sense of disappointment, as she realized that their two weeks of silence and seclusion were ending. She was *greatly* enjoying the wonder-filled hours of deep meditation with her great-grandmother by her side.

Catching Bellina's thoughts, Sabella said, "Our two inspiring weeks are over, dear one. We will have a relatively short meditation this morning, and then travel to a place where I will begin to explain our mission to you, at least as much as I understand it myself, so far.

"It has been my great joy to spend this time of silence and seclusion with you. I want you to know that. Your aura is radiant today—calm, pure, and saturated with divine light. I know you are ready!"

CHAPTER EIGHT

Oh death, where is thy sting?
O grave, where is thy victory?

— *Holy Bible,* First Corinthians 15:55

"Where are we?" Bellina looked around in wonderment. "What is this place? I have never seen anything quite like it!"

"We have traveled through time, as well as through space. We are at a place on earth called Forest Lawn Memorial Park, a very large cemetery in Glendale, California, on the North American continent. The year is 302 Ascending Dwapara Yuga (or 2002, according to the customary notation in this part of Dwapara Yuga)."

"What is a cemetery?" Bellina wondered.

"A place to bury the material remains of someone who is dead," Sabella replied simply.

"Why would anyone want to do *that*?"

"Oh, Bellina, you are teasing me now! I know you have studied history enough to know that the people on this planet once either cremated or buried a person's body after the soul had departed."

"Well, yes, I do know about ancient customs of dealing with dead bodies," Bellina said sheepishly. "But seeing this large 'city of the dead' in person and for the first time is somewhat startling. Although I have often time-traveled (as you well know, because you taught me how), I know I have never seen a place quite like this one. It's huge!

"How many dead people are buried here?" Bellina asked.

"All of them," Sabella replied and burst into laughter at her own slightly macabre joke. It took Bellina a moment to understand it, and even then, she was not sure it was appropriate to laugh so heartily in a place like this. The few people she saw milling about the grounds, staring down at gravesites, had very somber, sad faces.

"Bellina, everything is fine. Remember, they cannot see or hear us unless we choose to allow it. This place is much more amazing than you might imagine. Let me show you why."

She transported them to the inside of a beautiful, high-ceiling mausoleum. It had a cool, cavernous feeling and was sweetly fragrant with the smell of incense and fresh flowers. The marble halls echoed with the footsteps and soft murmurs of other visitors. A sign just outside one of the large building's enclaves described it as "The Sanctuary of Golden Slumber."

"What a pretty name for this dark and echo-filled place," Bellina said. Even as she spoke, she began to notice the extremely powerful and holy vibrations here.

"Why?" she wondered. "What is going on in this strange room filled with dead bodies?"

"Come and sit beside me on this little bench," Sabella said. "A casket containing Paramhansa Yogananda's body was placed in the vault in front of you, some months after his conscious exit from the body on March 7, 1952. It remained in an incorrupt state for many centuries, after which it vanished during the years of devastating mantric warfare."

"Yogananda! The great Avatar, Paramhansa Yogananda!" Bellina immediately knelt in awe. She could say no more. It became obvious why she felt such great waves of bliss rolling over both of them. All she could do was close her eyes and meditate gratefully in this holy place. Now she understood what she was feeling—oceans full of divine light, love, and peace were flowing through her entire being.

Both women sat for a while longer on the little bench, enjoying the stillness and indescribably powerful blessings here.

After their time of prayer and meditation in this holy place, Sabella transported them to a nearby hillside, where they could see several large mausoleums and thousands of gravesites all around them.

Bellina had a question: "It is my understanding that cremation was the usual custom for those who followed the Hindu teachings. Wasn't Yogananda a Hindu? If so, why wasn't he cremated?"

"First of all, Yogananda never called himself a Hindu, even though he was born into a devout Hindu family in India. He followed the tradition of *sanaatan dharma*, or the 'eternal religion,' which lies at the core of every true religion or belief system. He was also a great Master of Yoga, practicing the ancient yogic teachings, which can transcend, deepen, and enhance any religious tradition.

"In any case, a great yogi, who had achieved an exalted spiritual stature, was traditionally *not* cremated, because it was believed that his *prana* or unseen life force remained with his body for thousands of years, rendering the flesh itself incorruptible. Thus, the body of such a person was buried instead in a sealed tomb, which served as a place of pilgrimage and blessings, just as this site does."

"There is another reason Yogananda's body was buried rather than cremated. The physical body of a highly advanced yogi like Yogananda does not need to be purified in the fires of cremation, since it has already been completely purified through spiritual practices."

"I understand," Bellina thought softly. "It has been a great privilege to visit this holy place. Thank you for bringing me here!

Thus, it was at this time and place that Sabella began teaching Bellina more about death.

"Is death real?" was the first question Sabella asked her great-granddaughter.

Bellina, wanting to be completely truthful, replied, "It certainly seems to me that it is a real event in every lifetime. Nevertheless, most people still want to deny death's reality. I have also experienced that strange delusion in people I've met."

"Yes, you are right," Sabella said. "It reminds me of a story from the life of King Yudhisthira, which he related while I was visiting him in the Fifth Golden Chakra Pyramid:

"He told me the story in this way: 'When my four brothers and I were exiled from our kingdom and forced to remain in the forest for thirteen years, we experienced many supernatural encounters with gods, goddesses, saints, and gurus. Most of them helped us when we were in great need, but a few of them tested us greatly.

'Once on a very hot day, we were out hunting to provide food for ourselves. We all became exceedingly thirsty. Knowing there was a small lake nearby, I sent my youngest brother, Sahadeva, out into the wilderness to find it and bring us water. He found the lake and stooped down to drink from it.

'Before he could satisfy his raging thirst, he was challenged by a supernatural voice speaking to him from within the lake, informing him that he was not allowed to drink until he answered the entity's questions. Sahadeva was a strong and brave warrior, as were all my brothers. Paying no attention to the entity, he drank from the lake anyway and fell dead immediately.'"

Sabella said, "Yudhisthira continued to relate this fascinating story to me in this way: 'Meanwhile, not knowing what had happened, I sent Sahadeva's minutes-older twin, Nakula, to see why his brother had not returned with the sorely needed water. When Nakula failed to return, I sent his older brother... and then *his* older brother—until finally there were no more of my brothers left to send.

"I went out to find the lake myself, to see what had happened. Arriving at the lake, I was horrified to see each of my four exceptionally strong, courageous brothers lying dead beside the lake. Even as I stood beside their corpses, I, too, became overwhelmed with extreme thirst and knelt to drink from the lake. A powerful voice came to me from out of the lake, informing me that I was not allowed to drink until I had answered all its questions.

"Mastering my thirst and my great grief, and understanding that something very unusual was going on here, I shouted back, 'Very well, I will refrain from drinking the water. Ask your questions!'

"The voice asked many questions, some of them very tricky, like riddles. Most of them were quite profound. I was able to answer each one to the satisfaction of the unknown, inquiring entity.

"After the final question, the voice revealed itself to me as belonging to Lord Dharma, my very own father, whom I had never met before today. He told me he was pleased by my answers to his questions, and that I had replied with wisdom, selflessness, and bravery. Because of this, he brought my brothers back to life, and gave me the celestial weapons that I needed to win the upcoming war.

"You see, he wanted to know firsthand what kind of wise warrior-king his son had become, and whether or not I was truly worthy to be both his son and the emperor of our nation.

"Of all the questions he asked me, this is my favorite:

> 'Question: "What is the most wondrous thing that is?"
>
> 'My answer: "The most wondrous thing that is, is that every day people watch friends, loved ones, and strangers pass through the portals of death, and yet they remain convinced that death will never happen to them."'

"Oh yes, Sabella, I remember when you told me how King Yudhisthira recounted to you that amazing story from his life. Do you think it actually happened, or was it an allegory?"

"Of course it really happened, Bellina! Yudhisthira was reputed to be the most truthful man who ever lived. If he said something, then you could be sure that it was the absolute truth.

"However, the *Mahabharata*, the longest epic ever written on earth, is in many ways allegorical. It is the story of our own souls, and our search for freedom. It represents our need to engage in an inner war with our own negative tendencies in order to achieve that freedom.

"I wouldn't be at all surprised if King Yudhisthira knew, even when I first met him, about our future investigations into death and its ultimate meaning."

"Of course he knew! How could he not have known! He had reached a state of omniscience, that is, the capacity to know everything that there is to know about the past, present, and future!" Bellina took a definite stand on this matter. "He would have had the knowledge that we, who now live during this time of Ascending Treta Yuga, would be seeking ways to unlock death's mysteries for everyone, just as the High Council has asked us to do!"

"No doubt, you are right." Sabella said.

"Back to our original purpose. I brought us here to Forest Lawn Memorial Park in early Ascending Dwapara Yuga, so that we could see firsthand that most people in this time felt death to be a huge loss and the cause of much grief and suffering. For most of these people, the death of a family member or close friend could overwhelm them with grief.

"Things are much better in Ascending Treta Yuga, but even in our more spiritually advanced era, death is more of a mystery to people than it should be.

"Death is still feared by many. This fear is based on a deep-seated dread of the unknown. The High Council realizes that it is time to make the unknown known—to let the truth about death, and what follows it, become common knowledge for all on our planet! This knowledge will uplift us all and help to eliminate our fear of death almost completely, don't you think?"

"Yes, I do!" agreed Bellina enthusiastically, as she began to realize with more clarity the importance of their mission.

"We must be courageous, and face our fears in the way Sri Yukteswar did as a young boy," Bellina continued. "When his mother wanted her curious son to stay out of a particular closet in their home, she told him there were ghosts inside of it, who would 'get him' if he opened the closet door.

"He immediately ran to the closet, threw open the door, and

expressed disappointment that there were no ghosts to be seen in there. Never again did his mother try to frighten him by telling him scary stories.

"The moral of this story is, 'Look fear in the face, and it will cease troubling you.' Through familiarity with what we fear, we are able to overcome its paralyzing hold on us."

Bellina continued, "You asked me the question, 'Is death real?' I will have to answer both 'yes' and 'no.'

"'Yes,' because a person's death certainly has a strong sense of reality to it, especially to the ones who are dying and to those who are close to them. It may appear that death and the time after death are full of great unsolvable mysteries.

"A loved one may think, 'That corpse is obviously not her! Where did she go?' Later thoughts may come, 'Why is she not around anymore? It doesn't seem right!'"

"As time passes, those left behind may live immersed in the memories of the departed one for a while, but as the years pass, the memories eventually begin to fade away, like smoke drifting up into the sky. The grieving ones face their own deaths soon enough, and on it goes, seemingly throughout eternity.

"And 'no' because a few of the Great Ones have passed through the portals of death and returned to explain, *in great detail*, just what life on the other side is like. Death's primary reality is but a gateway to other realms: the astral worlds and beyond."

"Excellent and true statements!" Sabella marveled at the depth of her great-granddaughter's understanding of death. Most young people find death to be depressing, and avoid thinking or talking about it whenever possible. Bellina was more comfortable with death and dying than Sabella had expected her to be. It was a pleasant surprise!

"Bellina, look over to our right, down that hillside just a little ways."

Bellina did as she was instructed and was saddened to see a

young couple tearfully grieving beside the small, fresh grave of their recently deceased child.

"Oh, Gigi! I can't bear to see them grieving so deeply for their child. Can't we comfort them? Couldn't we just go to them and explain that their child is not truly dead? That there is no such thing as permanent death for anyone?"

"That is not for us to do. We cannot comfort them in a physical way, since we do not fully exist here in the past. It is time for us to leave this time and place and visit another important location in Ascending Dwapara Yuga."

"Sabella, we can't just leave them here like this! We could try to explain things to them mentally and...," Bellina was showing her stubborn nature, but it was her sympathetic sweetness that moved Sabella.

"Bellina, I'm sorry, but we can't do that! I must reiterate, we are not even really here, as you well know! This drama happened many centuries ago. However, what we can do is send them light, blessings and a sense of our Divine Mother's comforting presence. Shall we do that now?"

Sabella and Bellina stood calmly praying for the grieving couple, who were still deeply distraught and desperately clinging to each other. They surrounded the young parents with great waves of peace and healing light.

The calming effects of the blessings were immediately noticeable. They began to dry their tears and offer comforting words to each other. Slowly they turned away from the little gravesite and walked downhill. It was obvious that they were no longer feeling crushed by excessive grief.

Bellina was first to notice a small pattern of light floating nearby. It spoke to her in a tiny child's lisping voice. "Thank you for helping Mommy and Daddy! They are better and not so sad now. I tried so hard to show them that I am fine, but they could not hear me. I can go on now, to the beautiful place waiting for me, to rest and play with my friends there. Goodbye for now, and bless you, dear angel friends for helping us!"

"But we're not angels. We are just people, like you...," Bellina began, but stopped when she saw that the little bubble of light had vanished.

"Sabella, that little departed soul called us angels. Why? We're not angels, are we? And what exactly *is* an angel?"

"Good question, Bellina. No, we are not angels. Regarding what an angel is, you will have to wait to have that interesting question answered for you later. I am sure we will meet an angel or two when we begin to explore the astral lokas. Perhaps you can ask an angel that question directly. Fair enough?"

"I can interview an angel? Oh, that sounds amazing!" Bellina exclaimed. "Let's do it now!"

"Patience, Bellina! We are not ready for that part of our adventure yet. Everything in its proper time and place, dear one. For now, I have another important place to show you.

CHAPTER NINE

*A tiny bubble of laughter,
I Am become the Sea of Mirth Itself.*

— Paramhansa Yogananda

*I am free in Thy joy, and will rejoice forever
in Thy blissful presence.*

— Swami Kriyananda

(These two quotations are inscribed on the walls of Swami Kriyananda's Moksha Mandir)

In an instant, Sabella transported them to a magnificent garden, filled with thousands of tulips of every imaginable color, all in full bloom under pink-blossomed cherry trees. The tulips danced and swayed in a slight breeze. Pansies and other small flowers, alive with color, grew in abundance beneath the blooming tulips. The dozens of people walking about the gardens seemed intoxicated by the beauty surrounding them.

"Are we in the astral world now, Sabella?"

"No, but many who lived at this time felt that a visit to these gardens was as close as you could get to the astral plane while still on earth. These are the world-famous Crystal Hermitage Gardens at Ananda Village, in Northern California. The year is 317 Ascending Dwapara Yuga.

"The small building with the blue-tiled roof you see below us is the Moksha Mandir, and is the resting place of Swami Kriyananda's body. He departed this world in 313 Ascending Dwapara Yuga. Do you remember who he was, Bellina?"

"Yes, of course. He was a direct disciple of Paramhansa Yogananda, whose grave we just visited at Forest Lawn.

"However, this place seems very different, at least in its outward appearance. Yogananda's powerful and blessed presence was palpable at Forest Lawn, even there among all the other crypts in that dark, echo-filled mausoleum."

Enthusiastically, Bellina continued to describe what she saw and felt. "But here, there is so much more space, light, and harmony present all around us! This view, looking out across the forest-covered mountains and the river canyon far below is expansive. It is really quite amazing! Was this Swami Kriyananda's home?

"One of them. He had residences in two other Ananda communities, in Italia and India. He traveled extensively, sharing his Guru's teachings worldwide," Sabella explained. "However, this is where his loving heart longed to return at the close of his life."

Bellina enthused, "I would love to fly over these mountains and glide down to that sparkling river flowing far below us. What is its name? It seems very familiar, like it is calling me to come for a visit!"

Sabella smiled and replied, "At this time, it was called the Middle Fork of the Yuba River. Perhaps we can visit it later, if you like; but for now, I want you to join me inside the Moksha Mandir. That is the primary reason we have come here."

Bellina nodded her agreement and said, "First, let me ask this: What do the words *moksha* and *mandir* mean, Gigi? I know they are ancient Sanskrit words, but I've never really studied that language."

"*Moksha* means final liberation of one's soul from the bondage of continuous reincarnations. The soul's long journey has been completed victoriously, when it has merged back into God. Then, if the soul re-inhabits any loka—physical, astral, or causal—it is as a free soul, returning only by choice and by the will of God, to help beings there evolve spiritually."

"*Mandir* is defined as a consecrated temple or holy edifice used primarily for meditation and prayer," Sabella continued. "Come now, Bellina. You'll love being inside the *mandir*!"

Truer words were never spoken! Their forms were invisible to the few people silently meditating in the mandir. After some minutes of enjoying the glorious and expansive views through the floor-to-ceiling windows and feeling the great blessings and joy in the room, they joined the others in meditation.

At the front of the small golden, round room, there was a low, roped off rectangle, outlining the final resting place of the body of Swami Kriyananda, which was interred beneath the floor. Waves of great blessings poured into them, as they attuned to the essence of this great soul.

After many hours of blissful tranquility, they clearly heard a melodious, mental voice speaking to them. "Welcome, Sabella and Bellina. I know why you are here, and your mission brings me great joy. Some think me dead, and come here to honor or mourn me. I often try to tell them, 'I am not dead!' But if they cannot or will not listen, then I just quietly bless and help them in whatever ways I can."

Bellina, in her usual uninhibited way, said somewhat abruptly, "Hello, Swamiji. Are you here all the time?"

A rumbling chuckle made them both smile. He said, "No, I'm everywhere, all at once. That is one of the benefits of the state of *moksha*. However, I am often more fully here in certain ways, in order to help those who are disciples of my guru, Paramhansa Yogananda and followers of his path of Kriya Yoga.

"I know you both practice Kriya Yoga, so you understand. People often comment after meditating in this small *mandir*, near my physical remains, that they are able to meditate more easily and deeply here than any other place.

Bellina responded enthusiastically, "That is true! My meditation just now was effortless! This place seemed to meditate *for* me! This mandir feels infused with tremendous blessings!"

Sri Kriyananda said quietly, "Those are comments I hear often. I do my best to add energy to people's meditations. Sometimes, with God and Guru's help, I succeed, sometimes not. In any case, it is lovely here, isn't it?"

"A perfect tribute to a dear and great soul, Swamiji," Sabella said softly. "Thank you for greeting us and blessing our mission. Would it be alright with you if I asked you a question?"

"Certainly!" he said kindly.

"You said that you are here often, but wouldn't you rather spend your time in some more heavenly location?"

"Interesting you should ask that question, Bellina. Shortly before my departure from this earth, I wrote a simple note to many of my friends: 'From early childhood I've always felt that heaven was my true home. More and more, however, I am coming to realize that this world is, for one who wholeheartedly embraces God's will, no less heaven than anywhere else. Praise and calumny, success and failure, love and hatred—all these come to us as divine blessings. God alone matters! All else is a dream.'"

After hearing his inspiring words, the two women went deeper into meditation. The hours flew by. Many visitors came and left, completely unaware that they were sharing the mandir with people from another time and place.

Uplifted and blessed, Sabella and Bellina knelt for a while, close to Swami Kriyananda's body, while Sabella "AUM-ed" them from superconsciousness to consciousness.

Outside of the mandir, they stood for a moment, engrossed in the lovely twilight shadows and breezes, which played among the waving tulips and pink cherry blossoms.

"Shall we visit the river now, as you suggested earlier?" Sabella asked the beaming Bellina.

Knowing her answer, Sabella grasped Bellina's hand tightly in her own and they glided down the steep canyon to a tiny, sandy beach beside the boulder-strewn river. They were soon splashing about happily in the clear, blue-green water.

"Gigi, it is so picturesque and peaceful here and yet so familiar…wait a minute. Yuba River? Joyuba River? This place reminds me very much of the river-beach near your home. Is this the same river in a different yuga? No, it couldn't be, could it? Geography changes over the millennia, doesn't it?

"Bellina, we are only about 5000 years in the earth's past. The shifting about of continents, oceans, mountains, and rivers occurs on a scale of millions of years."

"Yes, of course you are right," Bellina said. "Nevertheless, I still want to know! Is this the same river?"

Sabella smiled, "Who knows? It might be. Dive into that pretty blue pool you see just a little ways upstream—the one with the bright rainbow trout swimming about and the orange-spotted leopard lilies and red and yellow monkey flowers leaning out over it from its banks. After you have done that and meditated for a little while, let me know what you think. Oh, and say hello to those bright red and blue dragonflies for me."

As Bellina followed her great-grandmother's suggestions, she was amazed to hear Swami Kriyananda's voice clearly speaking these words within her mind, "Behold this river, and think of it as the flow of your own thoughts. Affirm your mind's ability to adapt, like flowing water, to new situations and ideas."

"Thank you, Swamiji!" she thought back. "A wonderful suggestion for my life's path, and one which I will follow to the very best of my ability!"

The only reply was his radiant smile in her heart, accompanied by a faint echo of his distinctively beautiful singing voice:

> *There's joy in the heavens, a smile all around us, and melody sings everywhere. A heaven within us is ours for the finding...!* ©

Later, the full moon rose over the steeply forested canyon walls, filling the rippling river with points of shimmering, silver lights. Listening to the many frogs and crickets singing their happy nighttime songs, Bellina said to Sabella, "Thank you for this enlightening day of travel through time and space.

"By the way, I know that somehow, we *are* sitting beside the very same river I have known and loved all my life, because its sweet vibrations are identical!

"Although we have been visiting places devoted to death and burial today, I feel more alive and blessed than ever before in my whole life!"

CHAPTER TEN

To die, to sleep—to sleep, perchance to dream—ay, there's the rub,
For in this sleep of death what dreams may come....

— from *Hamlet,* by William Shakespeare

The next day, after meditation and a light breakfast, Sabella stunned her great-granddaughter with the question, "Bellina, are you ready to investigate what it feels like to die? We've both seen many forms of death in our time-travel experiences, but I'd like for us to observe and analyze the whole process in greater detail today."

"Wait, Gigi," Bellina thought with some trepidation, "Does this mean that one or both of us will die today?"

"Why not?" Sabella teased her light-heartedly. "Don't you remember how St. Paul revealed to his followers in the Judeo-Christian Bible, written thousands of years ago in Kali Yuga that he would 'die daily?' If he did it that long ago in a very dark age, then certainly we can do it now. I doubt that just one day's worth of dying will hurt us very much, don't you agree?"

"I always thought that St. Paul meant that he went deep in meditation, stopping his heartbeat and breath superconsciously, and then returning to ordinary consciousness. I didn't think he meant he was literally and permanently *dying!*"

"Yes, that's correct, Bellina. There *is* a difference in the way I am using the word 'dying.' I mean that I want us to experience a human's death process as realistically as possible, in order to understand what the death of the physical body feels like to a dying person. I plan for us to go through it as fully as we can. Nevertheless, I assure you that at the end of the day, you will still be more or less alive in your present form.

Sharp-minded Bellina asked, "More or less? What does *that* mean?"

Sabella laughed, "Bellina, today is not your day to leave your physical body. Please trust me. I've done this before."

"Well," Bellina mumbled, "I do trust you, Gigi. So, who *is* going to die today, while we observe and experience it, 'more or less firsthand?' Is it going to be anyone I know? I hope it is a stranger." Bellina said.

"Why do you hope that?" Sabella asked.

"Because...you know. I mean, if it's someone I know well...," Bellina paused, quite aware that she was revealing her lack of the important attitude of non-attachment.

If it was someone she did *not* know well, she thought she could be calmer and more objective about the whole process. Wasn't that the general idea, to study death, dying, and what happens after death, in the most objective and non-emotional way possible?

Sabella caught her thoughts immediately and asked gently, "Have you ever watched someone die, Bellina, and was there something about it that troubled you?"

Bellina always was amazed at her great grandmother's flawless intuition. "Yes, I did, quite some time ago. You are right. It was not a good experience for me or for my friend who died!"

"Why? What happened? Do you mind talking about it now?"

"Oh, Gigi! I was too young to process what happened. I guess Irissia's death did leave me with some emotional scars. I thought I had worked through it by now, but—well, maybe not."

"Sabella responded softly and compassionately, "Well then, dearest Bellina, let's take some time to try to understand what happened. Where were you and how old were you when this happened?"

"I was only fourteen years old and somewhat immature for my age. You probably remember how my mother and father always tried to shelter me from the world's unpleasantness."

"I do remember that I chided your parents often (especially your mother, who was my first grandchild), for being overly-protective of you and your brothers."

Bellina nodded and continued, "I was a student in the Halls of Wisdom. My best friend Irissia and I were very close—almost inseparable, for several years. One day, she became quite ill. Her health slowly faded over the course of the next six months.

"I visited her often, and weak as she was, we still laughed together and enjoyed each other's company immensely. I made up funny adventure stories and acted them out for her." Bellina smiled at the poignant, bittersweet memories.

"Although Treta Yuga has very few incurable illnesses, none of our best healers were able to save her life. I guess it was just her time to leave this world.

"Perhaps I was in denial, but I could not grasp what was really happening to Irissia. I am sure my parents did not know that her disease would be fatal, or they would not have let me spend so much time with her.

"One crisp autumn day, I was with her in her bedroom, when suddenly she began to choke and gasp for breath. I ran to her mother's quarters for help. Soon Irissia's room was filled with weeping, hysterical people.

"A healer was summoned. She did her best to get the situation under control, but she failed, both in saving Irissia's life and in calming down her family members.

"One sister in particular kept grabbing Irissia's frail form, actually shaking her and shouting wildly, 'Don't go, sister! You can't leave us. We love you too much to let you go! You can't go! Please, I beg you to stay. You are too young to die!'"

"There was complete chaos and confusion in the room. I do not think anyone cared or even noticed that I was there.

Naturally, I was horrified. The healer finally succeeded in calming Irissia's hysterical sister enough so that she quit shaking Irissia and yelling at her. Nevertheless, her sister remained sitting nearby, feebly attempting to stifle her loud sobs.

"I, too, was crying softly, as I watched Irissia's face contort in agony. I could see that she was struggling to breathe. Soon her face went slack, her eyes rolled up into her head, her mouth fell open, and she made a strange gurgling sound as she exhaled her final breath. I have learned since that this sound was called the 'death rattle.' What a terrible name for someone's last breath!

"I couldn't take it anymore and ran from her room, out of her house and into the nearby forest. I was shaken to my core in the face of my dear friend's death—a death I had witnessed in such a personal way, and for which I was completely unprepared.

"Later I told my parents what had happened, and they counselled me to put it completely out of my mind. 'Let it go! Don't think about it anymore!' they told me.

"I did try! Nevertheless, my first experience with death in this lifetime haunted me for many years.

"Finally, I took my troubles to my wisest teacher in the Halls of Wisdom. She comforted me, and we spent a long time discussing many things that she thought would help me understand death. I know she prayed for me also. Soon I began to let go of the anxiety I felt; and now I can remember, with joy, my close friendship with Irissia, un-shadowed by the horrors of her death.

"Since then, she has come to me twice in my dreams. Through these dreams, she assured me that she is very happy where she is and full of life and light. I know she was trying to comfort me, by letting me know of her continuing existence. I am convinced that we will meet again at some future time, perhaps in a beautiful astral loka.

"In fact, Sabella, I now fully expect that to happen! Is that a realistic expectation? And while we are on this subject, can the deceased really come to us in dreams?"

"They can and do, dear one. Irissia must love you deeply for her soul to visit you in your dreams. The always active and aware soul acts from its deepest convictions and highest desires—in this case, her loving connection to you. And yes, there is a more than excellent chance of a future reunion with your friend in an astral loka!"

Bellina smiled at that happy thought and said, "I never stopped feeling Irissia's love. She cares for me still, as I do for her. Death can never fully separate us." Bellina felt a tear roll down her cheek.

"Bellina, I will be frank with you. It was unfortunate that Irissia had to experience that degree of agitation at the time of her death. It was unnecessary and counterproductive for her relatives to carry on in that way. To be blunt about it, pure selfishness caused such outrageous outbursts of emotionally inappropriate behavior. Perhaps it was their desire for attention, through childishly insisting to those present to, '...look at me, look at me! I am sadder than anyone else is. Look at me! I am a caring person and need attention, too!'

"I'm truly sorry that you had to witness Irissia's joyless death scene, especially at such a tender and impressionable age. However, I am grateful that you were instructed and comforted, both by Irissia herself in your dreams, and through the wise words imparted by your teacher. I must have been away then, for I don't remember hearing anything about these events."

"Yes, Sabella. As I recall, you were gone for a very long time, visiting other planets. By the time I saw you again, I felt I was fine. I did not want to burden you with it. You were especially busy establishing all the new CP/AECS seminars and clinics during those years."

Sabella sighed and hugged Bellina. "Never too busy to offer you comfort and love. I do wish I had known then what you had gone through, and I am a bit miffed at your parents for not mentioning it to me. However, you are right. It was a time of non-stop activity for me. I am very sorry, dear one, for what you suffered.

"In any case, thank you for sharing your experience of Irissia's death. It will give us the context to understand better the death we are about to witness. But first, let me ask you, what bothered you most about the way Irissia died?"

"That's easy," Bellina said. "She needed a calm and peaceful atmosphere for her passing. Her relatives and loved ones did not serve her with their weeping and wailing. They should have sat quietly with her, praying and assuring her that God and the Great Ones were present there with her to assist her in her passage into the beautiful astral worlds. I know that chanting AUM in the right ear can help a dying person greatly. I first learned about this from Yogananda's teachings."

Sabella agreed, "You are right! Even in this advanced age of Ascending Treta Yuga, far too many people do not understand the many specific and powerful teachings about what occurs during the last moments of a person's life. They are not aware of the important aids available, both for the person dying and the people who are with them at the time.

Bellina thought this over for a moment and then said, "I remember a verse from the *Bhagavad Gita* which quotes Sri Krishna as saying, 'One who, at the hour of death, thinks only of me, enters unquestionably into my being.'

"That seems like straightforward guidance about the right way to die. Just think of God and you merge back into God, right?"

Sabella answered, "Unfortunately, it's not quite that easy, Bellina. It is true that people's final thoughts at death largely determine their after-death state. However, this does not mean that one can live any sort of life one pleases, then hastily summon up thoughts of God at the last moment of life and expect to leap over all hurdles of past karma and fly into the arms of God in perfect freedom. Many people hope by such a clever ploy to be able to live their lives ruled by lower desires, and then at the last moment of their lives think of God, call on God, and all will be forgiven, without effort on their parts.

"There is a story which illustrates this point. A rich thief who lived in India, having heard that anyone dying in the holy city of Varanasi would be freed automatically from all his sins, decided that this would be the best way of overcoming all his bad karma. Fearful of paying the price for his many sins, when he reached old age he had both legs cut off above the knees. Then, he settled down to die, determined never to leave that sacred city."

"That's a rather drastic solution," Bellina mused. "Did it work?"

"Patience, dear. The story will reveal what happened," Sabella went on. "One day someone riding by on horseback showed such an abysmal lack of horsemanship that his absence of skill raised gales of mockery in the former brigand.

'Why,' he boasted, 'even without my legs I could ride better than that!'

"He insisted that he be lifted up onto the saddle of the man's horse. As soon as he was seated firmly, the horse bolted. The city of Varanasi is bounded on one side by the Varuna River. Just as the horse crossed the river, it threw its rider, breaking the man's neck and killing him instantly.

"This story illustrates how one's thoughts at death cannot help but be influenced by the totality of one's life. Even were one to chant, 'Ram! Ram!' or 'God, God!' it would not mean that one's thoughts were immersed in the Divine. More than likely, there would be selfish thoughts present, such as, 'What favors shall I ask of God, when I soon reach his presence?'

"The deeper meaning of this story is that if, at death, one's whole consciousness is immersed in unconditional love for God, without any thought of ego-fulfillment or reward, then—and then only—will one merge in the Infinite. There must be no flicker of doubt, questioning, or worldly desires in one's mind or heart."

"The dominant thoughts that occupy one's mind while alive will be the same thoughts which predominate at the moment of death."

"So you see, in many ways, death is the most important moment of a person's whole life. It is 'final examination' time for the ending of that particular incarnation. And yet, one's life must be a righteous preparation for that exam."

Bellina sighed, "That sounds ominous! A final examination, like in school? What if you don't pass it? What if you fail miserably?"

"Answer your own question, Bellina! I'm sure you know what's true."

"Hm-m-m-m, well, pass or fail the exam, I think that death is not truly *final*, except for that one particular lifetime. If you have not lived a beneficial life (to yourself and others) or been aware of the primary purpose of living, then after death you simply rest unconsciously in an appropriate astral world. When your time of resting and rejuvenation is over, it's 'back to school again,' on a material planet encased in a new physical body!"

"What would it mean to pass your life's final examination?" Sabella asked.

"To *graduate* from the need for further human existence, of course," Bellina stated emphatically. "No more physical reincarnation needed—joy and happiness in the astral worlds, in heaven, for eternity, right?"

"No, although that's a common misunderstanding. The time that we spend between lifetimes, dwelling in the astral lokas, or heavens, is like a 'super-vacation.' It is a place of incredible beauty, harmonious and free from all strife. It is a perfect place for resting, healing and rejuvenation, readying and strengthening us for our next incarnation.

"However, because it is so peaceful, joyous and harmonious, without the suffering and pressures of a physical existence, we are not motivated to confront our karmic bonds and learn the necessary lessons quickly. So it is usually best to depart one's 'between-lives' respite as soon as possible, in order to reincarnate again on a material planet, in a physical body, which will spur you on to rapid spiritual progress. Do I have a clear understanding of this topic, Sabella?"

"In a way, what you are saying is true. Suffering, which is inextricably tied to occupying a physical body, is indeed an excellent incentive for one to find answers, to learn lessons, to work out all remaining karma, and to become free from suffering as quickly as possible," Sabella said.

"I must clarify, however," she went on, "that our soul's long journey through time and space is much more complicated than we could ever imagine. There are astral desires and causal karma, both of which can be dealt with much more easily in an astral or causal loka than on a material world like earth."

"Yes," Bellina agreed. "I am just beginning to understand that there are many more layers and dimensions of the afterlife than I had suspected."

"You have no idea!" Sabella laughed. "I would never presume to say that I was even *beginning* to grasp the intricacies, vastness, and complexity of the whole Cosmic Show with an inadequate tool like my little human mind. This is why we are focusing on longer, deeper meditations lately—to help expand our consciousness and intensify and enhance our abilities to embrace a reality that is infinitely vaster than our mundane, day-to-day experience.

"In any case, experiencing something firsthand is always better than merely talking about it, wouldn't you agree, Bellina?"

Bellina nodded in complete accord. With eyes twinkling, she asked, "So where are we going now, Gigi?"

CHAPTER ELEVEN

*When I die,
Look into mine eyes.
They will mutely say,
"I will be Thine always."*

— Paramhansa Yogananda, from *Cosmic Chants*, 1938

"We are going to visit an old friend of mine, whom you have never met. When I spoke with him recently, he told me that his time to depart this plane of existence is very near. Not only is he is not fearful, he is looking forward to his transition with eager anticipation.

"I asked him if you and I could be with him during his dying process. I explained the mission the High Council assigned us, to study death, dying, and the afterlife.

"He laughed when I petitioned him with my unusual request. Even though he is old, weak, and near death, he has maintained his healthy sense of humor.

"He answered me, saying, 'Sabella, I would be honored by your presence at my transition. It will be my joy to have your assistance at this crucial time, supporting me through your meditations, your prayers, and your enchanting and inspiring voice, singing and calling to God.

'Also, please do your best to keep my weepy, needy relatives away from me when my time comes. I do not want them holding me back, and I want to be able to take advantage of your and your great-granddaughter's presence and support. I hear she looks very much like you did, when you and I were together at school, all those years ago. I may be old and dying, but I can still appreciate having two lovely ladies with inspiring and lively spirits nearby!'"

"What is your friend's name, Gigi?" Bellina's eyes were soft with sympathy.

"His name is Loralon. He was a fellow student in the Halls of Wisdom, when Thomas and I were both young and very inexperienced. We were classmates during the time I told you about, when Simeon first introduced us to the art and science of time travel.

"Your great-grandfather, Thomas, never became friends with Loralon. Their conflicting personality types, or perhaps past karma, caused them to disagree quite often. Simeon worked hard to create harmony between them.

"Nevertheless, I liked Loralon. We got along well with each other, although I will admit, he could be annoying at times. Of course, I am sure he could say the same thing about me!

"As the years went by, I lost touch with him, but a few years ago, I heard that he had fallen ill. I have visited him several times since then. Yes, I am sad to see that he is near death, but he is happy with his life—I believe that he has very few regrets. Moreover, he is definitely ready to make his transition to the astral world, to enjoy a time of rest, recuperation, and a respite from his illness and the tests and trials of his present life."

Bellina wondered, "Does everyone need a time of rest after death? I mean, is dying always a hard thing to do?"

"Not always. The dying process, just like the living process, has infinite variations. Each is unique. Remember that many people, such as you and I, have experienced countless deaths and rebirths, encompassing a vast range of happy and horrible events, and everything in between.

"I sincerely believe that Loralon is an old soul, with no fear of death at all! Simeon taught all his students, clearly and carefully, that death is simply a process we all go through millions of lifetimes, until we are liberated forever from the cycles of reincarnation. That's why Loralon will be such an excellent candidate for us to observe." Sabella paused a moment, picking up Bellina's mental wish to discuss what it takes to achieve final liberation.

"Sorry, Bellina," she said, "that discussion will have to wait for another time. I received a mental message from Loralon just a few hours ago, saying that today is most likely his day to die. We must be on our way now, to be by his side when he makes his transition!"

Grasping Bellina's hand in her own, she transported them to a place on earth which had once been a country called Italia. Distinct governments, countries, boundaries, and different languages were non-existent in Treta Yuga, although some locations retained their same or similar ancient names.

They found themselves in a beautiful villa by the sea, in a large room with very high ceilings. The walls were transparent or open completely to admit the spicy sea breezes, and the ceiling contained numerous skylights with different colors of glass set with large prisms. The room was bathed in rainbow rays of light.

To enhance the vibrant effects of the rainbows, banks of flowers of every imaginable color and fragrance were displayed around the room. These were not cut flowers; rather they were flowers blooming on live plants, full of vibrating life force—so much so that there seemed to be a soft hum of energy, or even some kind of soft music, coming from the flowers.

Bellina knew immediately that it was Loralon resting in a large and luxurious bed, next to one of the transparent walls. He had his eyes closed and was breathing shallowly.

"What an incredibly beautiful place this is!" Bellina could not stifle her mental exclamation.

"Glad you like it!" Loralon's soft voice said. "Welcome Sabella and Bellina!"

Loralon's eyes fluttered open and he smiled at them in warm greeting. "You are just in time. I sensed you were coming and sent my troublesome relatives away on various errands, claiming that I needed to sleep. Ha! What do they know about the 'Big Sleep,' which I am approaching now?

"Sabella, it is wonderful to see you again! Bellina, you are, as I have heard, both beautiful and strikingly similar in appearance to Sabella when she and I were in school together. Thank you for being here with me for this important occasion.

"Forgive all the flowers—I realize that they are, perhaps, a bit excessive! However, you see, my family made a significant fortune in the flowering plant business. All my life, I loved plants and enjoyed nurturing and nourishing them, encouraging them to produce great masses of colorful, fragrant blossoms, such as these you see all around us. I suppose it's only fitting that some of my plant friends join me here at this important time."

As he looked at them, Bellina noticed that Loralon's smiling, radiant eyes were dark green, with tiny flecks of color in them—very much like the foliage of his plant friends. Although his eyes were beautiful, Bellina could see that they were slowly fading, as he withdrew his vision toward his inner eye.

"You are welcome here!" Loralon said. "Make yourself comfortable. I will be leaving soon, so you will not be waiting very long! For most people, the 'mystic summons' does not offer an exact timing. That would be the case for me, except that I cheated a little by inwardly asking Simeon to visit me.

"He came quietly last night, when I was alone and all was dark and quiet. What a thrill to see him again! He blessed me for my coming transition. It was a blissful occasion for me!

"Before Simeon left, he gave me a remarkable gift. He said that most people have to be considerably more spiritually advanced than I am to know the exact time of their departure from this world. Knowing that I had invited you to be at my side at this time, and wanting you to learn more, firsthand, about dying, he revealed to me the exact time of my death. He knew that your being present with me for my transition undoubtedly would help you with this aspect of your mission."

"...and because he loves you, Loralon—you know that! He never forgets any of his students." Sabella said quietly.

"Yes, Sabella. I do know that, and I am very grateful!

"My wife and many of my dearest loved ones have preceded me in death. Other relatives and friends will know soon enough that I have gone. So all is well. We are alone here, as I had hoped, and I am at peace with myself and with God." His mental words grew weaker and weaker.

"We are honored to be here at your side. What can we do for you now?" Sabella asked Loralon gently.

"Sabella, Bellina, come and sit here, on either side of me. Hold my hands and sing for me. That is all I want now. I will be gone very soon, slipping away into the land beyond my dreams. Pray for me...," Loralon finished his final words to them with a gentle sigh.

Following his requests, they sat on either side of him, and while each one of them held a hand, they began to sing to him softly:

In the land beyond my dreams,
Where no clouds come,
And golden dreams dwell,
I sit by life's well,
In the land beyond my dreams.

Sabella transmitted these words to Bellina only: "Although we will hold his hands, pray, and sing, as he has requested, I also want you to watch him closely. Sensitively and intuitively, tune into the physiological and psychological processes that he will go through, as he slips away from this material plane.

"Pay careful attention to the moment when his lungs are no longer able to inhale or exhale and his heart stops. It is at that time he will go through his life review."

Bellina was curious, "Will we also get to see Loralon's life review? How long will it take?"

"No, his life review is private—for his eyes only—at least while it is happening. Once he is in the astral planes, we can ask him to tell us more about it, and possibly even observe it later as a mind-movie, if he allows us.

"As for how long it will take, because there is no time and space in a superconscious event like a dying person's life review, to him and to us observing him it will seem to be almost instantaneous. We will talk more about this important part of a human being's dying process at a more appropriate time.

"When I know he has fully disconnected from his physical body, I will chant "AUM! AUM! AUM!" many times, in his right ear. Both you and I will bless him by anointing his heart and his spiritual eye with King Nakula's holy water. I brought it with me especially for this occasion. It comes from the Second Chakra Pyramid and has been blessed by Nakula himself.

"A few minutes after his life review is complete and he has fully disconnected from his physical body and this material plane, we will bless him in the ways I mentioned, pray for his smooth transition from this life into the appropriate astral loka, and then follow him to the astral plane.

"Loralon will not know that we are following him at that point. He will have more important things to focus on at that time. We do not want to distract him in any way!"

"Follow him into an astral loka?" Bellina's mental voice quavered slightly. "Are we going to die, too?"

"No, dear-heart, I thought you understood that we are only observing, not participating. Today is not our day to die! We will only pay a brief visit to an astral loka beyond this physical world—the one to which Loralon is going. His soul has been attracted to this particular astral world, because it is the one best suited to his present level of spiritual development.

"It will be an inspiring place to visit, for Loralon is a good man, and he made significant spiritual progress in this lifetime. You'll see what I mean soon enough."

CHAPTER TWELVE

*I may go far,
Farther than the stars,
But I will be Thine always.*

Paramhansa Yogananda, from *Cosmic Chants*, 1938

Much later, Bellina carefully recorded all that she had experienced observing Loralon's passing.

"Sabella asked me to watch her friend Loralon's physiological and psychological signs very closely as he died. This is what I perceived, as well as I can describe it:

"Sabella softly thought to me, 'Bellina, the process has begun.'

"I was glad she alerted me, even though I could clearly see what was happening. First, there was muscular paralysis and a withdrawal of the prana (life force) from the periphery of the body and from all the muscles and organs of his body, into his spine and chakras.

"His muscles and organs became inert, paralyzed by the departure of energy from the movement-making nerves in them. The paralysis moved quickly through his body, starting on the surface and moving towards his center. Energy was withdrawn from the feet, legs, hands, arms, abdomen (and all the organs therein) stomach, chest, lungs, neck and throat. Complete muscular relaxation, resulting from the gradual cessation of the transmission of sensations through Loralon's nerves, was obvious to me.

"His tactile nerves ceased to carry messages, and he lost his sense of touch. He could no longer feel the air moving across his body or even his body touching the bed.

"This is similar to how an arm or a leg can 'go to sleep'

temporarily, or how one can experience paralysis of part of their body from illness or injury. Loralon's whole body felt to him as though it had 'gone to sleep.' I perceived that he knew that he still had a body, but could not feel it or move any part of it.

"Loralon could no longer exercise control over any part of his body through his own will power. His body simply could no longer feel or do anything, just as a person with a paralyzed arm would not feel a severe burn to the limb.

"When this 'moving paralysis' reached Loralon's chest and lungs, I could see a slight expression of discomfort on his face. This, I knew was not true physical pain, but rather a mental struggle, giving him a brief feeling of suffocation, caused by his inability to bring another breath into his lungs. The struggle also awakened memories of the many deaths he had experienced in previous lifetimes. I was relieved that this part lasted only a few seconds.

"As brief as were Loralon's ineffective efforts to take another breath, I could not help but feel compassion and concern for him. I remembered a nightmare I had as a child, in which I experienced a frightening sense of asphyxiation. I smiled when I remembered how, when I finally struggled awake, I found my large tabby cat, Chew-Chew, sitting on my little chest, gazing lovingly into my eyes. No doubt, he wanted his breakfast, and soon!

"Sabella had explained to me that when a person's breath ceases completely, this dramatic shift of energy creates the sacred moments in which the soul experiences its life review: a holographic projection of every thought and action of his lifetime—good, bad, and neutral.

"This mental introspection appears as a series of rapidly moving life-tableaus. The life review process also helps determine the nature of a person's next incarnation, which will follow the astral world 'vacation' that is about to commence.

"I had the thought to tune in to what was happening in Loralon's mind, but remembered the private nature of this process. I did not interfere or eavesdrop in any way.

"When I realized that he had only enough physical energy for one more breath, I sensed he knew it also. I watched him let go and relax completely. He took a shallow breath, and then exhaled a long, slow breath, like a sweet, peaceful sigh, which caused a soft, rattling noise in his chest and throat. The breath did not return to his lungs after that exhalation.

"I then thought how most people think that life is predicated by breath, or the lack of it. The spiritually aware person, who has learned to slow or stop his or her breath at will using advanced meditation techniques, is bothered very little, or not at all, by the feeling of the cessation of breath at the time of death.

"Death is a lot like going to sleep. People don't fear that they will stop breathing and die when sleep overtakes them. In fact, falling asleep is often intensely enjoyable. At the time of death, the paralysis of the lungs may come as a slightly unpleasant surprise, but that part of the dying process is over so quickly as to be almost unnoticeable!"

A side-thought from Bellina: "In preparation for the mission, upon which Sabella and I have embarked, I have been rehearsing my own death, using certain yogic breathing techniques—especially the technique of *mantra* meditation called Hong-Sau. While practicing this technique with deep concentration, my breath rarely stopped completely. However, it often slowed down to the point that I felt as though I was barely breathing.

"When these close-to-breathless moments occurred—and how lovely and peaceful I felt at those times!—I inhaled very gently, and determined that after my next exhalation, I would not breathe (or think) again for as long as possible. Timing myself, I found that I could easily remain breathless and thoughtless for two minutes, or sometimes longer, with no discomfort or fear at all.

"At one point, I thought I had overdone it with this experiment and might be *unable* to inhale again. Of course, just having that thought made me take a breath, ending my experiment for that round.

"You can see from the details of my 'death rehearsal experiments,' that I was still using my brain to direct things. The physical brain does not function well without oxygen. Therefore, even one small thought was enough to force me to breathe again. I have learned so much from these experiments that I continue to perform them occasionally.

"I think everyone would benefit from experimenting for themselves in these ways. It is like having a dress rehearsal for the main event of your death, whenever that may come. It is a good idea to get comfortable with not breathing and to strive to release the fears you may still have about how that feels.

"I was pleased to see that during my experiments, I felt no anxiety at all. If God had called me to leave my physical body right then and there, in that calm, non-breathing state, I would be ready to go without hesitation!

"As another kind of mini-experiment, exhale and hold your breath out for 3 to 5 seconds. It is very easy to do—and remember, while you are not breathing, that this is *exactly* how long it will take you to leave your body at the time of your death! It feels like such a very short amount of time—amazing, really!

"Just before I began an experiment with slowing down my breath and rehearsing my death, I visualized releasing all the heartstrings, the likes, dislikes, habits, wants, needs, and attachments which tie me to delusion. I do understand, as everyone should, that letting go of the heart's desires is key to quieting the mind. I also did my very best to release the ego and all remaining sense of separateness from God and from all that is. I felt completely free. It was such a blissful feeling!

"Paramhansa Yogananda expressed this principle beautifully in a brief poem:

> *When this I,*
> *Shall die,*
> *Then will I know,*
> *Who am I.*

"Again I highly recommend that all sincere spiritual seekers have the courage to practice their own 'death rehearsal meditations' occasionally, for this can help you to be much calmer when the time comes for you to leave your physical body behind.

"I feel certain that it is important for us to surrender ourselves completely, by letting go of everything, including the breath and all awareness of our physical bodies, before we die. Then when we die, no letting go is required. Simply stated, we must learn to die before we die, so that when we actually die, there is nothing left to fear.

"I may be digressing here, but I am convinced that my suggestion can offer invaluable aid in helping people understand how it actually feels to die. Increased knowledge and experience should reduce anyone's fear of death!"

"Back to my description of Loralon's passing: I could see that his sensory nerves were shutting down in an orderly fashion. First, the senses of smell and taste ceased functioning. Next, Loralon's optical nerves stopped transmitting, and he became unable to see anything, at least anything in this physical world. Then, as previously described, the sense of touch and all feeling left the body, starting from the extremities and receding up into the head.

"At this point, Sabella placed her right index finger on his spiritual eye, exerting a little pressure. She softly whispered to him, 'Loralon, go into the inner astral light, which you see before you. I know you are seeing them now—the three tunnels of gold, indigo blue, and dazzling white light forming before your inner gaze.

'Go into and through the golden halo-like tunnel and know that what you are experiencing is your own life-force moving upward through your chakras and astral spine. Travel through that great golden tunnel into the astral world. Go with all our love, Loralon! Let go of this worn out body and brain. Let it all go!'

"Sabella sang softly into his right ear:

> *Go with love. May joyful blessings*
> *Speed you safely on your way.*
> *May God's light expand within you.*
> *May we be one in that light someday.* ©

"She then began chanting 'AUM, AUM, AUM, AUM, AUM...,' continuously into Loralon's right ear, for about three minutes.

"Sabella had explained to me that hearing is the last of the five senses to leave the consciousness of a dying person. This is why it is extremely important never to say anything negative in the presence of one who is passing.

"She told me that it is best either to say nothing, or if the person is brave and seems ready to die, he or she should be told, 'Cross the portals of this worrisome life into the vista of an everlastingly joyous life!'

"Otherwise, there should be only soothing sounds, such as one or more close friends chanting AUM, singing a devotional chant or sweet music, or a loved one offering words filled with unselfish love. The dying one should be encouraged to surrender and go peacefully into the Inner Light.

"When we could feel that the last of Loralon's physical senses had shut down completely, we released his hands and sat beside him in meditative silence, praying deeply for him.

"Such a glorious light suffused his sweet face. His jaw went slack, and his mouth fell open just a bit. His eyes relaxed completely, so that they appeared half-open and half-closed, as though he were looking inward and upward at the spiritual eye, as we do in meditation.

"Sabella then said to me softly, 'When the prana retires from the spine, brain, and finally from the medulla (the receptive pole of the sixth chakra), the heart stops and the dying process is complete. The soul is no longer encased in a physical body and is free to move into a different—and higher!—dimension.'

Still sheathed in its astral and causal encasements, the soul moves quickly into an appropriate astral loka. Not long after this, the physical body begins to change and decay rapidly, no longer of any use to the soul. The body is free to change back into its basic chemical elements. These elements are often referred to as "dust", as in the saying, "...it is from dust that we have come, and it is to dust that we must return."

The Great Ones tell us that death is the transition of the soul, where the nineteen elements of the astral body—intelligence, ego, feeling, mind (sense-consciousness), the five astral senses, the five pranas, and the five life forces— all depart from the physical body, to more fully occupy the astral and causal bodies.

Paramhansa Yogananda also tells us, in beautifully poetic ways, more about the nature of death, how it happens, and why it is not to be feared:

> *In death, the soul merely lays aside its fleshly garment. Death is only the switching off of the life force from the coil of flesh.*
>
> *Death is the change from the bodily automobile to the astral airplane of the luminous astral heavens.*
>
> *Death is the jumping of the grasshopper of life from the blade of one existence, to that of another.*
>
> *Death is a shortcut ordered by the pre-natal and post-natal karmas, to put out the bulbs of the senses, touch, smell, taste, sight and hearing, then heart, spine, and brain/medulla.*
>
> *Death is freedom from all physical pain and extreme tortures of flesh.*
>
> *Death is the consummation of life, at which time life wants to take its rest.*
>
> *Death is not painful; rather it brings the greatest happiness and freedom from all pain.*
>
> *A person may think that God is very cruel to take a loved one away from him or her through death, but remember that God is only saying, "All things I take away from you, that you may receive it again, more fully, from me."*

"'Bellina,' Sabella said to me calmly, 'now it is time for us to accompany Loralon's energetic essence, as he enters into an astral universe.'

"I asked her, 'How will we accomplish this, Gigi?'

"She answered, 'I will guide you carefully, as we follow Loralon through the golden tunnel of light through which he exited his body, and through which he entered into the astral realms.'

"I then ask her another question, 'Sabella, please explain to me more clearly what this golden tunnel is. I believe that I understand it is a part of the sixth chakra, and of what we refer to as the spiritual or third eye.'"

"'Yes, Bellina, you are correct. Light is one of the eight aspects of God. In meditation, we can begin to perceive the divine light of the spiritual eye, which appears in our foreheads. When the spiritual eye opens fully, many lokas of light, in the astral and causal worlds beyond this material world, are revealed to us.

'At the time of death, the golden halo around the spiritual eye elongates into a tunnel of golden light, leading us toward the great light of the astral universe, which we enter, to more fully inhabit our astral bodies. We leave behind the lifeless and useless physical body—now but a shell, soon to become only dust.

'Although it is rare, if a person is sufficiently spiritually advanced, they can enter a higher causal plane of existence, bypassing the astral realms. When this occurs, the blueish-purple field in the spiritual eye elongates to become a tunnel of indigo light, revealing, then delivering this person into oneness with, the light of the causal universe.

'Finally, when we achieve the deepest state of meditation called *samadhi*, or superconscious union with God, the whole spiritual eye is perceived clearly with its true shapes and colors, and we behold within it a five-pointed, silvery-white star of light, with the peak at the top.

'This image represents the final merging of the soul into

oneness with God. If at death, or at any other time, we are able to enter that star-shaped, third and final tunnel of light, then we are free forever, and all journeys are over. This is not death or even life after death. It is an ever-new, never-ending blissful state of immortality. It is the eventual destiny of everyone."

'Paramhansa Yogananda said that when the Bible states that we are made in the image of God, it is this star-like form that is the template for our physical bodies. If we stand upright, with our arms outstretched, our legs apart, and our heads uplifted, we physically *resemble* a five-pointed star. Thus, even our human bodies hint at our ultimate destiny—beyond life, death, and after-life experiences, in perfect freedom and oneness.

'Finally Bellina, let me remind you that we only need to be respectful and temporary observers of Loralon's passage from his body through the golden tunnel of his spiritual eye, and into the astral universe. We, ourselves, are not actually dying at this time. Are you ready, dear one?'"

"I assured her by saying, 'I am awake and ready, dearest Gigi!'

"'Then put all your attention at your spiritual eye, and off we go!'"

CHAPTER THIRTEEN

*Flowers and skies, and beautiful blossoming scenery
In the gardens of heaven—
They are but suggestions of divinity.
I enjoy them—I revel in them!
But after they remind me of Him,
These glorious messengers vanish,
And the beauty of my own,
Beloved infinity enthralls me.*

— Paramhansa Yogananda, *Whispers from Eternity*

The two women found themselves with radiant bodies of light, speeding through a glorious tunnel of golden light.

Bellina had often seen the spiritual eye in her meditations, but to be moving rapidly through its blazing golden tunnel of light—this was a new and thrilling experience—indescribable, exhilarating, blissful!

After what seemed like a short time, they emerged into a beautiful garden, more magnificent than Bellina could have imagined any place could be.

There were plants, birds, trees, sky, grass, and animals all around them, peaceful and apparently happy to see them. The whole scene shimmered—for everything was completely suffused with light! This ethereal setting was colorfully transparent, with light radiating into and through everything from an astral sun, brightly illuminating the whole scene with a heavenly radiance.

A brilliant light emanated from the inside to the outside of everything they could see around them, sending a bright glow throughout the heavenly gardens. Although it was amazing to perceive, at the same time it felt very familiar—a memory that this is the way things really *should* appear!

Bellina looked at Sabella and intuitively recognized her energy pattern, even though her body was different—made of light rays radiating from a heavenly inner light.

"My body must be made of light, just like hers," she thought, and lifted an arm to verify this incredible reality. Sure enough, it also was a shining pattern of light-energy, both visible to her and ethereal at the same time. She wondered if she could touch or lift something, if she tried.

"Go ahead," Sabella suggested, easily reading Bellina's thoughts.

Bellina floated over to an orchid hanging from a truly exquisite tree. The flowers of the orchid had an indescribably pleasant fragrance, and it seemed to be humming a sweet melody.

Bellina tried to touch the flower, but her hand passed right through it.

"I guess my light body is too insubstantial to touch the flower's light body. Things are very different here." Bellina was confused.

"Try asking its permission," Sabella suggested.

Bellina, feeling a little foolish, did as Gigi suggested. "O beautiful flower, like no other I've ever seen, may I touch you?"

"Thanks for asking," came a soft, melodious voice in reply. "I'm not sure why you would want to do that, but you seem to be a friendly entity. I will solidify myself a bit more, just for a short time, to make it possible for you to touch me. Remember, you will have to do the same with your own body. You must be new here!"

Bellina replied politely, "We are visitors, passing through briefly. Thank you for satisfying my curiosity. I will try to do as you suggest."

She sent a mental command to her arm and hand asking them to take on more substance, at least long enough for her to be able to touch and feel the flower's colorful petals. It worked! On her fingertips, she felt a sensation like the finest lush and fragrant velvet.

"I can both touch *and* smell with my fingers," Bellina exclaimed. "Remarkable!"

"And see with your ears, taste with your eyes, and so on. Astral senses, unlike the more familiar physical ones, can change or share their functions easily," Sabella reminded Bellina.

Sabella thoroughly enjoyed her curious great-granddaughter's interaction with the flower. "Bellina, we must not linger here much longer. Say goodbye to your new friend and come along with me."

"Goodbye, Matilda," Bellina smiled at the flower. "Thank you again, and I hope to visit you another day."

"How did you know my name?" the flower asked.

"I'm not sure! You just seem like a Matilda to me. My name is Bellina. It has been my great joy to meet, touch, see, smell, and speak with you."

"And you also, Bellina. Until we meet again...!" Matilda sang.

Off they flew, in the beautiful light bodies they now inhabited, trailing multi-colored sparkles of light behind them.

Their destination was a small pavilion dedicated to healing and revitalizing the energy bodies of those souls who had recently arrived from earth, helping them acclimate to their new home.

As they drew closer, they could see a great kaleidoscope of large astral butterflies fluttering all around, both outside and inside of the pavilion, their iridescent blue, gold, and silver wings catching the magical light of the astral sun. As they drew closer, one especially beautiful butterfly landed on Bellina's shoulder and whispered into her ear, "Follow me! Follow me!"

They soon realized that the butterfly-covered structure was

not a physical building at all. There were no walls, doors, or windows. It was made of sound vibrations and light rays; and it seemed to emit a constant low AUM sound.

Upon entering, Sabella and Bellina saw Loralon's astral form, lying on a high platform the size of his body. He was covered in a shimmering emerald green cloth. Golden light rays beamed down onto his light-body from a source above.

Beside him stood a being of light, who Bellina assumed to be a healing angel. The overwhelming radiance of this brightly beautiful being was so intense that, at first, Bellina's eyes ached to look directly at him (or her). Bellina could not tell the being's gender, if such beings even *have* a gender.

"Welcome Sabella and Bellina. My name is Ariella, and I know why you are here. Loralon will be in this healing pavilion for a while, resting and rejuvenating his energy body. When he arrived in this astral loka, many old friends and loved ones, including Simeon, were here to greet him.

"Loralon explained to me that the two of you, as visitors from Earth on a special mission to the astral realms, would be following along behind Loralon to visit him here. I am glad to assist you in any way that I can."

Bellina decided, from the vibrations she was feeling from Ariella, that Ariella must be at least somewhat more feminine than masculine. She also sensed intuitively that Ariella was *not* an angel. This made her want to meet a real angel, all the more.

Bellina sensed that Ariella was a human who was inhabiting an astral body and who was working through some karma by helping others adjust to this congenial place—a place so *very* different from earth. It seemed easiest to relate to her as an ascended female human being, so henceforth Bellina thought of Ariella in that way. Neither Ariella nor Sabella made any comments on the subject, seeming content with Bellina's assumption.

Ariella continued, "While the reunion was a gloriously blessed occasion for Loralon, it also took a great amount of energy. He has been through a lot. Consider the very recent death of his physical body after a lengthy illness on earth, the realizations that accompany one's life review, and the reunion and the intensity of the joyful feelings of oneness with all his loved ones, who were there to meet him.... You surely can understand how such an intense series of events would be overwhelming to almost anyone in the throes of the transition from the material world to an ethereal realm like this one.

"After the joyful reunion had gone on for a while, I ended it and brought him here for a prana recharging session. By that time, his aura was significantly depleted; but now his energy is being restored, and he will be ready to talk with you soon."

"Ariella, it is lovely to meet you," Bellina spoke inwardly and as quietly as possible, in order to not disturb Loralon's healing session. "May I ask the name of this loka?"

"Its name is Janaloka, and it is one of the countless planets in this section of the immeasurable astral universe. While it may not be the most spiritually refined of the astral heavens, it is a truly lovely place, especially for a spiritually inclined soul like Loralon.

"Janaloka is a world where souls retreat and rest between physical incarnations. Loralon has the advantage of having meditated throughout his life on earth. The garden-like setting will appeal to him and give him great comfort and joy, considering his sensitive attunement to flowers and plants during his recent life on earth.

"How long do most people stay in this loka?" Bellina asked.

"It varies. Perhaps one hundred to five hundred earth-years. Time is different here, as you soon may notice. In any case, souls dwell here as long as their karma dictates—long enough to rest, heal, and prepare themselves for their next physical incarnation, whether on earth or another planet in the material cosmos. Excuse me now," Ariella said. "I must attend to our friend, Loralon."

Loralon was awakening slowly. Bellina admired his new body

of light, which was every bit as beautiful as the astral bodies Ariella, Sabella, and she inhabited. It was easy to tell that it was Loralon, even though he looked much healthier, younger, stronger, and more handsome than he had, when she met him back in Italia. Bellina was impressed with the transformation and was a bit surprised that she so easily recognized him, because, unlike Sabella, she had never seen him when he was younger.

Ariella, hearing Bellina's thoughts, explained, "Every soul has unique energy and thought patterns, with an energetic signature, if you will, unlike any other pattern in creation. Most souls entering an astral loka, like this one, choose to dwell in a body that looks like a younger, more vibrant version of the physical body they most recently left behind.

"In the astral realms, beings can choose how they appear. However, whatever appearance they choose to have (Loralon might decide to change the way he looks, later—that will be his decision to make), they will, like all souls, maintain their unique and easily recognizable energy pattern.

"Loralon," Ariella addressed him in soft, sweet tones, "You look wonderful and fully refreshed after your time of rest and rejuvenation here. How are you feeling?"

Loralon lay still for a few minutes. His spiritual eye was wide open, while his physical eyes were half closed. He trembled slightly, a bit disoriented. Soon, however, he was able to focus, emitting peaceful, contented vibrations. His energy-body was beautiful to behold, comprised of swirling fields of brilliant, shifting colors.

As he gazed at Ariella, they seemed to be communicating privately. Then he looked carefully at Sabella and Bellina and said, "Yes, it is perfectly fine for them to be here with me, for they are dear friends of mine. I must admit, I am not sure how they are *able* to be here with me. I have a vague memory of Sabella saying that they'd be coming along behind me to explore this astral loka. I guess she was right, for here they are!"

He paused a moment to reflect, then said softly to Sabella, "I will never forget the many special ways that you and Bellina helped me at the time of my passing from the earth to this plane. Thank you!" He bowed gratefully and gracefully to both of them. He joyfully smiled at Ariella. It obviously pleased her that he was adjusting so rapidly to life on Janaloka."

Sabella said, "Loralon, a person's life review is a very private event, so we did not observe or intrude in any way. However, now that you have completed the review of your most recent life, for purposes of our investigation into the stages of death and dying, we are asking a favor of you and Ariella. Would you both feel comfortable having us share the experience of what you saw and learned in your most recent life review?"

"I don't mind at all, as long as I don't have to see it all again, myself!" Loralon seemed to be regaining some of his characteristically sardonic nature.

"That lifetime is over for me! Many things happened—some good and some not so good. It was what it was, and I learned many very important lessons from it. Nevertheless, for now, I am very happy to have completed that lifetime and to be in this beautiful place with family, old friends, and new friends, like Ariella.

"There were some parts of my life, which were..., well, let's just say, I'm not perfect yet! However, you are dear friends and I know you will not judge me for my mistakes. As far as I am concerned, please carry on as you want or need to do. Ariella, is this request also acceptable to you?"

"It is an unusual request, Loralon, but since you are comfortable with their sharing your intimate personal experiences, I am glad to help Sabella with what she has requested. Please rest here a little longer, and I will see to their needs. When I return with them, we will all take an extended tour of Janaloka."

Loralon seemed happy with these plans. He reclined back onto the comfortable platform, gave a contented sigh, and closed all three eyes in anticipation of another period of rest and energetic recharging.

Soon a pink and green mist surrounded him, in addition to the golden light, which was once again beaming down on him. Ariella motioned for Bellina and Sabella to leave the pavilion quietly.

CHAPTER FOURTEEN

What lies behind us and what lies before us are small matters compared to what lies within us.

— Henry Stanley Haskins

Sabella and Bellina followed Ariella out of the pavilion, which was still covered with shimmering butterflies, into the astonishingly beautiful gardens around it. Bellina was happy that her same butterfly friend (or at least she thought it was the same one) once again lit upon her shoulder and crooned a lovely little tune right into her astral ear.

Ariella smiled and transmitted a private thought to Sabella, "Bellina makes friends easily, doesn't she?"

"Indeed she does," Sabella agreed, joyfully watching her great-granddaughter flitting along beside them, looking very much like an astral butterfly herself.

After a few minutes, they arrived at a new, fascinating part of the gardens. They found themselves in a high-walled canyon with cliffs completely covered with green vines and tropical flowers, over which flowed a wide waterfall of rainbow lights.

The thunderous roar caused Bellina's butterfly friend to wink out of sight, but not before saying to her, "I hope to see you again later, but this place is just too intense for me—too noisy and powerful! Bye for now!"

Bellina understood completely. The waterfall's roar was deafening. This was unlike any waterfall she had ever seen, for it was not made entirely of water! Rather, it appeared to be composed of colorful light rays mixed in among the bright cascades of falling water. Every ray of light was composed of a rainbow of colors, showering everything around them with prisms of energy and a very large field of rainbow-colored mist.

The waterfall roared like AUM, which she often heard in meditation. She also could hear light strains of music, weaving its way through the rainbows, water, and mist. The music resembled the ethereal tune that her little butterfly friend had hummed to her, but magnified to an almost overwhelming volume, causing her whole body to resonate with its deep vibrations.

"Ah-h-h-h! How beautiful it is here!" Bellina said with pleasure. "Ariella, where are we? What is this amazing place?"

"I thought you might like it here, Bellina," Ariella said. "This waterfall is called the 'Veil of Life and Death.' The waterfall devas who inhabit these falls will allow us to use the mist as a screen upon which we may observe a holographic light projection of Loralon's recent life review."

Sabella added, "We've talked about how at death an overview of one's entire life flashes before his or her eyes. Things that seemed important when they occurred may be cognized during the life review as being quite insignificant. Conversely, things that seemed trivial at the time may be recognized now as having great significance for the person. All these things are beheld now as they *truly* were—whether good, bad, or insignificant—rather than how they may have seemed at the time they happened."

Ariella continued, "Ordinarily, a person's life review is private, or at least not open for general observation. It was very noble and selfless of Loralon to agree to Sabella's unusual request to allow us to observe his life review."

"We might also call what we are about to see: *The Life of Loralon: A Full-Length Feature Presentation, Complete and Uncensored*," Ariella said with a smile.

Bellina strove to maintain her composure and not giggle at Ariella's little joke. She asked, "Ariella, how long will the life review last? I think Loralon lived to be over 300 earth-years old...."

"Excuse me for interrupting you, Bellina. I should have mentioned that the whole presentation will seem to us to take about four seconds within our present perceptions of time, which is also how long it took Loralon to experience it. In one sense, it is like being in a realm of timelessness; but more accurately, it is a time-compression event.

"Life reviews are complete in every detail, just as even a small part of a hologram contains the whole. *Absolutely nothing* is omitted, from Loralon's first breath to his last breath of that lifetime. All the emotions generated by life events, the repercussions extending outward to others, the feelings of everyone involved in these events, what happened because of them, and the way these actions and emotions affected others, are there in plain sight, with nothing omitted—no pain, guilt, joy, sadness, pleasure, passion, or violence.

A life review offers us important learning opportunities. The great lessons we learn from it help to determine the major events and themes of our next lifetime.

Ariella said, "Please gaze carefully into the mists of the waterfall. Also, concentrate and focus at your spiritual eye. Look into and through it, and thus, into and through the mists of the Veil of Life and Death."

Bellina and Sabella did as they were instructed. The mists immediately parted like a curtain, revealing a tiny fetus swimming in his mother's warm, dark womb. Soon the baby boy emerged from his mother's body and was being held with great love in her arms.

"That baby is Loralon!" Bellina exclaimed. "His energy pattern is just the same when he was a baby as it was as an old man, when we watched him die and then awaken here in Janaloka."

"That is right," Ariella said. "A soul's energy patterns are easily recognizable, no matter what form the soul inhabits.

"Loralon just took the first breath of this lifetime on planet earth. Watch what happens now."

The little baby Loralon opened his big blue eyes and looked around, trying to focus and understand where he was and what he was seeing. Incredulously, he thought, "Oh, good heavens, where am I? I'm obviously not in heaven any more, am I?"

No one present seemed to be able to hear his completely reasonable question, for he had not yet learned to communicate well, either with his vocal cords or through thought transmission. He screamed stridently in frustration.

He waved his tiny arms and legs about wildly. His diminutive body felt alien to him—fundamentally different from the freedom and "lightness of being" he was used to in the astral loka from which he had just departed. Even floating around in the darkness of his mother's womb was much better than *this*! His body was not responding well at all to his wishes; it felt awkward and dense. He felt extremely disoriented, sad, and hungry, too!

Sabella commented to Bellina, "Remember when I told you why babies cry when they are born into a physical body? You can see what a dismaying shock it was for Loralon to find himself banished from an astral loka and from his light and beautiful energy body, only to find himself confined to this uncontrollable little bundle of matter. It would make anyone cry, don't you think?"

Bellina agreed completely, "And to contemplate that we have to go through this process millions of times! What a compelling motivation for us to find freedom from the endless, monotonous imposition of reincarnation."

Bellina smiled, remembering an old cartoon she had seen during her school days. There was a crowd of people holding up protest signs. The first one said, "Don't make the same mistakes twice!" The second one demanded, "Say NO to reincarnation!" This cartoon made a lot more sense to her now!

The red-faced baby Loralon continued to wail, attempting to communicate his extreme discontent to anyone willing to listen. Bellina thought sympathetically, "Oh, look at poor little baby Loralon! He is so sweet, cuddly, and cute, but in desperate need of comforting! His mother certainly loves him, I can sense that—but she obviously doesn't understand the true reason behind his present frustration!"

Then she recalled that she had just seen this same soul as a sick and dying elderly man, gasping for breath, passing from the physical to the astral realm. This memory helped to put things into perspective, as she observed the beginning of Loralon's life-movie.

A nurse came to take the baby from his mother's arms, so that she could get some much-needed rest. Baby Loralon continued to wail, expressing his indignation and discomfort, much to Bellina's dismay.

The "poor little thing" grew up quickly, right before their eyes. Bellina began to understand the process of life review, watching the amazing way Loralon's whole life actually was compressed into just a few seconds.

She observed that in his life there had been times of great sadness, as well as times of great joy—and everything in between. He grieved over committing grave errors of judgement, balanced by rejoicing in his successes. His life certainly was not what one would call an easy life. He had faced many extremely difficult challenges.

Observing this, Bellina remembered Yogananda often said, "An easy life is not a victorious life!"

They watched Loralon's years in the Halls of Wisdom, with Simeon and his other teachers instructing him in many important subjects, especially the most important one: the meaning and purpose of life.

They watched his wedding day and saw his charming new life-linked sweetheart smiling up at him with deep love and affection in her beautiful grey eyes. They saw her leave her body many years before Loralon and felt his grief and loneliness caused by her passing and of a life without her by his side. Their three children grew up quickly and were soon living their own, independent lives.

He spent most of his adult life successfully guiding the family flower and plant business in Italia. Because of his training as a student, he was committed to meditating as often as possible, but his busy adult life often took precedence over spiritual priorities. Nevertheless, Loralon justified this by clinging to the hope that someday he would have time to meditate longer and more deeply. Unfortunately, that time never came for him.

Loralon's life movie ended and the waterfall closed its misty curtain. Ariella explained to Bellina that Loralon's experience of his life review occurred in a moment outside of time and seemed to occur almost instantaneously. He had relived it all, vividly, completely, with all events seeming to occur simultaneously, in that mysterious sense of compressed time.

When people try to describe what they remember of a life review event, they often say, "My whole life flashed before my eyes in just an instant."

You could see that Loralon was able to look at the life he had just lived quite objectively. He clearly saw the ways he failed to measure up to his highest potential, and resolved to invest more attention and energy into his spiritual life in his next incarnation.

Sabella said to Bellina, "Did you notice that Loralon had the wisdom to refrain from judging himself for his shortcomings? In fact, *no* one judged him—not Ariella, who was beside him as his friend and guide and especially neither God nor the Great Ones. All of these beings of wisdom love him unconditionally, for they clearly realize that he is part of them and a part of all that is. This was a high quality life review! I give it five stars!"

Bellina really did not understand what Sabella meant when she said that she was giving Loralon's life review "five stars," but because Ariella and Sabella both laughed delightedly at this remark, she joined them in laughter. She began to get the general idea that Sabella was "rating" Loralon's life review by some sort of antiquated cinematic rating system.

Bellina said thoughtfully, "Ariella, Loralon's life review happened so quickly, I fear that I may have missed something. Is it possible to view it again?"

Ariella replied, "No, sorry, Bellina. Once is plenty, and

whether you are conscious of it or not, you absorbed all the vibrations you need to know about life reviews. Don't you agree Sabella?"

"Yes, absolutely," Sabella said softly.

Bellina was stubborn and not about to be denied. She protested, "But Loralon had a long and eventful life, even by Treta Yuga standards. That's a lot of years to compress into just a few seconds!"

Ariella replied patiently, "That's just the nature of life reviews. They are all over quickly, with no judgment or guilt, just a deeper and more complete understanding of how well the person succeeded in learning that lifetime's most important lessons. It is out of this deeper understanding that an appropriate plan is formulated for the person's next incarnation.

"Every life review is an important and necessary step in the soul's evolution. Contrary to what you might think, it is deeply comforting to the one whose life is being reviewed. Most often, they feel lighter and freer after it is over, and are able to let go of the experiences of that lifetime and enjoy the wonders and beauty of the astral world in peace."

However, I am sad to say that some people are not ready to release all their guilt, pain, and, most especially, their material desires. They carry these things around with them like psychic millstones hanging around their necks. These negative energetic burdens distract them from enjoying life amidst the heavenly beauty of the ethereal realms. They even carry these feelings and emotions when reincarnating. Naturally all this psychic baggage has an extremely detrimental effect on their next lifetimes."

"How long will Loralon reside in this particular loka, and what is generating the need for him to reincarnate on earth again?"

"Bellina!" Sabella said firmly. "You saw his life review. Did you not sense his unfulfilled desires, needs, and negative thought patterns?"

"Certainly, I sensed all those things, but I'm just wondering how the timing of one's rebirth is determined. Do small mistakes in your life force you to abandon heaven, only to reincarnate on earth sooner than you would have otherwise?"

Ariella stepped in to say to Bellina, "I can't answer your question specifically. The timing of reincarnation is influenced by many factors, primarily the weight of a soul's unresolved karma. The past karma of many lives is so complicated and convoluted that the Buddha once said that contemplating the intricacies of karma could be enough to unhinge one's mind!

"The length of stay in the astral worlds varies greatly from soul to soul. Some people, with an intense desire to work out their karma, return quickly to a material world. Or they are not yet capable of fully appreciating the finer points of subtler realms, and want the comforting heaviness of a material body and environment around them again."

"That is hard to imagine!" Bellina mused. "It is surpassingly beautiful and peaceful here. Everything and everyone is filled with joy, and everything glows with an inner light. How could anyone *not* enjoy it and want to stay as long as possible?"

"It would seem that way, wouldn't it, Bellina? However, the beauty here is highly refined. Souls who are not yet sensitive to its subtleties quickly become bored. Their desires draw them back to the excitement and down-to-earth feelings of what are often called the pleasures of the world. These desires could be for things as simple as a cigarette to smoke or a thick slab of cooked cow to eat."

"That sounds completely gross!" thought Bellina.

Ariella only smiled and changed the subject, "So far, you've only seen a small part of this delightful astral realm. Shall we return to Loralon and see if he is ready for the grand tour? I suspect he might want to wait until he is rested and more energetic."

Although Bellina and Sabella were enthusiastic about the tour, Ariella was correct in her assessment of Loralon's condition. He needed more time in the healing pavilion and assured them that he was enjoying himself immensely there.

Ariella placed her assistant in charge of Loralon's care while they were away. Her assistant was a tiny creature with golden wings, who, in a quiet voice shyly introduced herself to them. She fluttered her graceful wings and said, "Hello, earthlings. I am Peachie-tree from Peachie-loka. So blissful to meet you!"

"She's got to be kidding!" thought Bellina, causing Peachie-tree's smiling little face to blush a darker peach color.

Ariella replied, "That really is her name and where she is from, Bellina. Do not underestimate her because of her size and appearance. She is a gifted healer and will take excellent care of Loralon, while we take our tour of Janaloka. He can have his own special tour when he is ready. Come now, we should be on our way."

CHAPTER FIFTEEN

"O bird of paradise! Hop into My plane of omnipresence!
Fold now thy fluttering wings and ride with Me peacefully,
anywhere,
Everywhere in thine ethereal home!"

— *Whispers from Eternity*, 2008 edition, edited by Swami Kriyananda

For the next three glorious days, Ariella showed Sabella and Bellina as much of the wonders of this loka as time allowed. Janaloka is an astral planet, very similar to the one Paramhansa Yogananda described in his *Autobiography of a Yogi* in the chapter called, "The Resurrection of Sri Yukteswar."

Ariella began their tour by explaining, "We will only have time to visit certain parts of Janaloka on this expedition. Remember, Janaloka is only one of countless astral planets, teeming with astral beings. The inhabitants travel from one planet to another using masses of light to move faster than is possible when moving through the material universe."

Ariella paused to explain a little more about the entire astral cosmos. "The astral universe is populated with countless lokas, some like Janaloka, others very different from it. Astral lokas are formed by various subtle vibrations of light, energy, sound, and color. The whole astral cosmos is hundreds of times larger than the material cosmos. The entire physical universe hangs like a little solid basket under the vast luminous balloon of the astral sphere.

"Astral planets have astral suns and moons, more radiant and beautiful than their physical counterparts. These luminaries resemble the aurora borealis—the sunny ethereal aurora being more dazzling than the mild-rayed moon-like aurora. Days and nights are longer than those on earth."

As they continued the tour, it became apparent that Janaloka, in addition to all its amazing beauty, was clean, pure, and orderly. The earthly blemishes, such as wastelands, desserts, weeds, bacteria, diseases, biting insects, and poisonous snakes were wonderfully absent.

Ariella explained to them that, unlike the varying weather and seasons of the earth, typically astral lokas maintain the even temperature of an eternal spring. This perfect clime was occasionally punctuated by bright, but not cold, snow and rain, consisting of soft, soothing, radiating multi-colored lights. Janaloka teemed with opal lakes, vast shining seas, and rainbow rivers—all beautiful beyond description!

Bellina found it difficult to absorb all she was seeing, "It is all so peaceful, so lovely, so...unearthly and indescribable! Sabella, how will we ever be able to clearly communicate the wonders of this amazing place to the people on earth, once we return?"

"We'll just do our best, dearest."

Ariella continued, "The more ordinary astral planets, such as Janaloka, have millions of inhabitants who have recently come from a physical incarnation on the earth or a similar planet.

"In other astral lokas, you will find worlds which are predominantly inhabited by fairies, mermaids, fishes, animals, goblins, gnomes, demigods, and spirits, all residing on different planets in accordance with spiritual qualifications and karmic needs. However, as you will see, a few of these entities also live or visit here on Janaloka.

"The astral cosmos is very orderly. Various vibratory regions are provided for different levels of souls. Beneficent souls can travel about freely, but the ignorant and harmful beings are confined to certain regions. In the same way that human beings live on the surface of the earth, worms inside the soil, fish in water, and birds in air, so astral beings of different vibrations are assigned a suitable vibratory environment.

"As you see all around you on Janaloka, everything is shining and beautiful. The astral cosmos is typically closer to a state of Divine perfection than the physical universe. Every astral object is manifested primarily by the will of God, but more highly developed astral beings possess the power to modify and enhance the grace and form of God's creation. God has given all his dharmic children in these realms the freedom and privilege to change or improve their environment at will!

"What fun they must have, being able to modify their environment so effortlessly!" Bellina exclaimed.

Ariella and Sabella looked at each other knowingly. Sabella said, "Yes, it is fun for a while, especially for new arrivals, but...soon, the wiser ones learn to put their energy into spiritual pursuits instead."

Sabella was pleased to see that Bellina easily understood her meaning.

Ariella went on to explain, "The earth is rife with misery, warfare and murder, but most astral realms know only peace, harmony, and equality. Everything is quite flexible and can change form easily. Even flowers, fish, or animals can metamorphose themselves, for a time, into people. Astral beings are free to assume any form they choose and easily commune together. An astral tree can be asked to produce a mango or any other desired fruit, flower, or indeed, any object.

"Oh, can we do that now?" Bellina cried. "I'd love to talk, or perhaps even fly, with an astral eagle. And it would be heavenly to savor an astral mango! It makes me hungry just to think about it! Can we have an astral picnic soon—and what can we have to eat? I mean, what do beings here eat?"

Ariella smiled. Bellina's enthusiasm was contagious. "Luminous fruits and vegetables grow in abundance here in the soil. If they wish, inhabitants consume fruits and vegetables and drink nectar flowing from glorious fountains of light or directly from their source, astral brooks and rivers.

"Just as invisible images of those on earth can be perceived in the ether, viewed as a mental movie, then dismissed into space, so the God-created, unseen etheric blueprints of vegetables and plants can be made manifest by the will of this world's inhabitants.

"In the same way, astral gardeners can materialize their wildest fantasies, manifesting whole gardens of fragrant flowers through will power alone, only to return them to etheric invisibility later."

"Thank you for the explanation; all of this is a lot to take in! I'm not sure that I grasp all that you just said, but in any case Ariella, I'm becoming very hungry. Is it time for our picnic? Do I just tell that beautiful palm tree over there what I would like to eat?"

"By all means, Bellina!" Ariella laughed. "In the meantime, I'll see if I can summon my eagle friend, Garudina, to see if she can fly you around for a while and show you more of the sights."

"How will an eagle be able to fly me around? And what will it be like to commune with an astral eagle?" Bellina wondered to herself, she but remained silent, in anticipation of an incredible experience to come.

The picnic was delightful. The nearby palm tree was overjoyed to provide them with an abundance of every sort of fruit and vegetable imaginable, including heavenly sweet mangos without the usually bothersome large seeds. There were many other tasty edibles available that were delicious, even if previously unknown to Bellina and Sabella.

After they had eaten their fill, they relaxed beside a bubbling brook, which was tended by several fairy-like devas. It was entrancing to watch the tiny shining ones flitting in and out of the bubbles in the brook, singing their enchanting songs. The devas encouraged them to drink from their sparkling stream. Surprise after surprise adorned this magical place! The water was fizzy and tasted of a very delicious combination of sweet rose and orange blossom essences.

As they rested, Ariella softly called out to a large creature, perched calmly, high in the tree next to them. The eagle had been watching them eat, not making a single sound.

"Garudina, come and join us. Bellina especially wants to meet you."

On glistening golden wings, by far the largest eagle Bellina had ever seen silently swooped down to perch on a strong, lower branch, close to where they were sitting.

"Greetings, Ariella! Bellina and Sabella, it is a pleasure to meet you. My name is Garudina. I am a Spiritus Sanctus of these astral skies. Bellina, I understand you want to fly with me to view Janaloka from my lofty perspective. As you see, I am large enough to carry all of you easily. Hop on my back, and we'll be on our way."

The three of them enthusiastically agreed, and were soon soaring high above Janaloka. After Sabella and Bellina later returned to earth, they always remembered their adventure with Garudina as one of the high points of their visit. The noble eagle was gifted with the power to bestow 360-degree vision upon her guests. Throughout the tour, they could see everything above, below, and all around them, in perfect detail, no matter where they flew.

Garudina was a fabulous tour guide, pointing out several unusual features they otherwise would have missed. By the time they returned to their picnic spot, twilight was falling and the aurora borealis, stars, planets, and a multitude of moons of different sizes and colors began to light up the night skies.

Ariella politely thanked Garudina, then told Bellina that she and Sabella were returning to Loralon's healing pavilion. They wanted to allow Bellina time alone with her new eagle friend.

Bellina was appreciative, for she still had a few unanswered questions that she thought that Garudina might be able to answer. The eagle seemed ancient, wise, and willing to answer her questions in a friendly, but succinct, manner.

Bellina's questions were primarily about astral animals—not just eagles, but the many different beautiful and unusual animals that they had glimpsed on their aerial tour. In contrast to animals on earth, these animals seemed to have no fear of each other and did not flock together for safety. Many different species mingled peacefully while others walked, flew, or crawled about alone.

Among many interesting animal sightings, she had seen a little lamb frolicking with a lion cub and a tiny mouse riding on the head of giraffe, enjoying a vastly expanded viewpoint, while happily chattering into one of the giraffe's big ears.

Bellina made herself comfortable on the ground beside the brook. Garudina perched upon the same low branch where she had first perched earlier that day. The enchanting evening was alive with the nocturnal sounds of birds, frogs, and a myriad of vocal creatures.

"Dear Garudina-mata, thank you so much for the incredible aerial tour of Janaloka! I will never forget it! I feel that you have become my friend, and I sincerely hope you feel the same about me."

"Thank *you*, Bellina. I do feel a deep kinship with you, and am more than happy to answer your questions."

Bellina began by asking, "I see that the animals and people easily communicate with each other here. However, I noticed that animals also seem to talk to each other, too. If this is so, what do they talk about? Is there fear amongst the animals? Do they ever need to hunt and eat each other in order to survive, as is the case on earth? And what were those extremely unusual creatures we saw on our tour, and what can you tell me about them?"

Garudina spoke to Bellina mentally, "Communication is no problem among animal species here. We live together harmoniously, because we have no need to be in a hunter/prey relationship. We do not fear any animals, humans, or other creatures. We enjoy learning about other species, people, angels, plants, and all forms of life that inhabit this world. We live in perfect peace and harmony on Janaloka. We do not need food, because we are sustained by light rays.

"The unusual animals you saw today are the special

creations of causal beings, who are developing their abilities to create, manifesting new plants, animals, and even whole planets. Ariella told me that you will soon be visiting your great-grandfather Thomas on Hiranyaloka. Ask him to tell you more about this subject. He can explain these creative causal projects better than I can."

Bellina said, "I hope you don't mind my asking a personal question, Garudina. Are you here on Janaloka long-term, or will you soon reincarnate on earth or some other physical planet as an eagle, some other creature, or perhaps even as a human being?"

"I don't mind your question, Bellina. I am living in this form temporarily, as are all the creatures here. We, too, come and go from the material plane—though to be honest, we like it a lot better here. We also are travelers, like human beings, on the long, long journey through time and space, living, dying, and being reborn in many forms and places, but always evolving upward into higher levels of consciousness, and finally, into perfect freedom in God.

"My next incarnation will be as a human being on a material planet, perhaps earth, so we may meet again there."

"Oh, that would be wonderful, Garudina! I do hope that will happen soon!

"Everything you have explained to me so far seems clear, but how do people arrive on astral planets? Are they born from the union of a man and a woman or do they just materialize full-grown? I don't remember seeing any babies or children on our tour."

Garudina gave a low chuckle and said, "Many questions about human beings are beyond my ability to answer, therefore, I will fly you back to Ariella now. I'm sure she can answer this question to your satisfaction."

Once again, they were airborne, enjoying the beauty of the night skies. Shortly, Garudina spotted Ariella and Sabella at the butterfly-covered healing pavilion, and silently swooped down, landed softly, and let Bellina climb down from her great golden back.

Hugging her tightly around her neck, Bellina whispered into Garudina's ear, "Thank you, my new friend! My time spent with you has been great fun and most informative! I hope to meet you again on earth. Perhaps, then, I can be of service to you."

Nodding in agreement, Garudina silently flew away, with multi-colored moonlight glinting off her giant golden wings. Bellina watched with a grateful heart. Their time together had been deeply satisfying and a unique experience in her life.

She turned to Ariella, who was smiling at her, and said, "Thank you for arranging for our air tour of Janaloka. I will never forget it. Garudina was an excellent guide, but suggested that I ask you my questions about...."

Ariella interrupted, "Yes, I know your questions. They are about how souls are born into this place, what their astral bodies are like, and why you have not seen any babies or children. Is that correct?"

Bellina smiled and nodded her assent.

"People are not born of the flesh, as is true on earth. Beings materialize into groups that are suited to their karmic needs and similar in vibrational patterns. Those entering an astral world are drawn into a familiar family, attracted by harmonious mental and spiritual tendencies.

"There is no need for a soul to begin life in these worlds as a baby and then endure the long process of growing up."

Astral bodies are not subject to cold, heat or other natural conditions. Their energetic core, the *sushumna* (or energetic spine) is comprised of the thousand-petaled lotus of light (the crown chakra) and six other chakras. The astral heart and brain draw in cosmic energy (prana) and light, and send it to the nerves and body cells through 72,000 *nadis*, or energy channels. Astral beings can affect their bodies through *mantric* or sound/light vibrations.

"Typically, people's astral bodies are close replicas of their last physical form. Most beings prefer to appear as they did in their youth in their previous earthly sojourn. Occasionally some choose to appear as they did in old age. Some take on a completely new appearance altogether.

"In these realms, information is knowable through the all-inclusive sixth sense of intuition. We see, hear, smell, taste, and touch primarily through intuition. The two 'physical' eyes are closed partially, while the third eye, the main organ of perception, is open.

"As you see, while astral beings have all the outer sensory organs–ears, eyes, nose, tongue, and skin–they can employ their intuitional senses to experience sensations through any part of their bodies. These senses are interchangeable, and they can see through the ears, or nose, or skin and can hear through the eyes or tongue, and can taste through the ears or skin, and so forth.

"Whereas the physical body is subject to countless threats, and it is easily hurt or maimed, the astral body is harmed only occasionally, very slightly, and can be healed at once through will power.

Bellina felt the need to ask Ariella another question. "Excuse me, but it seems like every person and creature I see around me is beautiful. Are all astral beings always so beautiful to behold?"

"Beauty in the astral realms is seen as a spiritual quality, and is not based on outward appearances. Therefore, astral beings attach little importance to the way things look, but still have the ability to costume themselves at will with new, colorful, energy bodies. Just as on earth, a person might wear a costume or a new set of clothes for a party or special event, so astral beings can decorate themselves with an array of appearances, each appropriate to the occasion.

"We talked about how friends from other lives easily recognize one another by their distinctive vibrational pattern—no matter their present outward appearance. Rejoicing in the immortality of friendship, they realize the indestructibility of love, often doubted at the time of the sad, delusive partings of the physical world."

Bellina asked, "Can people communicate from an astral loka to those who are living on a material planet?"

"The highly developed intuition of some, though not all, astral beings can pierce the veil between the ethereal and material worlds and observe human activities on earth. Earth's residents ordinarily cannot view the astral world unless their intuition is highly developed. Still, many earth-dwellers have glimpsed an astral being or world, primarily in visions or dreams.

"It's good you have raised this subject now, Bellina, for I believe there is someone nearby who wants to greet you."

Irissia instantly appeared at Bellina's side and whispered in her ear, "Hello, dear friend. I am so *very* glad to see you again!"

"Irissia!" Bellina shouted with joyful surprise, as she saw her dear childhood friend floating beside her. "I was hoping that I would see you on this mission. Sabella hinted at the possibility of our reunion. Oh, Irissia, my sweet friend! I have missed you so much! How are you? You look radiant. Are you happy here? Oh, let me hug you."

"Like always, Bellina, you ask too many questions all at once," Irissia chided her friend playfully, giving her a big astral hug, which was very different from a physical hug. It felt to Bellina to be more like a swift merging of their vibrational patterns, with completely harmonious mental and emotional empathy.

Irissia continued, "I missed you too, Bellina. I am glad that I was able to appear to you in your dreams, after I left earth, to reassure you of my undying love for you. Of course, I am very happy to be here on Janaloka. You can see what it is like—so beautiful, peaceful, light-filled, and full of joyful activities for all who live here!"

"That reminds me what I was going to ask Ariella. Please excuse me, but do you know Ariella? I know you have met my great-grandmother, Sabella."

Irissia smiled at Ariella and Sabella. "Hello, Sabella. Nice to see you again. I hope you don't mind my surprising you like this. Yes, Bellina, I know Ariella very well. She contacted me recently, to let me know of your impending arrival here. She graciously agreed to let me show up unannounced. Ariella also suggested that I could help answer some of your questions about Janaloka.

"Ariella was a great help to me during my first year here on Janaloka. It was dear Ariella who helped me contact you through your dreams, during those first weeks after my arrival here.

"For a long time, I mostly slept or rested in a healing pavilion. I was still in a state of great confusion. My death, as you know, was not without some distressing challenges, especially my family's excessive excitement and grief. I'm sure you remember all the terrible commotion at my deathbed!

"In fact, it took me quite some time to even realize that I had died! Then it took even more time to relax into my new energy body, to heal my psyche, and to acclimate to this peaceful environment.

"In time, I began to engage in many of the joyful activities that I found most interesting. All is well now, and here we are together again, my dearest friend Bellina. What other questions do you have for me?"

"Irissia, I am completely thrilled and delighted to see you again, so much so that I can barely remember the questions I wanted to ask. I think it was concerning something you were just mentioning....Oh yes, I know now. You said something about your joyful activities here on Janaloka. I had just been about to ask Ariella what astral beings do to fill their time. Do you work, play, sleep, dance, sing, study, create things, or what?"

"As you continue your tour of Janaloka, you will observe beings involved in many activities. Residents here may engage in all or none of the things you mentioned, depending on past karma, needed lessons, and any unfulfilled desires they wish to satisfy during their stay here between physical lifetimes.

"Personally, I spend as much time as I possibly can in deep

meditation. Many here do that, you know, though not everyone. I also love to sing, and often join in singing with my angel friends in a heavenly choir."

"Irissia, are you saying that you actually have angel friends?" Bellina enthused. "I recently mentioned to Sabella and Ariella that I *really* want to meet an angel while we are visiting Janaloka! Would it be possible to meet some of your angel friends? And can we hear your heavenly choir sing?"

Irissia looked at Ariella and Sabella, silently communicating Bellina's question to them.

Sabella answered, "Go ahead and enjoy yourselves however you like, as long as you don't take too long. We do not have much time remaining in Janaloka, and there is still much more to see, learn, and experience. Irissia, when can we meet again?"

They all agreed on a time and place for another meeting. Irissia gave Bellina another hug and instantly disappeared from their presence, leaving these words lingering in Bellina's mind. "See you again, dearest sister of my heart. I'll go now and ask my angel friends to prepare a special concert for you and Sabella."

"Ariella," Bellina said, "Aren't you the sneaky one! You knew Irissia was going to find me here and...."

"Bellina," Arielli interrupted, "Your friend very much wanted to surprise you, so I went along with her wishes. I hope you don't mind."

"Of course I don't mind! It was such a great joy to see her again in this most beautiful place. She seems completely at home here—filled with light and spiritual purpose. However, she was gone before she could answer a question that arose as we were conversing. She said that the souls who dwell here in Janaloka might, '...want to satisfy unfulfilled desires while residing here between lifetimes.' What did she mean by that? What desires are satisfied better in the astral realms?"

"Excellent question, Bellina!" Ariella laughed with delight.

At the same time, Ariella thought privately to Sabella. "Your great-granddaughter is very sharp. I don't think she misses much, and she is definitely not afraid to ask the tough or even inconvenient questions, as soon as they arise in her highly inquisitive mind. You have trained her well!"

"I can't take the credit for much of her so-called 'training', for she is and always has been her own person," Sabella said. "However, I do agree with you about her sharp wit and brilliant intellect. The more we are together, the more I admire her spirit of fearless and open-minded inquiry into everything that comes her way. Besides being my beloved great-granddaughter, I can see more and more that she is a dear and great soul—more than I ever knew!"

Ariella said to Bellina, "That is an excellent question and will take some time to answer. We have had a long and fruitful day, but all beings need to rest and regroup their energy patterns from time to time. May I suggest that we do this now, and I will answer your question later, after all of us have had a little time to rest? Besides that, I can sense that Loralon needs my attention now. I have prepared a comfortable place, an 'astral resting-nest,' for you and Sabella. Let me take you there, and then I'll see you tomorrow!"

Bellina knew that Ariella was correct in her assessment that she and Sabella needed to recharge themselves by sleeping, or at least resting for a while. An 'astral resting-nest' sounded like a delightful place to be. Once Ariella transported them there, they could see that it was truly perfect. Ariella quickly departed in order to be with Loralon and attend to his need for further healing and rehabilitation.

CHAPTER SIXTEEN

*We are influenced by beings in the astral universe.
Disorder and confusion on the material plane appeal to lower astral entities.
Material beauty and serenity attract the blessings of saints and angels.*

— Swami Kriyananda, from *The Promise of Immortality*

Bellina awoke from her refreshing sleep. Before she began meditating, she took a few minutes to enjoy the exquisite lavender and gold astral dawn. She realized that in this place, it did not take much sleep in order to feel completely rested and recharged. Even sleeping was different in an astral loka.

The first thing she noticed after her time of meditation was Irissia sitting beside her with a big smile gracing her radiant and loving face. "Good morning, Bellina. I am so glad to visit you to deliver good news to you. My angel friends have arranged for you and Sabella to attend a special concert this evening, prepared especially for your enjoyment and in honor of your mission and your visit to Janaloka. Sabella asked me to tell you that she and Ariella are with Loralon now, but will join us later at the concert hall.

"In the meantime, please join me for breakfast. Ariella commissioned me to help you understand the nature of angels. It is a complex subject, and I am honored that she thought me capable. If you have questions that my angel friend or I cannot answer, Ariella will be available to talk to you more about it later.

"Perfect!" Bellina said, "I was hoping to spend more time with you, Irissia, before I return to my life on earth!"

"And I also, with you, dearest Bellina! Here, take my hand

and let me take you to one of my favorite places for us to have breakfast together."

In the wink of an eye, they were transported to a beautiful garden setting, filled with blossoming trees and banks of multicolored flowers. There were comfortable cushions scattered about on the grass. They sat beside a low table filled with an abundance of cloud-like pastries, fresh fruit, and sparkling, colorful beverages.

Bellina looked around curiously and asked, "Where are we now, Irissia?"

"I thought you might enjoy visiting my astral home."

"Your home? I don't see any buildings. Where is your home?

Irissia laughed delightedly, "Well, I could manifest one now, if I felt the need to, but my 'home' is right here, in this garden! Since coming to Janaloka, I discovered that I prefer the natural shelter of trees and sky to buildings of any kind.

"There are no inclement weather conditions or biting insects to bother me here, so why *not* live outdoors in a natural setting? It is sublimely beautiful here, isn't it, Bellina? I have come to enjoy this thoroughly satisfying lifestyle! Shall we bless the food and eat?" Irissia smiled at her friend from earth.

The food was absolutely delightful and satisfying. She thanked Irissia for her kind hospitality, and felt such joy in this reunion with her friend, especially in Irissia's lovely Janaloka garden-home! She would treasure the memories of their time together. Everything was so soothing and comfortable that she almost forgot that Irissia had said that they were going to talk about angels.

Easily catching Bellina's thoughts, Irissia said, "Yes, by all means, let's discuss the fascinating subject of angels. I thought that the best way to do this would be to ask one of my dear angel friends to join us. I would have invited her to join us earlier, but angels do not eat food as we do. Therefore, I decided it would best to wait until now to call her. I told her all about you and what I believe you want to know about angels. I will take you to a place where she will feel most at ease."

Taking Bellina's hand again, Irissia transported them to a... what was it? Bellina could only describe it later to Sabella as a "cloud swing." It felt like a comfortable, puffy bench-swing for two people, but it appeared to be made of pastel-colored mist and clouds, swirling and floating high above Irissia's garden home. Soft breezes rocked them gently.

"Bellina, please meet Sofieli. She is here to answer your questions about angels. I will leave you two alone for a while. When it is time for us to leave for the concert, Sofieli will escort you there, and I will see you then! I'm looking forward to enjoying the concert with you."

Materializing in the center of the dazzling light-cloud that had just appeared in front of them was the most spectacular being Bellina had ever seen, or could imagine would exist. She was shaped like a human being, though larger, and was radiantly beautiful in an ethereal way.

Bellina was a bit stunned to notice that she could see right through Sofieli. She wore diaphanous robes, which seemed to be made of lemon yellow rays of light. Her long hair resembled delicate, sheer spun gold, streaming out behind her, lifted gently by a subtle wind, which Bellina could not feel. Matching her robes, her eyes were golden-yellow and shone like radiant beams of energy.

An unusual voice sounded in Bellina's mind. Although Bellina was used to mental communication, she had never heard a voice like this one! Singularly and liltingly beautiful, Sofieli's musical voice sounded more like a song being played on a flute or a lute or some strange, otherworldly musical instrument. Bellina found that listening to Sofieli's song-like speech was a truly enjoyable experience!

"Hello, Bellina!"

"Hello to you also, Sofieli. You have a beautiful name—one I've never heard before. What does it mean?"

"Thank you, O Mortal One! It means 'one who instills a love of nature in all hearts.' What would you like to know about angels?" Sofieli came right to the point, a quality that Bellina appreciated.

"Well, I suppose I want to hear anything you can tell me! I am hungry for information. The subject of angels always has fascinated me. I would like to learn as much as I can during our time together.

"However, since I think this might be a vast subject, perhaps you should begin by telling me whatever you would like me to know about angels."

Sofieli laughed with delight. She answered, "Wise decision, Bellina! Yes, there is a lot to know! I will summarize as best I can. I am a young angel and there are many things I don't know yet, such as how, when, and why we came into existence."

"Well, that's fine, Sofieli. I am a young human being, too, so we may be well matched. And just for the record, I'm not really sure how or why my species came into being, either!" Now it was Bellina's turn to giggle.

Sofieli laughed with delight at this amusing being, speaking to her so sincerely. Her sweet laughter echoed in Bellina's head, like tiny silver bells, ringing through the treetops. "I think it would be correct to say that angels are advanced astral beings. Angels, called by many different names on the earth, are also called *devas*, which means 'the shining ones.'

"There are archangels, mighty warrior-like angels and lesser angels, guardian angels, messenger angels—so designated according to their primary assigned duties. There are even very small, childlike angels called cherubs.

"On earth, myths about angels abound. One common image is that all angels have halos and wings, which they use to fly around heaven, while playing on their harps."

"That's true! Now that you mention it Sofieli, where *are* your wings, halo, and harp...?" Bellina stopped communicating instantly, realizing that she might be asking an embarrassing question. She thought that perhaps Sofieli was a lower ranking angel who had yet to earn these accoutrements.

Sofieli smiled at Bellina, "Well, I could manifest some wings right now, if you really want me to, but we have no need for them, except for decorative purposes. I can fly or teleport from place to place, as I wish, without wings, which I have found generally to be cumbersome appendages. I have the ability to teleport interdimensionally, unlimited in where I can go instantly. Do you have these abilities also, Bellina?"

Bellina could see that her new angel friend was not bragging. Sofieli was curious about her too, as a representative of the human species.

Bellina replied. "Although I am studying advanced transdimensional travel skills, I would not have been able to be here in Janaloka without the assistance of my great-grandmother."

"Oh, you'll learn soon enough, Bellina. It's not hard to do." Sofieli said kindly.

"As for the halo, it is my understanding that people on the material plane, especially the saints and masters, have beautifully shining auras of light around them, which some people can perceive. Their auras radiate especially brightly around the chakras in their heads. In ancient times on earth, many great painters of saints or angels must have been able to perceive halos, for they appear with great regularity in those paintings."

"I can see your vibrant aura as we speak, Sofieli," Bellina said. "It's hard to tell where your aura ends and your skin begins. And your aura keeps shifting and changing colors as we talk."

"I can see your aura, too, Bellina. It speaks a hidden language that tells me more truthfully than words ever could, who you really are."

"That's a frightening thought," Bellina thought to herself, she hoped.

"And just why would you think *that* of yourself?" Sofieli said. Obviously, Bellina could not shield her thoughts from her new angel friend.

"You, too, are a beautiful, shining child of God! It is true that you and I are different kinds of beings, created by the Divine, but we are both divine in our eternal essence. You *do* realize that, don't you, Bellina?"

"Intellectually yes, but thank you for the reminder. It helps to hear it often, for I fear I sometimes forget."

"It is the same for angels, Bellina. We can and often do make mistakes in our perceptions."

"That is a little hard to imagine," Bellina said. "I was under the impression that angels were perfect in every way."

"Well, we try, but no—if we were perfect in every way, we would immediately merge back into our Creator. We too have a spiritual evolutionary process to go through, on our return journey to oneness with God. In that sense, we are no different from everything and everyone in the material universe."

Bellina had another question, "There is another myth on earth that if you are a good person and behave rightly, then, when you die, you go to heaven and become an angel or at least enjoy their company. Is this true?"

"Well, yes, the second part of what you have asked is true, just as I hope you are enjoying my company at the moment, Bellina!" Sofieli laughed entrancingly. "But no, humans do not become angels and angels do not become humans. Angels are a completely separate creation of God and have their own unique evolutionary pathways.

"There exist much more spiritually advanced angels, who I have not mentioned yet. You may have heard of the traditional hierarchy of angels. There are the nine orders, ranked from lowest to highest: angels, archangels, principalities, powers, virtues, dominions, thrones, cherubim, and seraphim."

Bellina replied, "Yes, I learned about the different groups of angels and their names when I studied ancient history during my school years on earth, but there was much that was not clear to me then."

"It can be confusing, but the names and ranks of angels generally designate an increasing level of spiritual development and the more increasingly powerful ways in which an angelic being can function, including the considerable and important responsibilities that they have serving in the three universes." Sofieli explained.

"The highest types of angels are extraordinarily advanced beings, who have vast creative powers. The Infinite Consciousness works through them to design, create, protect, and guide the three universes: causal, astral, and material. These are the vastly mighty angels, whom God designates to bring into existence an infinity of lokas. In contrast, I am a new or lesser angel."

"I think you are a wonderful angel!" Bellina told Sofieli.

"And I think you are a wonderfully sweet human to say that," Sofieli sang softly.

She continued, "There are guardian angels assigned to protect those who live on planets in the material universe. There are messenger angels, too. You may remember the famous angel, Gabriel, whom God sent to visit Mother Mary of Nazareth, to tell her that she soon would be giving birth to the great Avatar, Jesus. Messenger and guardian angels often appear in the dreams and visions of human beings, to guide them or warn them of impending danger.

"It is right and good for human beings to offer love, honor, and devotion to angels and the nature spirits or *devas*. At the same time, it is wise to respect what the great Avatar, Lord Krishna, says in the *Bhagavad Gita*: 'Those who worship the lesser gods go to their gods. Those who worship Me [which is to say, the Cosmic Infinite Consciousness] come to Me.'

"In the material lokas, unenlightened humans express Infinite Consciousness more fully than do the lower animals, who are less self-aware. Similarly, above the human level, there are the angels and other advanced astral beings, who more fully express their Divinity.

"However, these *devas*, no matter how highly evolved they might be, are less highly evolved than a spiritual Master, even if the Master is still living on the material plane. For as I have said before, the devas are still evolving spiritually, whereas a Master has transcended evolution itself.

"Paramhansa Yogananda expressed this principle very well when he said, 'There is no end to evolution. You go on until you achieve endlessness.'

"Human beings have achieved some measure of self-awareness, and therefore have a responsibility to help uplift less evolved creatures. For example, kindness to animals fosters their spiritual unfoldment, and guides them to increased attunement to God, the Source of all love.

"The devas or angels, in their turn, hasten their own evolution by reaching out to help human beings. To ask an angel for help need no more imply lack of faith in God or the Masters than would a request for help from an older brother or sister, instead of taking all of one's problems to one's parents.

"The Supreme Spirit seldom, if ever, intervenes directly in the affairs of human beings. This seeming detachment is analogous to an ancient electrical power station, where the voltage had to be stepped down by transformers, in order not to incinerate the electrical wiring in people's homes.

"The universe abounds with innumerable entities who actively direct the growth of plants and animal life, the manifestation of new species or whole planets, and the unfolding of individual and group karma.

"No created being is comparable to God. No angels, devas, or astral entities should be regarded as deities. They should be called, more correctly, nature spirits or astral functionaries. On the other hand, these spirits thrive on love, and can give human beings much more energy, if humans would, in turn, offer their love and appreciation to them.

"For example, if nature devas feel unloved and ignored, they withdraw their energy and help in much the same way people do, when their expressions of good will are not well received or appreciated."

Bellina had a question she wanted to ask now, but hesitated, not wanting to be impolite. Finally, she said a quick prayer and went ahead, "Sofieli, all that you have told me is fascinating, but I would like to ask a question that I hope will not be offensive to you. Do angels have any strong desires?"

Sofieli sweetly replied, "Bellina, I would never be offended by your pure-hearted questioning. Ask whatever you like, any time! An angel's deepest desire, where human beings are concerned, is to help those who are willing to receive—it is as simple as that. We do not offer aid unless people first reach out consciously for help, for we feel that it would be presumptuous to intrude."

Bellina thought this over for a moment then asked, "Could an angelic being enter a person's mind that was passively open to receiving angelic messages?"

"I have heard that the darker astral beings or 'fallen angels' employ such tactics, but never the bright angels or the Great Masters. Highly evolved souls know that it is against every important divine principle to use human beings against their will, or through their ignorance or passivity.

"Inviting the presence of divine beings in deep meditation is the polar opposite of indulging in a mental void or becoming passively open to whatever entity might want to occupy one's inner being. Deep meditation is a state in which one is so intensely aware, so powerfully focused, that all mental restlessness subsides. In such a meditative state, devotees may invite God, the angels, and Great Masters to enter and uplift their consciousness and fill them with grace. An uplifted state like this naturally protects the meditator from any dark or negative entities.

"However, be aware that it is possible for human beings to be influenced by other forms of astral beings. Disorder and confusion on the material plane appeal to and magnetically attract lower astral entities, whereas material beauty and serenity attract the presence and blessings of saints and angels."

Bellina looked puzzled, "Sofieli, you have referred to dark or lower astral beings more than once now. Can you tell me what they are, where they live, and what is their purpose and effect on humanity?"

"I will do my best, Bellina. An astral heaven such as Janaloka is an ideal place for human beings to dwell for a time, but it is not the *only* loka astral beings inhabit. There are heavens far higher and more beautiful than this one, worlds that really cannot be described in words. Conversely, there are other astral regions far darker than an earth-dweller could ever imagine.

"In an astral loka, whose primary essence is light, any absence of light is extremely oppressive in a sense that cannot be easily grasped in material or human terms. There are dark astral regions, in which beings are constantly longing for something beyond their reach; they are unable to grasp anything fully! As you can imagine, this keeps them trapped in feelings of helpless rage, frustration, and pain.

"The inhabitants of those regions, like creatures in the less evolved regions of the physical universe, know no peace—only discord, hatred, and warfare. They experience perennial regret over what they cannot have and what they *think* cannot be changed, either in their environment or in themselves.

"Darkness, like a filthy mist, hangs heavily over dull, empty plains and barren valleys. Because the inhabitants' emotions there, as in higher astral regions, are intensified by their freedom from bondage to matter, their misery is far greater than it would be on earth, where human beings at least have some distractions that can dull their minds to suffering.

"Inhabitants of the higher astral regions, both angels and some advanced astral beings, have the freedom to descend into these dusky, hellish places. They go there with the purpose of helping those whose suffering has brought them to the point where they desire to reach upward, however tentatively, toward the light.

"For you see, these wretched beings eventually tire of dwelling on the past injustices inflicted on them. It is their erroneous viewpoint that allows them to view the errors they themselves have committed in this way. Once they begin to accept personal responsibility for their sorry plight, they begin to realize that only by accepting responsibility for changing themselves, can they begin to alter their living conditions for the better. It is only at this point that the angels can, and do, come to help them.

"Beings living in the dark astral regions are unable to ascend to higher regions without help and guidance. Thus, merely to be an inhabitant of an astral world does not necessarily endow them with a state of wisdom beyond their current state of evolution. One may live in a lower astral world and be convinced that there are no angels, saints or masters, and that there is no reality to the idea of spiritual evolution. They may be convinced that they have nothing in the future to look forward to—even though the truth is that they eventually will return to a material plane.

"Many earth dwellers who, upon dying, pass on to an astral plane are, in fact, even less aware than they were on earth. Having lived on earth in total identification with their physical senses, they did not develop the intuitive power to perceive the subtler realities of the astral world. The emotions they feel may be intense to them, but they resemble the emotions one feels in nightly dreams: strong perhaps, but somehow never brought into clear focus.

"When a person dies, he leaves the physical shell behind. This, however, is only the outermost of the three bodies. He retains the astral and causal bodies. Physical death, then, does not mean that one merges into a great sea of consciousness, as some people wrongly believe. That destiny awaits us all, in fact—but not, as some choose to believe, in eternal unconsciousness, and certainly not upon the mere act of leaving the physical body behind in death. Rather, it comes with release from all three bodies. It comes with a conscious self-expansion into the Infinite, into complete oneness with God. This is the state of self-mastery and permanent bliss, which all Great Masters have attained.

"To the extent that people are able to be conscious of the afterworld, they retain their personalities, good or not so good. Very few humans are truly evil. Perhaps they are not always well-meaning, because of their innate self-absorption and the meanness of their hearts, but their selfishness usually is due more to ignorance than ill will.

"Such souls are not punished with intense suffering after death—except in the sense of feeling bewildered and disoriented. After a time in an astral world suited to their present vibrational level, their material desires draw them back to the physical plane and into new bodies and new learning experiences once again. In this way, they feel relatively refreshed and prepared to cope yet again with the challenges of a material incarnation—this being yet another step in their long climb out of the swamps of material attachments."

"Sofieli, please tell me, is there such a thing as hell? Is that what you mean when you refer to these dark astral regions?"

Sofieli answered carefully, "If you use the term 'hell' to designate a place of eternal suffering, where sinners are sent by a vengeful God for eternal punishment, then no, there is no such place. Our Creator is loving and always forgiving.

"Unfortunately, souls can move very far in the direction of darkness, for all beings have free will. However, the dark astral regions, though they do exist, are only *temporary* homes. Souls reside there for a time, according to the amount and weight of their karma, especially their bad karma—that is, the patterns and amounts of negative energy and harmful actions stored within their astral bodies and chakras.

"Remember this, please, Bellina! Souls *never* stay in such places forever! Even while residing in dark worlds, they are being ministered to, loved, and helped by angels. Soon their karma is mitigated, at least enough to allow them to ascend into higher regions of light or to return to the material world for another chance at redemption through working out their karma.

"Does this answer the question to your satisfaction, Bellina? I hope so, for if you feel the need to visit such a dark realm, I cannot help you to do that. I think I need a few thousand years of significant spiritual growth and strengthening to be able to endure such places."

Bellina looked shocked. "No, Sofieli! I do *not* wish to experience that kind of astral loka—at least not now! I, too, need more time for spiritual growth and strengthening before attempting a sojourn into a dark realm, such as you have described."

Sofieli shined her blazing angelic smile at Bellina. "Thank you for your understanding. However, I can relate a bit more information, from the little I have learned so far about the dark lokas.

"Evil beings, demons, dark angels, and other maleficent creatures are confined to specific areas, and cannot move about freely. Among the dark beings expelled from other worlds, friction results in energetic warfare using weapons such as lifetronic bombs and mental mantric vibratory rays. These beings dwell in the gloom-drenched regions of the lower astral cosmos, working out their evil karma, toward their eventual release from these shadowy nether regions."

"I've met a few confused, immoral, or morally misguided people on earth," Bellina said sadly. "While these people don't seem nearly as dark as the evil beings you have described, it was not at all a pleasant experience for me. Sofieli, have you ever met a dark or fallen angel?"

"No, Bellina, I have not, nor do I have any desire to meet one!"

Bellina sensed that Sofieli wanted to drop this subject. Thus, she refrained from further comments and inquiries about the lower astral regions.

"Sofieli, I know our time together is almost over, and I don't want to end our visit on a dark note. So, let me ask one last question. What advice would you, an angel and a being of such great radiance and joy, give to a mere mortal from earth?"

Bellina was quite surprised when Sofieli stooped to embrace Bellina's feet, kissing them with soft angelic kisses. Then she arose, looked straight into Bellina's eyes and deeper, into her very soul, and said, "You are not a 'mere' mortal, Bellina. Please forgive me for being flippant when I addressed you as

'O Mortal One' when we first met. You are immortal, just as I am and everyone is. I can see that clearly now, and I sense that we will be friends forever!

"I have been taught that as I evolve as an angel, the power to help humans will grow ever stronger within me. Will you do me the honor of calling on me whenever you need help? I promise to be there for you and assist you in whatever ways I can!

"In addition, I offer you this gift. In the future, you will always be able to feel my presence whenever you are in nature. Remember that my name means, 'one who instills a love of nature in all hearts.' This is a very special gift that I think we both have, and I offer my blessings to enhance this ability within you.

"I have peered into your soul today, sweet Bellina, and I am deeply touched by what I have seen.

"I now believe that our Heavenly Father created you and every human being as a special kind of angel. You are angels of energy, though encased in solid flesh; you are dazzling currents of life force, flowing through the material bulb of the flesh.

"Too often, as a human being in a material world, you focus on the frailties and weaknesses of the flesh, forgetting to feel the immortal, indestructible aspects of Eternal Life Energy shining through the changeable flesh.

"One of our elder angels once told me that someday I would meet a human from earth who would show me the glory and the true essence of a human being and their glorious potential.

"He predicted that, in this moment, I would bow my head to honor the nobility, courage, and magnitude of spirit that humans have within themselves, in the face of the many enormous challenges which they must go through over the course of almost countless incarnations on the material plane. I am grateful that the moment he predicted has now arrived. I give you my unconditional love—now and always!"

Bellina strove to find words to answer Sofieli. What an amazing promise this radiant being had just given her! What a blessing and a joy to have an angel for a friend and to hear her say that she would love her, bless her, and watch over her! It seemed almost too overwhelmingly generous for her to accept.

"Sofieli, my heart is bursting with love for you, too. I will hold the joyful memory of this moment within me forever, and will remember your angelic promise to help me whenever I need it."

Bellina continued, "You are right! Being human is fraught with many dangers. While I have learned to trust God, and know that things turn out for the best in the end, I am grateful to have all the help I can get! Henceforth, I trust you also to be a part of God's blessings and protection for me and to be one who assists the Divine in bringing forth the best possible plan for my life. I don't know how humans can help angels, but if I ever find an opportunity, I will not hesitate to help you also."

No more words or thoughts needed to pass between the two beings. Their bond was sealed and their friendship would last forever. A merging of minds and energy had occurred between them. Their union as friends seemed to both of them to be preordained, divinely blessed, and indescribably perfect.

Bellina clearly sensed that it was important to hold what had happened between them as a precious secret in her heart.

"Bellina, it is time to join your friends for the concert. Please remember that this concert is being presented in your honor, as an esteemed visitor to Janaloka. Are you ready?"

"I am ready!"

CHAPTER SEVENTEEN

Angels we have heard on high
Sweetly singing o'er the plain
And the mountains in reply
Echoing their joyous strains
Gloria, in excelsis Deo!

— Traditional Christmas Carol

Bellina recorded her thoughts and impressions of the concert of angels soon after returning to earth. It took more time than she expected to feel grounded enough to articulate what she had experienced on that magical final day in Janaloka. Here are her words:

"Even after taking time to reflect on the experience of the angelic concert, it will not be easy to express what I felt in words. I can assure you, it by far surpassed any earthly music I have ever heard, even Sabella's (excuse me, great-grandmother) exquisite musical productions.

"Although I did not inherit her exceptional musical talent, I always found listening to good music extremely enjoyable. Nevertheless, to say this was 'good music' would be a gross understatement! It was truly heavenly in every way. Many times during the concert, I wept tears of joy. I was moved to my core and never wanted those blissful sounds to cease. But I digress. Let me start at the beginning.

"Sofieli, my angel companion, flew me to an astral pavilion filled with enthusiastic Janaloka residents—human and otherwise. Apparently, word had gotten out about the concert and the crowd was huge. I could not even begin to count them, but I would guess they numbered in the thousands or even tens of thousands.

"My enormous astral eagle friend, Garudina, was there, perched on a huge pedestal in the back of the hall. She was joined by little Peachie-tree, the healing fairy, sitting beside her, on a tiny perch of her own. Both winked at me as we entered.

"The crowd grew quiet as Sofieli escorted me to a comfortable seat between Irissia and Sabella. Loralon sat next to Sabella—old friends reunited. Ariella sat on his other side, keeping close watch on him. I knew this was his first public outing since arriving in Janaloka, and beginning the treatments he needed in order to heal from the traumas he had received from death, as well as his most recent life on earth.

"I could sense that Ariella was concerned that Loralon was still a bit fragile. I also could perceive that she felt sure that a heavenly choir concert would fill him with the best kind of healing vibrations. This was obviously her primary motive in encouraging him to join us.

"Sofieli said a loving goodbye to me and went to take her place with the other angelic choir members.

"I greeted Sabella and the rest of my Janaloka friends. Irissia whispered in my ear, 'Bellina, you are covered in golden angel dust and sparkling ribbons of astral colors spanning the rainbow. You are glowing with light and more beautiful than I have ever seen you appear. Did Sofieli 'decorate' you for this occasion or give you a makeover or astral spa treatment? I can see also that you must have benefited greatly from your special interview with an angel. You look stunningly radiant!'

"Only now did I remember that I should have attended to my appearance before showing up at such a special occasion, presented in my honor, but dear Sofieli had already assumed her role as my personal helper-angel. I never would have guessed that her duties would include such a small detail, like dressing me appropriately for this important event, but it seems she had done so, without my even noticing it. Inwardly I sent her my gratitude.

"Let me try to describe the concert hall. It was enormous and seemed to be floating on a gigantic fountain of rainbow lights and to be made of shining vapors. A prolonged sunset and several moonrises were happening all around us, easily observable through the transparent walls of the pavilion. Heavenly bodies appeared with the setting sun, including stars, planets, smaller moons, and whizzing comets, as the darkening velvety sky took over from the daylight of this wondrous place.

"The heavenly concert that unfolded before us that evening was equally indescribable. The waves of consciousness they lovingly sent through their music embraced and included all my senses. It was simply sublime! Heavenly! Once more, words fall short and are almost meaningless unless you have already had a similar experience.

"A huge and mighty angel floated into the hall and took his place as conductor before the massive choir and orchestra. How many musicians were there? Too many to count! Rows and rows of many varied devas of all sizes and shapes. There were so many that they not only stretched to the top of the pavilion, but seemed to continue beyond its boundaries, into the night sky as far as one could see.

"Irissia whispered to me mentally. 'The conductor-angel is of the Principality Rank.'

"'I don't know what that means!" I whispered back.

"'I don't know exactly either, but I do know that he is one of the most powerful angels in Janaloka! We are honored to be in his holy presence.'

"The Principality spoke in a booming voice, 'Welcome to all, and angelic joy to everyone. A special welcome to Bellina and her great-grandmother, Sabella Lovingheart, who are here on an important mission from earth. Bellina requested this concert, and it is to her and her quest for the highest truths that we dedicate this music.'

"He turned, lifted a mesmerizing baton of light, and cued the musicians to begin the concert. This was not like earthly music, presented only for the enjoyment of listening and observing the musicians performing the music. The nuances of angelic consciousness were communicated through *all* our senses. There were a variety of lovely fragrances and tingling, blissful feelings transmitted directly into our energy systems.

"Many times during the concert, hundreds of radiant angels danced and flew gracefully around, above the audience, the choir, the orchestra and in the skies beyond the hall—their amazing dances and movements all perfectly and gloriously synchronized with the music. Color-sound rays and fragrant flower petals descended upon the audience. Every sensation blended with the glorious harmonies of the angelic voices.

"I wept, laughed, and almost lost consciousness at one point. It was truly overwhelming! I could feel Sabella giving me the strength to bear it all. I spotted Sofieli in the choir, and I could feel that she also was sending me her special, angelic energy. 'Too much joy!' I thought. 'Oh, much too much joy!'

"The conductor brought what I thought was the last piece of music to a close, but then he turned and addressed me, 'Bellina, for our finale, we offer you a special gift. This music was composed on earth, early in the most recent Ascending Dwapara Yuga, by someone you know. It is a heavenly composition, and was inspired and channeled through him by the angel chorus here.

"'Please enjoy 'Life Mantra/Chant of the Angels,' by Sri Sri Nayaswami Kriyanandaji.'

"A hush filled with vibratory anticipation went through the crowd and all the musicians. The conductor lifted his baton and the music began softly. The angel choir sang these words to us, both as hearable sounds and as mental/visual transmissions:

> *God is life. God is joy.*
> *Life is God's: Life is joy.*
> *God is life. God is joy.*
> *Life is God's: Life is joy.*
>
> *God, who is infinite, is life.*
> *God, who is in all life, is joy.*
> *Life is a mission from on high.*
> *Life is a quest for inner joy.*

> *Joy, joy, joy, joy!*
> *God is life. God is joy.*
> *Joy, joy, joy!*
> *Life is God's: Life is joy.*
> *Joy, joy, joy, joy, joy!* ©

"After an instrumental interlude embracing the melody, the choir sang the words again and again, the sounds and feelings growing stronger and more powerful with each repetition of the mantra. I cannot say how long the piece continued, for before it ended, I closed my eyes and the music carried me into the deepest superconscious state that I have ever experienced.

"More time passed, and I finally opened my eyes to see everyone in the vast and completely silent concert hall, smiling radiantly at me. Sabella gently gave me a mental nudge. I felt she was telling me that I should express my appreciation to the conductor, choir, and musicians.

"I immediately wished I had a large bouquet of astral flowers to give to the conductor. Almost as quickly as I had this thought, a giant flower bouquet appeared in my arms, humming with life-force, incredibly fragrant, and containing every color of the rainbow and even a few more.

"Well then, what else could I do? I put my shyness and hesitation aside and walked toward the giant hovering angel conductor. I lifted my bouquet up to him, and with this gesture, did my best to transmit my deepest appreciation to all who took part in the concert.

"Suddenly there was a thunderous roar all around me—not exactly applause as is traditional on earth, but a great hum, like the booming oceanic sound of AUM. The conductor stooped down (*way* down) to receive my gift, and to my surprise, lifted both the flowers and me up into his arms.

"Then we descended to an exceptionally bright soul sitting in the front row, not far from where I had been sitting. The conductor kneeled before the ascended human and humbly presented him with the bouquet, saying, 'Thank you, Swamiji, for the privilege of presenting your exquisite music to Bellina and to everyone here tonight.'

"Yes, it was he, Nayaswami Kriyananda. Sabella and I had visited his beautiful Moksha Mandir not long ago. While I had not seen his astral form then, I had felt his presence strongly, and had heard his voice welcoming me to that holy place."

Now I knelt before him, mute with awe. Finally, I gathered my courage and said, "Thank you for composing this inspiring music, Swamiji. May I ask how it was written?"

Nayaswami Kriyananda gave me a big, blissful smile, 'Hello and welcome to you, Bellina. I was glad that you and Sabella could visit my Moksha Mandir to meditate with my physical remains. I no longer inhabit a body of any kind these days, but I materialized an astral one to join you on this special occasion. It is a reasonable facsimile of what I looked like in my last lifetime on earth.' He chuckled a delightful and utterly contagious sound, which made me laugh, as it did all those around us who heard him. I later learned that every being in the audience also heard his words, through some sort of mysterious sound-vibration projection process.

'I would love to tell you how this music came to be. In my last lifetime on earth, I was musing about what an angel choir might sound like and was inspired to compose a choral piece. I wanted it to be a composition for an angel choir, but not so much for the angels in heaven, as for human beings on earth, who could sing as if they were angels. Suddenly, words and music came pouring over me, like a refreshing waterfall of sound.

'I heard the whole of the choral piece, all at once, complete within itself. I experienced it as though angels were singing to me. Writing down this music came effortlessly, and I was able to write it all out, in a single day! The only editorial change I made later was to extend the duration of a single chord from one to two measures.

'Then, I thought to write an instrumental interlude between the choir pieces. This insertion would, I expected, come easily. After all, the primary musical score itself already had been written. Therefore, the melody line had only to be shifted to the soprano part, wherever it had been assigned to the lower voices. The interlude turned out to be less than half the length of the original. Even so, it took me several days to complete it.

'Only then did I realize how entirely the choral piece had been given to me. I had been the conduit, merely, for the projection of an astral, angelic choir into the material plane of existence. So please understand that I, as the human being called Swami Kriyananda, *did not write it.*

'Instead, I inwardly listened to an astral choir, much like the one that just sang so beautifully tonight. Then I did my best to record everything I was hearing in musical annotation.

'This heavenly music expresses the essence of what all human beings need to bring more consciously into their lives. The form it takes is not important. The highest human aspiration is to live life as a mystical experience, with their energy continually aspiring upward, toward who they *really* are: immortal children of God. Bellina, we are all manifestations of the Divine—God's creations, and co-creators with God!

'The more human beings can resonate with this truth, the more fulfillment they will find. The less attuned they are with that truth, the more they will suffer. Music, more than most human creative expressions, has the potential to resonate with the highest realities of love and joy. One of my goals in my life as Swami Kriyananda was to be a creative channel, offering musical compositions as doorways to the inner kingdom of heaven, our one true home.

'Something wonderful occurred during an early rehearsal of this piece. Only six core members of our choir were working on it at first. At one point during a practice session, they were taking a break. Unexpectedly, a sweet voice was heard, seemingly out of thin air, repeatedly singing a section of the music: "Life is a mission from on high. Life is a quest for inner joy!"

'Three people in the group clearly heard the etheric voice. We understood this to mean that the angels themselves were indicating their blessings and approval for this work. All throughout the process, I was thrillingly aware of numerous angelic presences, guiding and blessing my efforts.'

"I expressed my sincerest gratitude again to this dear and great soul, for all he had revealed to me. He patted my cheek, like an affectionate grandfather, and disappeared before I could say or do anything else. I was a little disappointed to see him vanish so quickly, but I felt blessed and uplifted at being able to meet and talk with him. I said a prayer to God and Gurus, requesting that we might be able to meet again someday.

"This concludes my report of what happened at the concert on my last evening in Janaloka. Respectfully submitted by Sabellina, great granddaughter of High Council Member, Sabella Lovingheart, to the High Council of Planet Earth, Milky Way Galaxy, within the Material Plane of Existence."

CHAPTER EIGHTEEN

When Spirit first manifested the universe,
A portion of its consciousness moved in the form of thoughts.
Out of these thoughts evolved the causal, or ideational, universe—
A universe not made of forms, colors, and textures,
But of pure ideas.

— Swami Kriyananda from *The Art and Science of Raja Yoga*

It was exactly midnight, when the concert was over. The small party of friends, including Sofieli, had returned to Irissia's garden at her invitation, to partake of a late night snack. Bellina had no appetite, for she was feeling sad. She instinctively understood that the time was coming very soon, when she and Sabella would have to leave this heavenly place.

As they were departing from the pavilion, Ariella noticed that Loralon was looking a little more transparent than usual. Therefore, Sabella and Bellina felt to say their good-byes to him and Ariella.

Bellina expressed her sincerest thanks to both of them for the parts they had played in their visit to Janaloka and all their learning adventures in this heavenly place. Loralon and Ariella insisted that no thanks were needed, and that they would all meet again someday.

While Bellina was sure that they would indeed meet again, her soft human heart felt tender saying goodbye to these dear ones.

Leaving Irissia was even harder, because of their deep karmic bonds from this lifetime. Even though Irissia had shed her human form, she was no less a true sister in Bellina's eyes.

"Bellina, dearest sister of my heart, you won't forget me, will you?" Irissia asked gently.

"Never!" Bellina said to her friend. "I carry your friendship with me always, and I look forward to meeting again someday soon."

Sofieli took her turn saying her brief farewells to both Sabella and Bellina, but at the last moment, a quiet angelic whisper spoke to Bellina's mind alone, saying, "Remember, call on me any time. I will be there with you instantly. This is my promise to you, Bellina. Never, ever forget it!"

Finally, Bellina turned to her great-grandmother, saying, "Well, Gigi, what happens now?"

It was then that she noticed how joyously radiant Sabella looked, even as Bellina was feeling very sad at this time of bittersweet goodbyes. So what was going on with her great-grandmother?

Suddenly the answer came. Well, of course! Sabella was anticipating seeing her life-linked mate, her beloved Thomas. She also would be helping Bellina explore and investigate the inexpressible subtleties of his home on the high astral planet, Hiranyaloka.

"Yes, Bellina," Sabella twinkled at her, "It is finally time for us to visit with Thomas in Hiranyaloka! Are you ready, dear one?"

"Why do you ask me questions like that, Gigi?" Bellina laughed. "How could I possibly know if I'm ready or not? Nevertheless, I trust that with you as my guide, I'm as ready as I'll ever be!"

Sabella smiled at her great-granddaughter and then instructed her to sit down, right where they were—in a slightly more private area of Irissia's picturesque garden-home.

"Meditate with me, Bellina. Concentrate your attention fully at the spiritual eye and focus on the bluish-purple tunnel of light within the golden halo. This is our passageway from the astral universe to a causal loka."

The next thing Bellina knew was that she had shed her astral body. She had grown accustomed to being without her physical body, while they were visiting Janaloka, but now she had escaped even her astral body. And what a great body it had been, all shining and filled with colorful lights! She felt somewhat lost without it, even though she had only consciously inhabited it for a few days.

It was bewildering to feel that she possessed no body at all and began to wonder if she were even still alive.

"Well, wondering if you are alive, Bellina indicates that you can still think and question what's going on around you. Therefore, you must be still alive in some way, wouldn't you say?"

"I might say so, if I had a mouth, but I'm sure I don't, Gigi. What am I now?"

"You are still alive, of course, but your soul is inhabiting only its most subtle container, your causal body, known also as the ideational body. At this moment you exist only as the *thought, idea, or mental concept* of Bellina's essence, don't you see?"

"I don't see anything, Gigi, for it seems that I don't have eyes anymore either!" In the face of this disorienting experience, Bellina was confused, slightly irritated, and perhaps even a little afraid.

"You actually *do* see, my dear great-granddaughter, but in a different way. Cast your mind over in that direction."

Bellina could feel Sabella's distinct mental nudge and tried to cooperate. It worked, for she instantly knew that she was with Thomas, her beloved great-grandfather.

While this form of cognition was unfamiliar, she clearly perceived both of her great-grandparents, as they joyfully entwined their thought patterns of greeting and reunion, here on the causal plane of existence.

"Tom-Tom!" Bellina mentally called out her childhood nickname for Thomas. There was no doubting that his presence was fully here, welcoming and embracing both of them.

Nor was there any way to mistake the powerful essence of Thomas and the intense feeling of the love he was offering them at this moment!

"Great-grandfather Thomas! You *are* here with us! I have missed you so very much. I love you!"

Their reunion was unusual, to say the least. Thomas had neither a physical nor an astral body to hug, and even if he did, she had no arms with which to hug him! While it was only the thought of Thomas, expressing his presence to thought-essences of herself and Sabella, the experience of his being was exceedingly powerful!

The experience was mystifying, but Bellina was beginning to grasp the workings of a causal loka. Regardless of how strange the experience, she felt free and blissful.

Being in the causal universe triggered a memory of one of her classmates who, perhaps as a joke, always mispronounced the word "causal" and kept referring to the "*casual* universe." Silly classmate, silly joke!—but come to think of it, there might have been some truth to the term *casual*.

Things were extremely casual around here, so casual in fact, that it seemed there was *nothing going on at all*, in the ways we usually relate to reality. There was nothing to see, hear, taste, touch, or feel—no sense stimulation at all!

Bellina took a moment to gather her wits about her and then transmitted her question to Thomas, "I thought that we'd be meeting you on Hiranyaloka, which, as I understand, is a place of much higher consciousness than Janaloka. I mean, Hiranyaloka is still an astral planet—isn't it? Yet it seems that we have arrived somewhere else, a causal loka, a different dimension altogether. Is that true? Where are we? I'm confused?"

"Yes, what you say is true. So sorry that you are confused, dearest Bellina, but there is a reason I brought you here first, which I will explain later. Meanwhile, I welcome you to this nameless, formless loka in the causal universe, far beyond Hiranyaloka, which you correctly placed in the astral universe.

"As you know from your studies, Hiranyaloka is one of the highest of all the astral planets, but it still exists as light and energy patterns. We are in one of the extremely subtle causal lokas, which has no physical or astral component. Nevertheless, it truly does exist! It is an important loka, which all beings inhabit before they achieve final liberation—that moment, which frees them from all incarnational necessities, physical, astral, or causal.

"Our visit here will be brief," Thomas continued. "Sabella visited me here once before, but I know this is your first time visiting the causal realms.

"I understand how disorienting it can be to be completely aware and yet free of the body and senses, existing without the usual benchmarks of reality, but still able to think clearly and remain a cognizant, separate entity.

"I wanted you to enjoy the experience of a causal loka before we go to back to Hiranyaloka, my primary place of residence and service."

Sabella took this moment to express her gratitude, gently saying, "Thank you, Thomas. I am sure Bellina has gained a deeper understanding of what it is like to be in the causal universe. Please take us to your home on Hiranyaloka, where I think she will be more comfortable."

"I agree. Off we go, on wings of pure thought."

Bellina saw that the three of them once again were cloaked in their more familiar astral bodies. However, recalling her recent experiences on Janaloka, Hiranyaloka was obviously a very different sort of astral world.

She observed that Hiranyaloka was simple, possibly even a little stark, in contrast to the lush, almost gaudy beauty of Janaloka. Still, Bellina was aware that it had its own unique kind of splendor, a pure, unadorned loveliness that was deeply satisfying on many subtle levels.

Thomas offered them ethereal nourishment. It was not like they had been given to eat on Janaloka, but it satisfied her hunger. The meal was simple—a piece of fruit she had never encountered and a small container of refreshing, cool water.

Tuning in to her curiosity, Thomas said to Bellina, "The fruit is called a Hiranyalokan rose-peach. While we have the most exquisite foods available to us, most residents have given up eating altogether, and are nourished by cosmic light rays alone. I rarely bother to deal with food or drink any more, unless I have a special guest to welcome, like you! I could feel that you were hungry—naturally enough, for you've come a long, long way to be here with me."

Having finished her meal, she felt satisfied, but very tired. "Great-Grandpa, do you have an astral resting-nest that I could use? I think I have been up all night, but I am not really sure about that, with the astral days and nights being much longer than what I am used to on earth."

Thomas laughed and assured her he would materialize a suitable spot for her to rest for as long as she needed.

She realized that her astral body was crying out for an extended period of deep rest. The many spectacular and unusual events she had experienced in such a short amount of time had left her quite tired. Also, it was apparent to her that her great-grandparents wanted to be alone for a while. This thought made her smile, for she felt they were both very, *very* old.

"Never too old to be in love, Bellina!" Sabella said. Bellina was embarrassed to feel the gentle tickle of Sabella's thought, as it trickled into her mind.

Sometime later, refreshed from sleep and meditation in the cozy nest that Thomas provided, Bellina went looking for Thomas and Sabella. She found them quietly sitting on a nearby plateau, shoulder to shoulder, gazing off into a clear astral sky. She wondered if it would be appropriate to interrupt their inner communion with each other. In its simplicity, it was deeply profound to see them together in this way.

"Please join us, dearest one," Thomas said. "You are not interrupting us."

Bellina sat on the soft ground on the other side of her

great-grandfather and happily held his hand. They all sat in silence for some time, simply enjoying each other's company, in utter stillness. She realized what a great blessing it was to be with these amazing souls.

Eventually Thomas said, "Go ahead and ask your questions, Bellina. I know you are bursting with curiosity."

"I will, for you are right. I want to know as much as I can about Hiranyaloka, but before I can focus on that subject, I must admit that I still feel stunned by our visit to the causal loka. Please begin by helping me understand what we experienced. It was all so foreign to me, that I am having trouble integrating what we encountered there."

"Very well," Thomas smiled at his lovely yet earnest great-granddaughter, thinking with great pleasure of how much she resembled Sabella when he first met her, so many years ago on earth.

He continued, "I think that it would be helpful now to review some basic principles that you first learned as a student in the Halls of Wisdom.

"In the beginning, when God brought the Universe into creation, he chose to encase human souls in three bodies: the thought or causal body, the most subtle; the astral or energy body, the location of human emotional nature; and the dense material or physical body. These bodies exist in God's creation in the corresponding casual, astral, and material universes.

"On the material plane, a person is equipped with a physical body, brain, and physical senses.

"An astral being works through his consciousness and feelings with a body composed of energetic *lifetrons*, also called prana or life force.

"A being, with a formless causal body, dwells in the blissful realm of ideas."

"It's true," Bellina agreed. "When we arrived in that causal loka, I didn't know where I was at first. It was deeply unsettling to realize that I had no form at all, but even in my confusion, I felt extremely blissful and took great comfort in the fact that I was there with you and Sabella.

"And yes, I certainly remember studying the foundational concepts of the three bodies and their corresponding universes. As fascinating a subject as it is, intellectual understanding is one thing, while the actual experience is quite another!"

"You are absolutely right about that, Bellina!" Thomas said.

He continued, "Let me explain more about the causal realms. The seed, or blueprint of a person as an individualized soul is rooted in the causal body. It is a matrix of ideas used by God to form the subtle astral body and finally the gross physical body.

"God, in the aspect of Creator, became a fountainhead of ideas that he projected out from himself into different levels and vibrations of reality and consciousness. Coming from the central point of complete stillness and moving outward, vibratory forces condense, first subtle, then gross. God determined that our causal, astral, and physical bodies would be separate and different from each other, but still fully integrated and able to function together as a seamless whole.

"When you were with Loralon, as he exited his physical form, you were able to observe that after a person's desire to live in a physical body is severely shaken by disease or other causes, death inevitably arrives. At that time, he or she sheds the heavy overcoat of flesh. I believe you were then able to perceive that Loralon's soul continued to remain encased in his astral and causal bodies, after his departure from his physical body.

"The binding force which holds all three bodies together is desire. The great power of unfulfilled desires and attachments holds the three universes and their corresponding bodies in existence. Desire is also the root cause of all suffering!

"Physical desires are rooted in egotism and sense pleasures. The compulsion or temptation of *physically* oriented sensory experience is more powerful and binding than the forces of desire connected with astral attachments or causal perceptions.

"As you saw on Janaloka, astral desires differ from physical desires in that they are based on the enjoyment of vibrations. Astral beings appreciate the ethereal music of the spheres and are entranced by the sight of all creation as endless expressions of light and sound. Astral beings also smell, taste, and touch light and sound. Astral desires are thus connected with an astral being's power to perceive all objects and experiences as forms of light, sound, and vibrations of energy.

"Causal desires are fulfilled by perception only. Because the nearly free beings who are encased only in the thinnest veil of the causal body see all universes as pure expressions of the Divine Idea, they can materialize anything and everything by thought alone.

"Causal beings consider the enjoyment of physical sensations or astral delights to be dense and suffocating to their finer sensibilities.

"Causal beings quickly work out all their desires by materializing them instantly. Those who find themselves covered only by the delicate veil of the causal body are able to bring whole universes into manifestation. Because God first manifested all creation out of cosmic thought, the soul, thinly clothed in a causal or thought-body, can enjoy and take direct part in vast manifestations of divine creative power.

"The soul is insubstantial and can be distinguished only by the presence of an encasing body. Therefore, the mere presence of any of the three types of bodies signifies an indwelling soul and is the product of unfulfilled desires.

"As long as a soul is encased in three, two, or even just one 'container,' sealed tightly by the 'corks of ignorance and desires,' it cannot merge with the great Sea of Spirit or God. When the physical body is abandoned in physical death, the astral and causal bodies continue to exist, preventing the soul from immediately becoming one with God.

"When complete desirelessness comes to us through meditation-acquired wisdom, the enormous power of attachment is released and disintegrates all remaining bodies. All 'corks of ignorance' are popped and removed; the human soul emerges from its restrictive encasements, free at last, becoming one with all that is, one with God!

"The lofty, mystifying causal world, which you briefly experienced, Bellina, is ineffably subtle. In order to realize it fully, beings would have to possess such phenomenal powers of concentration that they could visualize the astral and physical cosmos, in all their vastness—the enormous luminous astral balloon, with its solid basket of matter hanging beneath it—as existing as ideas only.

"If by such superhuman concentration, they arrived at a unified world view, resolving the two cosmoses (material and astral) with all their complexities into sheer ideas, they would reach the causal world and stand in a world of fusion between mind and matter.

"There, they would perceive all created things—solids, liquids, gases, electricity, energy, all beings, gods, angels, humans, animals, plants, bacteria—as forms of consciousness. In a similar fashion, human beings can close their eyes and still be aware of their existence, even though their bodies are temporarily invisible to their physical eyes and are present only as an idea.

"Please remember, Bellina, that whatever a human being can imagine, causal beings can *manifest*. The imaginative human intelligence is able, in mind only, to range from one extreme of thought to another, to skip mentally from planet to planet, to tumble endlessly through the corridors of eternity, to soar rocket-like into the galaxy-filled canopy, or to scintillate like a searchlight over milky ways and starry spaces.

"However, encased only in a causal or thought body, these beings have much greater freedom, and can *effortlessly manifest* their thoughts into instant objectivity, without any material or astral obstruction or karmic limitation."

"Tom-Tom! Since we were last together, you have become

so eloquent and poetic! '...scintillate like a searchlight over milky ways and the starry spaces?' How lovely that sounds! But I've never known you to use such fancy language before!" Bellina giggled.

Thomas glanced sternly at his mirth-filled great-granddaughter and thought how very young she looked, and often acted.

"My dear," he said quite seriously, "I'm quoting Sri Yukteswar, when he explained the abilities of causal beings!"

"Oops, sorry. Will I get to meet him, while we are here on Hiranyaloka?"

"Perhaps. We shall see about that later. I will continue my lecture on the causal world, if you have finished teasing me, Bellina."

"Please continue, Tom-Tom. All this is fascinating information!" Bellina enthused, stifling another small laugh. She thought she might have caught a faint mental chuckle from Sabella, also.

"Very well, in spite of your disrespectful mirth, my dearest ones, I shall continue. Souls in the causal world recognize one another as individualized points of joyous Spirit. Their thought-objects are the only things which surround them. Causal beings perceive any distinctions between their bodies and thoughts to be merely ideas.

"Just as in meditation, we can perceive a dazzling white light or a faint blue haze, so causal beings, by mind alone, are able to see, hear, feel, taste, and touch. As I have said before, causal beings can create anything or dissolve it away through the intense concentration of their cosmic minds.

"Both death and rebirth in the causal world exist in thought only. Residents feast only on the ambrosia and cosmic light rays of eternally new knowledge. They drink from the springs of peace, roam on the trackless soil of perceptions, swim in the endless ocean of bliss.

"See their brilliant thought-bodies zoom past trillions of Spirit-created planets, fresh bubbles of universes, wisdom-stars, spectral dreams of golden nebulae, all over the sky-blue bosom of Infinity!"

"'...the sky-blue bosom of Infinity,' indeed! Sabella, these fancy poetic descriptions, whether original, from Sri Yukteswar or Yogananda, or from some long-deceased earthly editor, certainly have a ring of power from one who has experienced that reality. I am enjoying it all very much!" Bellina thought to Sabella.

Thomas continued to offer insights into realms Bellina knew little about, "Many beings remain for thousands of years in the causal cosmos. By deeper ecstasy, eventually the freed soul then withdraws itself from even the insubstantial causal body and expands into the infinity of the causal cosmos.

"All the separate eddies of ideas, particularized waves of power, love, will, joy, peace, intuition, calmness, self-control, and concentration melt into the ever-joyous Sea of Bliss. No longer does the soul experience its joy as an individualized wave of consciousness. Finally, it merges into the Cosmic Ocean of Bliss.

"When a soul breaks free of the cocoons of the three bodies, it escapes forever from delusion and becomes ineffable and eternal. Behold the butterfly of omnipresence, its wings etched with stars, moons, and suns! The soul expanded into Spirit remains alone in the region of lightless light, darkless dark, and thoughtless thought, endlessly intoxicated with its ecstasy of joy, within God's dream of cosmic creation. It truly has become a completely *free soul*, forever!"

"These concepts are stunning and have greatly helped me to begin to perceive the finale of my cosmic destiny, dearest Thomas. Thank you for these most precious insights! Can it really be true that this path ends in complete freedom for me and for everyone in existence?"

"Of course! It is your absolute destiny—as it is every soul's destiny! The question is not if it will happen, but when. That part is up to you."

"Up to *me*? What do you mean?" Bellina asked.

"I mean that as far as *your* spiritual progress goes, you can accelerate the process more than you would imagine. Or not—it is your choice. It takes sincerity of purpose, daily deep meditation, energy, devotion, and a God-realized Guru to guide and help you move forward."

"Okay! Sign me up right now!" Bellina blurted out enthusiastically. Then she paused, remembering her recent, somewhat less-than-respectful behavior towards Thomas.

"Oh, Tom-Tom, do forgive me! I did not mean to be frivolous or silly. I want freedom! I mean, I really, *really* do! I deeply appreciate your efforts to show me the way to find perfect liberation for my soul, but it all seems so vast, overwhelming, stunning, and.... Oh dear, I find I suddenly have become very hungry. Can we eat soon? And I don't mean causal food either!"

Thomas roared with laughter at his wonderfully precocious great-granddaughter. Soon, all three of them were immersed in waves of light-hearted laughter—sincerely appreciating the deep love they felt for each other.

CHAPTER NINETEEN

As prophets are sent on earth,
To help people work out their physical karma,
So I have been directed by God,
To serve on an astral planet called Hiranyaloka,
Or "Illumined Astral Planet."

— Sri Yukteswar, from *Autobiography of a Yogi*

Bellina said, "Thomas, Gigi tells me we have only one or two astral days to spend here with you. I wish we had more time together, but I suppose it will have to be enough. I hope we can take a tour of Hiranyaloka, but first, please tell me about the inhabitants of this lofty plane."

Thomas agreed that their visit would be too short for his liking, but that he would do his best to be a good host and travel guide. Wasting no time, he began to describe the denizens of Hiranyaloka.

"The inhabitants of this loka have already passed through the ordinary astral spheres, such as Janaloka, the astral world to which you followed Loralon after his death, and which I understand you thoroughly explored for several days before arriving here."

"Wait a minute, Thomas," Bellina objected. "How can you call Janaloka an 'ordinary world?' It was sublimely beautiful, full of shining angels, openhearted astral people, and quite an interesting variety of creatures. Even the plants there talked to us and produced a variety of delicious food for us to enjoy—not that I'm complaining about the food here, but...."

"You are right, Bellina. Perhaps I should not have called Janaloka ordinary. I can imagine how beautiful it must have appeared to your astral vision, accustomed as you are to seeing only through your earth-eyes, at least more recently. Nevertheless, energetically, Janaloka is not on the same lofty level as this world. That is the simple truth!

"Hiranyaloka is where great Avatars, such as Sri Yukteswar, are aiding advanced beings to rid themselves of any remaining astral karma, and attain liberation from astral rebirths. The inhabitants are very highly developed spiritually. In order to reach the elevated state necessary to reside here, one must have acquired, through meditation, the power to exit the physical body consciously at death.

"In addition to that great power, souls cannot dwell on Hiranyaloka unless they have passed beyond the state of *sabikalpa samadhi* into the higher state of *nirbikalpa samadhi*, while dwelling on a planet in the material universe.

"In *sabikalpa samadhi*, the devotee has progressed spiritually to an inward state of divine union, but cannot maintain that level of consciousness unless they remain immobile in a trance-like state of meditation. By continuous meditation, a devotee reaches the superior state of *nirbikalpa samadhi*, enabling them to move about freely in the world and perform outward duties without any loss of God-realization.

"In the astral universe, there are countless planets like Janaloka, where most beings from material planets go after death. It is there that they can complete the process of burning up many seeds of material karma. The process continues, and in order to free their souls from remaining traces of confining karma lodged in their astral bodies, cosmic law eventually draws them to be reborn on Hiranyaloka, the highest of all the astral heavens.

"There are also many highly advanced beings here who have descended from the superior, subtler, causal realm."

Bellina had to ask, "Thomas, why would someone advanced enough to leave Hiranyaloka for the causal universe ever come back to live in the astral universe again, even a place as spiritually advanced as Hiranyaloka?"

Thomas answered her, "For the same reasons souls move

back and forth between the physical and astral universes. There is simply more karma that needs to be dissolved away. As a rule, astral karma can be released most easily in the astral realms, just as physical karma must be worked through in the physical world. On Hiranyaloka, advanced beings receive help to rid themselves of all astral karma and attain liberation from astral rebirths."

Bellina asked, "Thomas, please help me to understand. Once a soul loses its physical body and is reborn in a beautiful astral world like Janaloka, why can't they just stay in the astral realm and work out their karma from there? It seems so cruel to be forced to return to a material world filled with suffering and sorrow, after one becomes accustomed to living in such peace and harmony, especially in such a beautiful, wonder-filled world. By contrast, inhabiting a physical body on a material planet like the earth inevitably feels like being tortured."

Thomas replied, "The physical karma of human beings must be *completely* worked through before a permanent stay in the astral worlds is possible—or really, even desirable. Two kinds of beings live in the astral spheres: those with earthly karma and those without. Those with earthly karma *must* re-inhabit a physical body in order to pay their karmic debts on the material plane, while those without material karma have overcome the need to reincarnate on a physical planet.

"Beings with unredeemed physical karma do not have the capacity, after astral death, to go on to a causal sphere, but must shuttle to and fro, between the physical and astral worlds only, conscious of alternating cycles of material and energetic bodies.

"After exiting their physical bodies, spiritually undeveloped beings remain for the most part in a deep stupor and are barely conscious of the beautiful astral sphere. After resting, these souls return to the material plane for further lessons, gradually becoming accustomed, through repeated comings and goings, to the lovely astral worlds, woven of subtler vibrational textures.

"Long-established residents of the astral universe have forever shed all material longings, and have no need to return to the heavy, stultifying vibrations of the material plane. These beings are limited only by their remaining astral and causal karma.

"At their time of exit from the astral realms, they pass to the infinitely finer and more subtle causal world. In accordance with cosmic law, after their allotted time in the causal realm, these advanced beings return to a high astral planet like Hiranyaloka, in order to work out what little may remain of their unredeemed astral karma. Souls from lower physical planets like the earth, if they retain *any* vestiges of material karma, are not able to rise to the elevated level of Hiranyaloka.

"Most people on earth have not attained the heights of meditation and intuitive vision necessary to appreciate the superior joys and advantages of astral life. Thus, after death, they retain the desire to return to the limited, imperfect pleasures of earth.

"So it is also, that many astral beings, during the normal disintegration of their ethereal bodies, fail to envision or appreciate the advanced state of spiritual joy in the causal world. They still desire what the flashier, gaudy astral worlds have to offer; thus, they are compelled to revisit these astral paradises. All astral desires must be fulfilled before they can achieve a longer stay in the causal lokas, which are only thinly partitioned from the Creator.

"One must exhaust all desires for pleasing-to-the-senses astral experiences so that they cannot be tempted to return, before they can release all causal karma and burn all seed-thoughts of desires. Soon enough, the confined soul pops the last of the three corks of ignorance, and emerging from the subtlest container of the causal body, commingles with the infinite, eternal Spirit of God.

"Bellina, does this answer your question?"

"Absolutely, Great-Grandfather Thomas! Your answers have dispelled my confusion!" Bellina said. "May I ask another question? I notice that you have not taken time to rest or sleep since we arrived at Hiranyaloka. Do the beings here require any sleep or rest?"

"The inhabitants of Hiranyaloka mostly remain awake in ecstasy during the long astral days and nights, helping to work out complex problems of cosmic government and the redemption of matter-bound souls. When they do occasionally sleep, they may experience dreamlike astral visions, but usually their minds are completely engrossed in the superconscious state of nirbikalpa samadhi.

"As odd as it might seem to you now, astral beings are still subject to mental pain. This is especially true on Hiranyaloka, because the extremely sensitive minds of the higher beings here feel keen pain or even agony from errors in conduct or even just wrong perceptions of truth. In order to avoid this mental suffering, Hiranyaloka residents tirelessly endeavor to attune their every action and thought with the absolute perfection of spiritual law."

Bellina was surprised to hear this, but could see how it made sense. She had another question—and wondered if her questions would ever end!

"Thomas, how do astral beings communicate with each other?"

"Communication happens entirely by telepathy. Therefore, there is none of the confusion and misunderstanding engendered by the written and spoken word which earth-dwellers in the lower ages of Kali and Dwapara Yuga must endure."

Bellina seemed satisfied with this answer, but found she had still another question. "Thomas, you said you don't care to ingest food or beverages these days. What is it that sustains you?"

Thomas smiled kindly at his inquisitive descendant. He answered, "Just as persons on a movie screen appear to move and act through a series of light pictures, but do not actually breathe, so astral beings walk and work as intelligently guided and coordinated images of light, without the necessity of drawing power from food, drink, or even air.

"Beings in the material universe depend upon solids, liquids, gases, and energy for sustenance. As I've said before, astral beings sustain themselves primarily by cosmic light."

Bellina paused, then said, "I don't understand how you do that! Do you actually eat, drink, or breathe cosmic light?

Thomas smiled at her, "Not in the way you imagine. It's a process of natural absorption and is difficult to describe."

"I think I understand, but even air too? I *thought* I noticed that you are not breathing much, if at all. Amazing! Anyway, another question comes to my mind, dearest, *patient* Great-Grampa. When souls graduate permanently from one universe to a subtler one, is there a celebration of any kind?"

"Oh, yes, indeed!" Thomas enthused. "Joyous festivities take place when a being is liberated from the astral world. On the higher astral planets like Hiranyaloka, when a being is ready to enter the causal world, the invisible Heavenly Father and the saints who are merged in him materialize bodies of their choosing and join the astral celebration.

"In order to please His beloved devotee, God takes a form that is near and dear to the devotee. If they enjoyed worshiping God through compassion or loving devotion, they may see the Lord as some form of the Divine Mother. To some, like Jesus, the Father-aspect of the Infinite One was appealing beyond all other conceptions.

"Our divinely endowed individuality makes every conceivable and even inconceivable demand on God's endless versatility!"

Bellina was growing tired again. It was difficult for her to maintain an energy level high enough to match the energy of Hiranyaloka's rarified atmosphere. However, she still had one final (she hoped!) important question to ask her great-grandfather. "Thomas, when one lives on an astral loka, how difficult is it to communicate with people on earth?"

Thomas answered, "The highly developed intuition of many astral beings can pierce the veil between worlds, and enable them to observe human activities as well as communicate with people on the material plane, providing these humans are open to such communication. For example, Sabella and I effortlessly stay in contact with each other. For the majority of human beings, regular, deep meditation is essential to develop one's intuition, as you well know.

"Most humans, while inhabiting physical bodies, cannot view the astral world or communicate with its inhabitants. Those few who have developed their power of intuition may communicate with subtler realms. Nevertheless, thousands of earth-dwellers have at least momentarily communicated with an astral being, an angel, or had glimpses of an astral loka."

Sabella knew it was time to step in and close this discussion. Both she and Bellina could feel that their time in the astral universe was ending.

Their final hours together included a somewhat rushed, but very enlightening tour of a portion of Hiranyaloka, climaxed by a brief visit to Thomas's mentor, Swami Sri Sri Yutekswar Giri.

Sri Yukteswar, being an Avatar of few words, had very little to say to them. He offered each of them, privately and individually, a few words of profoundly wise advice—words they would treasure always. He gave Sabella and Bellina a loving farewell, and wished them success in their new project on earth. He indicated that he knew all about it—thus, any further conversation seemed superfluous.

Bellina was speechless in his august presence, entranced by his beautiful eyes. He blessed her and Sabella by touching each of them at the spiritual eye, just before departing from their presence. It was an unforgettable moment and without question, the most sacred in young Bellina's life.

It was over now—the greatest adventure she ever could have imagined. Bellina was not sure how to feel about that. She knew she did not like saying goodbye to her beloved Great-Grandfather Thomas.

She thought Sabella must be even more distraught about their parting, until she saw them gazing at each other fondly for several minutes. She realized that they did not feel separate from each other at all—almost as though, somehow, they did not live in different universes!

Bellina could only wonder if it was her own destiny to find such a strong and enduring life-linked partner in her present lifetime on earth. Seeing the beautiful example before her made her desire a relationship like theirs even more! Ah well, no time to dwell on *that* subject. It was time to go to their present home loka. Off they flew on wings of light.

CHAPTER TWENTY

God is no tyrant....
One who has been accustomed to drinking nectar,
And then eats stale cheese,
Soon grows dissatisfied with it and throws the cheese away,
Crying for nectar again.
If he longs with all sincerity for God's love alone,
The Lord won't reject him.

— Paramhansa Yogananda, from *Conversations with Yogananda*

In no time at all, Bellina and Sabella were sitting on the deck of Sabella's small pyramid home, overlooking the sparkling Joyuba River. Both were still and silent; they would remain that way for several days.

It was a big adjustment, having physical bodies again. These dense bodies felt heavy and uncomfortable, not unlike wearing a thick overcoat on a warm day. With time, they got used to the heavy feeling of being in a physical body again. On top of that, they were still adjusting—mentally, emotionally, and spiritually—integrating their otherworld experiences.

After some time, they began to communicate mentally again. They had been so deeply and profoundly moved by their experiences that at first, they could only converse in short phrases.

Sabella asked Bellina to record her thoughts and impressions of their recent adventures, whenever she felt ready and able to do so, "... but don't wait too long, Bellina. I don't want you to forget *anything* that you experienced; record it in the greatest possible detail!"

Bellina felt ready soon after Sabella made the request. Before beginning, she prayed deeply for help and guidance. She then began to relive and record her memories and impressions of the astral and causal worlds they had visited.

How long had they been away in normal earth-time? Bellina really couldn't say. Days? Weeks? Finally, she asked Sabella.

"Oh, for heaven's sake, silly one! Look at a calendar! You remember what day we left, don't you? Well, today is...." They worked it out together and were both somewhat surprised to find they had been away from earth for a little over a month.

"Time passes in different rhythms in other universes, doesn't it, Gigi?"

"So it would seem!"

A few days after she completed her intensive sessions of remembering and recording, Bellina transmitted them to Sabella and asked if she would review them and correct any errors. She also asked for some time off, to go on a short vacation. She felt a bit overwhelmed by the whole experience and was ready for some quality downtime.

"Of course, dear one! You deserve it! Where do you plan to go?"

"Well, there's that special beach you once told me about—the one where you and Issoweet spent time reviewing your adventures in the Water Chakra Pyramid. I would like to visit it myself, and just be there alone and in silence, for at least a week or more. I think you mentioned a hammock under palm trees and the clear, turquoise lagoon where you swam among the colorful tropical fish.

"Does this plan work for you? Please contact me if you need me while I'm away."

"That sounds perfect, Bellina. Enjoy it for me!"

Several weeks passed with no communication between Sabella and Bellina, for none was needed.

Bellina spent her time alone, thoroughly enjoying the tropical paradise, meditating for long hours, and (she couldn't help herself) formulating more questions she hoped to be able to ask Thomas, Sabella, or the others she met on her most fantastic journey.

She also found herself combatting a slight feeling of sadness at finding herself back in her material body on the earth again. Beautiful as it was here on the tropical beach, everything was radically different from the astral and causal lokas they had visited. Even though their time there had been brief, she felt mildly depressed, much like feeling homesick.

Swimming underwater with a myriad of tropical fish in the turquoise lagoon helped to keep her spirits high, for they reminded her of the bright and colorful world of Janaloka.

She spent time reviewing what she had learned. It particularly struck her how souls must be aware enough, spiritually speaking, to allow them to be awake sufficiently after death, even to *begin* to appreciate a place like Janaloka. Thus they would avoid just sleeping through their time there and all too quickly reincarnating on a material planet.

She also recalled that Thomas had mentioned to her that living on Hiranyaloka was possible *only* for those who had achieved nirbikalpa samadhi while still living on earth. She assumed that this meant not only on earth, but also on any planet in the material universe.

In any case, these memories were deeply inspiring to her, and were a great aid to increase the length and depth of her daily meditations.

Bellina did her best not to let the still-fresh memories of her recent adventures overwhelm her. The whole of creation, including physical, astral and causal universes, are infinite. She now understood how it was all beyond comprehension to a normal human mind like her own, at its present limited state of evolution. Nevertheless, in certain ways, she felt comforted in the realization that everything she had experienced (and far more) was still out there and available to her, within her own inner being.

One day, while resting in a comfortable hammock strung between two palm trees, she received a mental message from Sabella.

"Bellina, the High Council members want to meet with us soon. I have reviewed your recorded reports and now want to go over them with you, to clarify a few points. I also sense that you have more questions. Do you feel ready to return soon?"

"Yes," Bellina replied to her great-grandmother. "I'll be there with you in about 24 hours. Would that be soon enough?"

"Of course, dearest. See you then."

Bellina realized that she needed just a little more time to put her thoughts and questions in order—and perhaps time also for another swim or two in the lagoon.

A little over a day later, Bellina sat comfortably with Sabella on the scenic deck outside her home. They ate together and spoke of simple things. Bellina, looking radiantly refreshed, described her time in the tropics and reminded Sabella how lovely it had been when she, too, had been there with Issoweet, so many years ago. Sabella had always meant to return for a vacation, but now Bellina had done it for her, which was almost as satisfying!

Bellina understood that the time had come for she and Sabella to concentrate and prepare themselves to meet with the High Council. Sabella explained that the Council had asked for a thorough report on their recent adventures and all that they had learned.

She also told Bellina that they needed to be ready to present a comprehensive plan to complete their assigned mission, by finding new and dynamic ways to disseminate useful information about death, dying, and the astral and causal realms.

"Bellina, you mentioned that you had other questions and observations. Please tell me of your thoughts."

"Yes, Gigi. Unfortunately, it is not a pleasant topic, but it is one that I feel compelled to explore thoroughly. It is a subject, which I believe is not fully understood by most people. Everyone *needs* to understand the truth, so they have the right information to make a dharmic decision. In any case, I know that I certainly need to understand this challenging subject well, so that I can help those who face difficult circumstances in their lives.

"The question is this: morally or spiritually speaking, is suicide ever an acceptable action, under any circumstances, especially when one is in great physical or mental suffering, or rapidly approaching a painful death?

"Similar to that question, is there ever an acceptable reason for assisting people to end their lives deliberately?"

Sabella gave an approving smile to her somber great-granddaughter. She agreed that Bellina would need to be prepared to tackle such tough topics.

"Bellina, these are thorny questions about important subjects. Your lack of fear in facing difficult questions about them will serve you well in this mission.

"I have a great idea. Let's see if my beloved mentor, Issoweet, is available to enlighten us about these matters. Does that sound like a good plan?"

Bellina answered, a little hesitantly, "Gigi, I'd be very happy to see Issoweet again, but I thought you'd know the answers to these questions."

"I appreciate your confidence in me, Bellina, and I *do* know a fair amount about the questions you have asked, but just to be sure, I'd like to double-check with Issoweet. Besides, I would love to see her again.

"Do I hear my name being tossed about wildly by you two?" Issoweet's sweet voice rang in their minds.

Bellina was startled, but Sabella calmly turned to look over her shoulder at her beloved mentor, sitting quietly nearby. "Issoweet! You didn't even give me a chance to call you!"

"Am I not always with you, Sabella? Besides, I already had the idea that you would want to consult with me at this point in your major research project. I was in the neighborhood, so here I am. Lovely to see you again, dearest—and you too, Bellina!"

"'In the neighborhood!' Ha-ha! That's a good one, Issoweet. You were probably hiding behind the sunbeams, waiting to appear just when we needed you. Would you care for a cup of herbal tea? It is Simeon's "Thyme Travel" tea blend, fresh from my herb garden," said Sabella.

"That sounds perfect!" Issoweet said.

They sat in Sabella's herb garden, sipping the freshly brewed tea. At Issoweet's request, Bellina enthusiastically shared a few of the stories of their recent adventures in the astral lokas. Issoweet smiled and nodded appreciatively.

Bellina was grateful to have a wise soul like Issoweet to listen to her rehearse her presentation to the High Council. After Issoweet's many years of service on the Council, she was a valuable resource to help Bellina understand what they would expect of her.

"While you should be clear about what you want to say, a formal presentation is not the best way to work with the High Council, Bellina. Just be yourself. Speak your mind and speak from your heart. These are sensitive beings who will be receptive to your thoughts and intentions and will clearly understand what you are attempting to convey."

"And *that* is supposed to make me feel more relaxed, when I'm speaking before them?" Bellina laughed.

Issoweet smiled, but then became serious, saying, "You'll do fine! In any case, I know you have some questions, so let us address them now.

"First, about suicides. People often judge souls harshly for what they label 'throwing away their lives.' However, God and the Great Ones never judge in that way. They empathize and understand completely. We have all had past lives where suicide seemed to be the only way out of intense suffering—whether mental, physical, or emotional. And in some cases, we actually did end our lives prematurely!

"That doesn't make suicide right or a beneficial course of action by any means! While it is true that the consequences for such an act are severe, we are not affected at the level of our innate immortality. Compared to the great length of the soul's journey, the repercussions of a suicide are relatively short-lived."

Bellina asked. "I know, Issoweet, but why would God punish such sad, suffering souls for ending a tortuous life? Surely their suffering and self-inflicted death is punishment enough!"

"Always right to the point, aren't you Bellina? Well, there *is* some truth in what you have said. Making a big mistake like taking one's life is just that—a huge error in judgement, based on ignorance of the law of karma and the consequences of suicide.

"A suffering person might think, 'Surely *anything* must be better than the excruciating emotional pain I am feeling right now!' Or 'Please, give me oblivion instead of this unbearable physical pain.'

"Nevertheless, ignorance of the universal laws of karma is not an acceptable excuse. Remember that whatever suffering we go through, we ourselves created the cause of the suffering in this, or some other lifetime. Blaming God for our karma does not help us to escape pain and suffering. Past karma often brings us intense suffering. Moreover, because suffering is so difficult to ignore, it is a good teacher, perfectly designed to help us learn and correct our harmful actions, ensuring that we will not make the same mistake again.

"When Paramhansa Yogananda spoke of suicide he said, 'Life is a school from which you must graduate into Infinite Consciousness. If you are truant from this school, you will return to life repeatedly, until you learn life's supreme lessons.

'All beings want to be happy. Even if a person commits suicide, it is rooted in the desire to be happy. They think that by destroying their material bodies they will be happier than when they were living.

'Based on ignorance, suicides wrongly believe that they can escape the pain that is plaguing them, by terminating their lives. Their goal is perfectly right and common to all beings. However, attempting to reach happiness through suicide does not work. Through ignorance, a person committing suicide chooses a long detour on the path to a permanent state of bliss.'"

Issoweet continued, "*Each* lifetime is a very important gift from God and is never meant to be squandered or heedlessly discarded. Even though life can be intense and uncomfortable, every life we live is precious and important in the grand scheme of things!

"Suicide is an even greater karmic mistake than murder. To kill another person is to deny one the remainder only of that particular lifetime. The act of suicide implies the total rejection of the magnificent gift of life itself, bestowed upon us by God. Essentially, suicide is the ultimate denial of *all* life!"

"But most importantly, suicide is not an escape, for the ego survives physical death. The wholesale rejection of life will require significant hard work to expiate all that negative energy.

"If we want to grow spiritually, we must understand that, in objective reality, life and death are all the same thing. Paramhansa Yogananda once spoke to Swami Kriyananda about how Divine Mother 'eats people.' What he meant was that God does not really care whether we live or die, physically, because our Creator sees that we never truly die anyway! Whether we are in a physical body or not, we maintain that same infinite spark of God-consciousness."

"At another time, Swami Kriyananda also asked Yogananda an intriguing question about suicides, 'If the primary thing that keeps us bound to this world is our desire for it, why don't people who commit suicide become liberated? Surely, they at least have no desire to remain here. Just look at the extreme measures they employ to escape the world!'

"Yogananda chuckled at this absurdity and then replied, 'But there must also be a positive desire for God!'"

Bellina asked, "So exactly what happens to a person's soul

after suicide? Where do souls go, after they have taken their own lives? Does God cast them into some hellish astral realm, as the result of such a grave error?"

Sabella stepped in to say, "Bellina, it is incorrect to view ourselves or anyone as victims! God does not *do* anything to anybody! We do it to ourselves. God created us with free will, and to guide our free will, God also created the laws of karma, of action and reaction. When we err, we must expiate the negative energy patterns we create and pay the penalty for doing that, but not an *eternal* penalty. A finite action cannot cause an infinite reaction.

"True, our Creator set these universal laws into motion. You can get upset with God for doing things this way, as many do, but it doesn't help, because that attitude only mires you deeper in delusion.

"It would be much wiser for us to strive to understand and attune ourselves to Divine Law. Doing that minimizes our suffering and quickly brings us into the bliss and oneness with God that is our one *great* desire, behind all our other desires.

"To elaborate further on your question, in the Judeo-Christian Bible, suicides are labeled as 'unclean souls.' Here is what Paramhansa Yogananda says about such souls: 'Unclean souls are those who leave their physical bodies in a state of grave ignorance and error. Murderers, thieves, drunkards, treacherous people, and *those who ruthlessly and foolishly commit suicide*, all are considered to be unclean souls in the astral world.

'These souls roam about among the darker astral worlds, compelled by their karma and imprisoned in their causal and astral bodies, but finding no rest or joy. They remain in a very confused state and are often tossed back and forth between the conflicting desires of never wishing to be reborn on earth and intensely desiring to have a new physical lifetime, in which to try again to set things right.'"

Bellina said, "Thank you, Gigi. Let me ask both of you another related question. When we were visiting Janaloka, I was blessed to spend time with a beautiful angel named Sofieli. She mentioned that all angels eventually evolve to a higher state than she had reached—a state in which they are able to help the very needy residents of the lower astral worlds. Would these be the 'unclean souls' about whom Yogananda spoke?

Issoweet glanced at Sabella, who indicated that Issoweet should answer Bellina's question. "Yes. These souls have to roam about in a deeply confused state, dwelling in the gloom-drenched lower astral worlds until some of their bad karma can be dispelled by what they have learned from the experience, or until they receive assistance from other, more evolved astral beings, including angels.

"In the case of suicides, these beings must begin again to appreciate the true value of a human body and brain. They must create within themselves an intensely strong desire to live another life in a human body.

"As a consequence of the negation of not only a lifetime, but of life itself, once their desire to live again as a human being is sufficiently strong, they likely will still have thwarting karma that prevents the fruition of that life. Some may enter a human mother's womb only to leave again quickly through a miscarriage or an abortion.

"Trying again, they may repeat this cycle numerous times. Their great desire to be born and continue to live grows stronger and stronger through repeated denial. The ordeal may continue, and even though they achieve a live birth, the ripples of karma might result in being stillborn or only having a brief life.

"Another way the karma may express itself is, as these souls eventually begin to be able to hang on tightly to the precious human body into which they have reincarnated, they might suffer from severe insomnia. You see, they very much wanted oblivion through suicide. To balance that energy pattern, they may be forced to stay awake, thus becoming denied the oblivion of sleep.

"The fruits of these life lessons are that people who commit suicide eventually come to treasure life very much. Whether they are conscious of the causes or not—and it is doubtful that at this stage of evolution they *would* be that wise—they begin to work at living in accordance with the laws of *dharma*, or righteous living."

Bellina interjected, "This information would be helpful for grieving parents who have lost a little one. It must be agonizing to wonder why a baby would come into their lives, only to be taken away after such a short time."

Sabella took this moment to offer her thoughts on the subject at hand, "In some cases, you would be right, Bellina, but not all grieving parents are spiritually mature enough to receive or understand such information. We must be sensitive and prayerful in what we say to those who grieve.

"Since grief is so intimately related to the subject of death, we will talk more about how to help someone who is grieving for the loss of a loved one. However, the time for that discussion will be later. For now, remember that the soul's journey from bondage to freedom is a long and arduous process and never quite the same as anyone else's—every soul's karma is unique and intricate."

Bellina asked, with tears in her eyes, "Sabella, most people, myself included, know someone or the family of someone who has committed suicide. Is there anything that we can do to alleviate the suicide's suffering after their death—long wanderings in the lower astral hells, sadness from the frustrated desire to inhabit another body, or any of the other scenarios you described? What compassionate things can we do to help them?"

"Bellina, your sweet, tender, loving heart is beautiful to behold. We should always remember that because most of us have lived millions of lifetimes, the odds are that we committed or at least attempted suicide many times. That fact alone should be enough to fill us with great compassion for those lost souls.

"Regardless, we *must* realize the full truth of this matter. Suicide is an ultimately selfish act! A person who chooses to die that way rarely considers the impact their death makes on the grieving ones left behind. They think only of themselves and of death as a supposedly effective way to end their own suffering.

"Even worse, they might become vindictive and think thoughts like: 'That'll show them!' Alternatively, 'This is a good way to punish those who have hurt me.' Or 'No one will miss me anyway!' Or 'This is how I can stop all my physical, mental, or emotional suffering!' Or simply, 'I hate my life, and I want out, *now*!'

"Suicides may think that their self-imposed death is a way to resolve their suffering and turmoil, but the truth is, their misguided solution only makes things worse for them. Some people, when contemplating suicide, might be given this information as a reason *not* to commit suicide. However, they may easily doubt this information, thinking, 'Well, I don't believe that things *could* get any worse for me!'

"Unfortunately they are wrong! Things definitely can and do get worse, at least *temporarily*, if they choose suicide as a solution to their suffering.

"Please remember the word *temporarily*!' Suicide is not the end of the line for the soul. It is merely a setback—a serious one, that is true, but still only temporary.

"To answer your question, we can say healing prayers for suicides, surrounding them with divine light, sending them our love, and praying deeply that they move out of the darkness and uncertainty into which they have unwittingly plunged themselves more quickly than they could manage to do alone.

"Our prayers do help greatly! Do not abandon someone just because he or she has made a grave error. Do not judge them harshly either, for you most assuredly have made the same mistake at one time or another.

"In addition to offering your prayers, call on the healing angels of light for help. They most definitely will give it! You told me that your angel friend Sofieli said that this is one of the primary duties of high-ranking angels—to help fallen or unclean souls come back into the light, as quickly as possible."

"Yes, Sofieli did tell me that." Bellina said thoughtfully.

Bellina paused for a few minutes, to assimilate all the information she had just received. She then said, "Issoweet, thank you for taking the time to explain this challenging subject to me so thoroughly.

"I now more clearly understand the precious nature of a human lifetime and how it is critical that we, as human beings, appreciate being alive and the over-arching Divine Intention inherent in the grand scheme of things.

"What an unbelievably grand cosmic show is going on all around us. As Yogananda said, life's purpose is for our education and entertainment—that is, until you realize that your life really is just a magic shadow-show and that, in the long run, it is all just a small part of the vast Cosmic Dream."

"Well said, dear one! You are obviously wise beyond your years. I understand now why Sabella requested your assistance and companionship on this particular mission. But I believe you have another question?"

CHAPTER TWENTY-ONE

In a very true sense,
The most important moment of life,
Is its last moment.
If our last, lingering thought is one of regret,
For the mistakes we have made in this life,
Our direction will be downward.
If that last thought is of God,
Then it is upward to God that we shall go.

— Swami Kriyananda, "The Final Exam"

Bellina frowned, "I think I know the answer to my question, but I'd really like confirmation from you. I wanted to know about the spiritual implications of assisted suicides. Are there any conditions where it is acceptable to help someone in great physical pain to leave the body and avoid prolonged suffering and an unpleasant exit?

Issoweet mentally sent Bellina this message, "Yes, I believe you do know the answer to that question. Tell me what you think."

Bellina took a few minutes to focus her thoughts, "Issoweet, it's easier to express my understanding through a story that you may already know. This story speaks to a deeper realization of the high cost to all concerned in participating in an assisted suicide.

"There was a very great saint, a priest of the Catholic Church, who lived in the southern part of Italia in early Ascending Dwapara Yuga. During the course of his life, he performed countless miracles, including many healings.

"One day he was called to the hospital to comfort a very sick, old man, whom he had known well for many years. It was obvious that the man was terminally ill and in great pain.

"As the saint sat with him, blessing and praying for him, the man summoned up the strength to speak. He said, 'Holy Father, I know that my time to die is rapidly approaching. I do not feel it right to ask you or God to heal me, but I am very tired of all this suffering. I know that God works miracles through you when you ask. Please, won't you ask God to let me die right now and leave this ailing, pain-filled body behind?

"The saint smiled compassionately at the man and said, 'No, my son. I cannot ask that of our Heavenly Father. You see, for you, there is still just a little more chaff left to burn.'

"The dying man had been a farmer. He understood quite clearly what the priest meant by 'chaff to burn.' Chaff is the seed coverings and other debris separated from the edible grains of wheat by the threshing process. Removing the chaff leaves the grain clean and ready to grind into flour. Sometimes chaff was fed to the farm animals, but often it was simply swept away and burned.

"It is clear that the saint was saying that his friend was in the process of burning up karma through his present state of intense suffering. Often a person can dissolve large amounts of difficult karma in the last months of a lifetime.

"The saint was trying to explain to his dying friend, in a simple and understandable manner, that what he was going through was sometimes a necessary part of the process of life. If he avoided this suffering now, at the end of this life, it might compel him to reincarnate more quickly, driven by the urgency of unfinished business. In addition, due to the weight of this wrongfully avoided karma, he would not be as capable of enjoying his respite in the astral world.

"The saint clearly perceived how much wiser it would be for his friend to endure and outlast this karma, here and now. Even though it was a difficult task with his old, worn-out body, it was best for him to complete this test and burn up the karma as soon as possible!

"The saint knew that if this test were not successfully completed *now*, the cost in the future would be much higher. It definitely would not be a favor to anyone to interfere with this process of purification."

Issoweet smiled at Bellina in approval and said, "Yes, Bellina, I know of this incident in the great saint's life. You told the story beautifully. It is an excellent illustration of the need to work out karmic debts, especially at the end of life. As a rule, deliberately cutting the process short causes dire consequences, karmically speaking.

"In a sense, when one person assists another in killing himself, the karmic debt is doubled, because the crime is doubled—the assistant also generates the bad karma of taking a life. Whatever the justification, it is still murder and as such will have negative karmic repercussions in a future life. Moreover, the suicide has not only chosen to negate the power of life itself, but has also involved another person in this dark drama.

Bellina asked, "But Issoweet, many argue that it is the compassionate thing to do, to assist a suffering person to die and avoid much great suffering. I mean, it has been common wisdom through the ages to euthanize a very sick or suffering animal."

Issoweet answered, "Animals do not accrue karmic debts as humans do, for their nervous systems are not yet sufficiently evolved. They do not have highly developed astral bodies, brains, and chakras, and cannot store karma in their subtle nervous system as humans do. They do not have strongly developed egos yet and rely much more on instinct, or group minds. So no, it is not the same at all!

"It is *not* compassionate, even if a person is ignorant of the laws of karma and reincarnation, to end a life prematurely. It matters not whether it is his own or someone else's, for it causes intense future suffering."

"An exception to this law is when the killing is done for selfless or dharmic reasons, such as defending one's homeland from invaders. For example, the *Bhagavad Gita*, one of the greatest scriptures ever written, is set on a battlefield. The fifth of the Ten Commandments in the Judeo-Christian Bible has been mistranslated over the millennia. It really says, 'Thou shalt not *murder*,' not 'Thou shalt not *kill*.' Killing for dharmic reasons is one thing, but killing as a selfish act will inevitably attract a karmic backlash.

Issoweet continued, "A favorite story of mine on this subject is about a Bodhisattva, who, in the Buddhist tradition, is someone who is able to attain Nirvana, or final liberation, but who delays doing so. Motivated by his great compassion for all suffering beings, he devotes his life to helping them move towards their own Nirvana."

"One day as the Bodhisattva was sitting on a ferry crossing the river, by means of his highly developed intuition, he suddenly and clearly realized that the man sitting next to him was planning to kill everyone on the ferry, stealing their belongings and then dumping their bodies into the river!

"He was deeply distraught, thinking about the mountains of bad karma this man would accrue through his actions, how long it would take him to burn it all off, and the torment he would have to endure while ridding himself of such karma. He realized that the only way to stop the would-be mass murderer, save innocent lives, and spare the murderer his grim karma, was to kill him.

"In a completely selfless act, he decided to take on the terrible karma of murder by killing him immediately. Through the sincere contemplation of this noble act and in that instant, the Bodhisattva was finally and completely liberated. The massive waves of bliss emanating from him caused the would-be murderer to lose his will to carry out his plans, and all the ferry passengers were saved!"

Issoweet looked at Bellina and said, "While it seems that we have satisfied your two areas of greatest concern, I sense you still have some other questions. Now's the time to ask, while we here are together, discussing these subjects!"

"Thank you for telling me that story about the Bodhisattva, Issoweet, and for your loving support of me in my investigation of some unpleasant topics. It is a great honor and a rare privilege. I deeply appreciate you sharing these sacred lessons at this pivotal point in my life."

Bellina took this moment to kneel before Issoweet and touch her feet, honoring her in an ancient gesture of respect and devotion. She felt immense gratitude toward this great soul.

Rising to her feet, Bellina said, "Shall I ask my questions now?"

"Yes, by all means, Bellina. Ask away!"

Bellina began, "We have spoken often of how we all carry karma between lifetimes in the material worlds, with astral respites between physical lifetimes. Just how do we carry that karma between lifetimes? How does a soul in the astral world know when it's time to be reborn into a human body, and how does it recognize its parents?"

Issoweet slyly winked at Sabella and thought privately to her, "Sabella, look at this truly lovely descendant of yours! Wouldn't you say that her energy is very much in tune with yours, when you were her age?"

Sabella thought back wryly, "Yes, you certainly are on target there! I am beginning to appreciate all that you went through training me. How did you *ever* survive my endless questions? You were so lovingly patient with me, my dear mentor. Thank you!"

"I loved every minute of it, Sabella, just as I love being with your sweet and intelligent great-granddaughter today. Her natural curiosity draws answers from me, effortlessly."

Bellina missed this mental exchange between Sabella and Issoweet, for they were very careful to be discrete.

Issoweet said to Bellina, "You have asked several questions, and we'll answer them in order."

Bellina smiled. "Thank you!"

Issoweet continued, "You first asked how we carry karma through life, death, life after death, and rebirth. We store it in our astral bodies and more specifically in our chakras and astral nervous systems.

"Our karma is the sum total of all of our actions, activities, thoughts and ideas from this and every past lifetime. Karma is the spiritual expression of the universal law of cause and effect.

"A single increment of karma is called a *vritti*, which is a tiny whirlpool of committed energy. These countless vrittis, which make up our karmic patterns, are stored in the chakras. Each vritti finds its own level, by being magnetically drawn to the appropriate chakra; like attracts like.

"Although there are a few physical expressions of these subtle centers in our physical bodies, our chakras primarily exist at the level of our astral and causal bodies. Because we cast aside our material bodies at the time of physical death, and because our karma still resides in our astral and causal bodies, we keep all that latent karma with us, where it waits to be mitigated at the right time—usually an unimaginably *long* time!

"The old saying, 'you can't take it with you' is true only in the sense that nothing from the physical realm, be it material possessions or your physical body, survives the transition of death. However, you absolutely *do* take your karma with you after you die."

Issoweet continued, "All our unresolved karma is still a part of us, stored in our subtle bodies. When we release our karma through meditation, service, devotion, attitude adjustments, and learning all of life's lessons, the seeds of karma are destroyed and we are free of them forever. Powerful yogic practices such as Kriya Yoga can burn through one's karma at a greatly accelerated rate!

"*Astral* karma can be resolved while in the astral world. I believe you discussed this while you were on Janaloka. Isn't that true, Bellina?"

Bellina replied, "No, we never did, I *did* ask Ariella about astral karma while we were there, but even though I know she meant to answer me, we ran out of time and did not get to discuss the subject. Thomas also spoke briefly to me on this subject. However I would appreciate your answering this question for me more clearly now. What is the difference between material and astral karma? It seems to me that understanding this difference would be extremely helpful!"

"Yes, it *is* important." Issoweet said. "Material karma is created by any desire to possess something made of matter, including another human being. As we have said, when material desires remain unfulfilled, karma is created and stored in our chakras as vrittis. Every vritti must be dealt with, either by satisfying the desire or transmuting the energy through spiritual methods. Attempting to satisfy every desire rarely works out well, because there are simply too many of them. Moreover, once a desire is satisfied, very often many other desires rush in to take its place.

"Astral karma is somewhat different from material karma. While it still involves desires, they are lighter, more ethereal, and not nearly as binding as material desires. These kinds of desires are *much* more quickly satisfied in the astral realms. They do not cause other desires to spring up in their place once they *have* been satisfied.

"An example of an astral desire is wanting to enjoy beauty, music, color, joy, and harmony among all beings.

"Nevertheless, desires, whether material, astral, or causal, are still desires and must be dissipated in some way. As an old adage says: 'Chains, though of gold, still bind!' The good news is that such desires are much more quickly and easily satisfied in the astral or causal universes than they are here on earth!

"If, when we die, we carry strong material, rather than astral, desires with us—desires for things that provide sense pleasures, be it food, alcohol, sex, drugs, or possessions that offer pride of ownership, we are forced to return again and again, through countless lifetimes, to pain-filled material planets, to deal with them. That is because these types of heavier, more materialistic desires can only be satisfied while residing in a physical body on a material plane.

Bellina was astonished. "It's hard to imagine having to hurriedly reincarnate back on earth, just to enjoy eating physical food! Astral food tasted a thousand times better than anything I ever ate on earth!"

Issoweet replied, "I agree with you about astral food. However, repeatedly pursuing and satisfying desires for physical pleasure over many lifetimes creates a strong impetus within us to return to the physical universe, compelled to action by the force of our momentum, in spite of any thoughts to the contrary.

"Material desires *cannot* be fulfilled on the astral or causal planes. We reincarnate for countless lifetimes, until we grow excruciatingly tired of the endless monotony of the process. Or a state of intense satiety sets in, making us feel physically sick, heartsick, or utterly bored and unhappy. We simply become fed up with the material universe and all that it falsely promises to give us, to make us permanently happy. Again, no wonder a baby cries at its rebirth on earth!"

Bellina's mind reeled from the implications of this information. She thought about how hard it would be for a new mother, gazing at her newborn with deep love, to comprehend that even at this early time in life, her cute little baby is carrying within it all the karma, all the dark desires of the heart, from who-knows-how-many past incarnations.

"Yes, Bellina. It *is* hard to understand. Every soul goes through the long, arduous journey of many lifetimes, deaths, and rebirths, for an unimaginable length of time.

"I might add that this long, long journey can feel like not only a very lengthy journey, but also a lonely one. For as Swami Kriyananda says, 'The soul is solitary. It comes into the body alone at birth. It leaves it solitarily at death. During its earthly existence it appears as if surrounded by others, but in fact, in its essence, it is ever apart from them....'

"Remember though, that we are all *immortal* beings and that eventually we fully realize and merge into our original state of blissful immortality and oneness with God, for eternity! What a drama! What a show! Wouldn't you agree?" Issoweet's eyes were shining with joy, as she uttered these words.

CHAPTER TWENTY-TWO

She saw a mother smile,
As she tended her baby;
A widow weep that love had to die.
The joy of new friends,
And the sadness of parting:
All these made her ask God—Why? ©

– "Why?" from *Songs of Divine Joy*, by Swami Kriyananda

"But why, Issoweet?"

Bellina then turned to Sabella, almost in tears, asking, "Why, Gigi? Why all this suffering and misery? Why the journey? Why the drama and in my opinion, the overly long show? Why did God create it all this way? Surely creation could have been designed according to different laws, avoiding the weight of unbearable suffering completely!"

Sabella smiled, "Ah, yes! I wondered when this question, perhaps the ultimate question, was going to come up in our discussions. Paramhansa Yogananda sometimes answered this question by saying, with a wry smile and a bright twinkle in his eyes, 'You will know, when you know God.'

"There was another answer he often offered his disciples. He explained that a drama must have highs and lows, villains and heroes, happiness and sadness, for it to be interesting to the audience. If everything were always calm and perfect, the audience would become bored in short order. The juxtapositions of light and dark create infinite dramas in 'The Grand Movie.'

"God is the ultimate and finest possible playwright; therefore, all possible expressions of duality are present in creation; love, hate, health, disease, life, death. The trick for us is not to get caught up in this drama, thinking that it is real—but rather to step back, through meditation, intuition, and introspection, in order to see what is *really* happening—the play of light and shadows, smoke and mirrors: the magic shadow show!"

Bellina still felt a bit irritated by the whole subject. "I'm sorry, I just can't imagine how creation would not be improved by eliminating all this suffering."

Sabella and Issoweet both laughed. Sabella said, "Bellina, if you want to tell God how you disagree with the ways he created everything and how it all functions, then go right ahead. In fact, Yogananda often scolded God for this very thing.

"He said, 'God doesn't mind our arguing or scolding him for the way creation turned out. God actually likes this, understands our complaints, and is sorry for all the inconvenience; but God will not go against his own natural Divine Laws, which were put in place as a necessary means for keeping the great show going.'

"If you can figure out a better way to do it, then by all means, let God know all about your ideas." Sabella and Issoweet could not help chuckling together at the absurdity of this thought.

Bellina simply shrugged and said, "Well, I'll work on it."

This made the two older women laugh even more. They were quite amused at this delightful young woman's "divine presumption." Bellina didn't mind. She knew their laughter was kindly, and that they loved her, as she loved them.

Sabella winked at her great-granddaughter. "As long as we are on the subject of complaining to God about how things are set up, let me tell you another story of Yogananda's. He often told this tale, to illustrate how people wander through the corridors of time on their long journey of countless incarnations, trying to satisfy all desires.

"There was a man who had achieved a certain degree of spiritual advancement, but at the same time had a few unfulfilled worldly desires. At the end of his life, an angel appeared to him and asked, 'Is there anything you still desire that you didn't get in this past lifetime?'

"'Yes,' the man said. 'All my life, I have been weak, thin, and unwell. In my next life I want a strong, healthy body.'

"In his next life he was born with a strong, large, healthy body, but he was poor and found it difficult to keep his robust body properly fed. Finally—still hungry—as he lay dying, the angel appeared to him again and asked, 'Is there anything more you desire for your next lifetime?'

"'Yes,' he replied. 'For my next life, I would like a strong, healthy body, and also a robust bank account!'

"Well, the next time he not only had a strong, healthy body, but was wealthy as well. In time, however, he began to grieve that he was alone and had no one with whom to share his good fortune. When death came, the angel asked again, 'Is there anything *else* you desire?'

"'Yes, please. Next time, I would like to be strong, healthy, and wealthy, and also to have a good woman as my wife.'

"Well, in his next life he was given all those blessings. Although his wife was a lovely woman, she died shortly after they were married. For the rest of his lonely days, he grieved her loss. He worshiped her gloves, her shoes, and other precious memorabilia. As he lay dying of grief, the angel appeared to him again and said, 'What *now*?'

"'Next time,' said the man, 'I would like to be strong, healthy, and wealthy, and also to have a good wife who lives a long time.'

"'Are you sure you've covered everything?' demanded the angel.

"'Yes, I'm certain I've remembered *everything* this time.'

"In his next life he had all those things, including a good wife who lived a long time. The trouble was she lived *too* long! As he grew older, he became infatuated with his beautiful young secretary, to the point where he eventually left his good wife for his secretary. As for the girl, all she wanted was his money. When she had gotten her hands on it, she ran away with a much younger man. At last, as the man lay dying, the angel again appeared to him and demanded. 'Well, what is it *this* time?'

"'Nothing!' the man cried. 'Nothing ever again! I have finally learned my lessons. I see that, in the fulfillment of my every desire, there is a catch. From now on I want nothing else. Nothing but God alone!'"

They all had a hearty laugh together, appreciating this amusing story and the great truth it illustrated.

"Moving along to your next question, Bellina," Issoweet said. "You asked how a soul in the astral world knows when it's time to be reborn into a physical body and how it finds its new parents.

"The timing of people's rebirth from the astral world back into the material world is determined by the weight of material desires and attachments still embedded in their astral bodies as unresolved karma.

"Yogananda put it this way, 'In sleep every night, we discard the consciousness of a tired body and a care-worn mind to find temporary peace. Likewise, in the greater sleep of death, souls forsake the disease-torn body and the attachment-corroded mind for a restful vacation in the astral world.

'However, in every sleeping soul arises a natural desire to be more awake and aware. As this desire returns repeatedly and the sleeping person comes back into wakefulness, so also arises the desire for a body and a physical environment, propelling the disembodied soul to rush once again into a new embryo in his future mother's womb.'"

Issoweet continued, "There is a divine understanding, a kind of contract between the soul and God. Thus, in the astral world, when the time comes for us go on to the next stage of the soul's long journey through time and space, we begin to feel uncomfortable where we are. It is kind of like an energetic tug. It is the irresistible pull of unfulfilled material desires and our stored up material karma demanding that we reincarnate on the material plane to attain resolution. This pull cannot be ignored for long.

"Some humans who have reached a higher level of spiritual awareness *really* don't like the idea of reincarnating into the material world and often try to figure out a way to avoid it.

"Paramhansa Yogananda also mentioned the soul's reluctance to reincarnate, in his poetic interpretation of the *Rubaiyat of Omar Khayyam*: 'One day [in a state of ecstasy] I beheld that place from whence souls are sent to earth. Gazing with inner vision, I beheld the Divine Energy shaping the little bodies that would serve souls as their earthly residence. I saw new forms being condensed and molded out of the blazing furnace of life force. As disembodied souls were being thrust into their new earthly casings, I observed their uneasiness over their impending imprisonment, and the swift approach of their birth throes.'

"One great saint described the necessity of reincarnating in this way: 'Life is a school. However, if you have not successfully passed all the tests of your previous lifetimes and learned all the needed lessons, you may get to have a nice summer vacation in the astral world, but then it's 'Back to school again!'"

They all laughed. Sabella chose this moment to re-tell a story that Thomas had shared with her many years ago, while he was traveling through time, experiencing many dimensions and past lives. In one scenario, he was enjoying himself very much in a beautiful astral loka, when a strong intuitive feeling burst upon his consciousness—a feeling it would soon be time to reincarnate in a new body on earth.

"Thomas felt intensely resistant to this idea! He simply did *not* want to be reborn on earth again so soon, or perhaps ever—he was thoroughly enjoying his time in this pleasant astral loka! He looked around and noticed that several close friends seemed to be 'popping' out of existence from this astral plane.

"'Where are all of you going?' he cried out to them! 'Surely not back to a life on earth! That's crazy! We are having a wonderful time here! Why, my dear friends, would you ever be foolish enough to want to leave this enchanting place?' He was truly mystified.

"His spiritual teacher, who was there with him in the astral loka, saw his bewilderment and lovingly explained how it really *was* the right time for him to reincarnate on earth. 'You, along with your close friends and I, are part of a special astral family. It is time for us to create and develop an important spiritual community on earth, to aid in the earth's transition through the chaotic times of early Ascending Dwapara Yuga. Thomas, you are an integral part of this project. You and each one of your friends have essential parts to play in in this community's formation!

"His teacher continued encouraging him, 'It will be fun for you, plus you'll learn great lessons and burn through mountains of karma. And of course, I'll be going along with you, too.'

"'Oh, all right!' Thomas said grudgingly. 'If you are going and if you really think I should join you, then I will do it. It seems that you and all my friends are leaving now, anyway. I will admit that it is true that I would not want all of you to leave me behind, even as lovely as it is here.'"

Sabella went on with the curious story her life-linked mate had told her. "Thomas was intrigued, and even though he still complained a bit at the prospect of reincarnating on earth, he agreed to go with them.

"Continuing to explain his experience to me, Thomas added that when he discovered himself confined in his mother's womb, he went into a state of complete panic. When he felt the rumblings of his mother's birthing labors finally begin, it became alarmingly clear that he did not want to have to deal with the challenges and discomforts of physical incarnation—no indeed! Not at all!

"So he dug in his fetal heels and refused to come out of his mother's womb! In those days, there was a barbaric process practiced by doctors assisting births. When they saw that the baby was having a hard time exiting the womb, they used an implement called forceps, which was a large metal device, with broad pincers, used to encircle a baby's head and drag the baby out of its mother's womb into the world."

Bellina could not keep herself from exclaiming, "Oh Gigi! Poor great-grandfather Thomas! What a terrible story. Did he survive that particular birth experience?"

"Oh, yes, he did, but it left him with an injury to one of his eyelids, caused by the crude roughness of the forceps. For that was sometimes a part of a physical body's birthing process. In this case, the stubborn little Thomas had to be dragged, kicking and screaming, into the world. It was not an easy birth for his mother either, as you might imagine!"

"Sabella, I understand how that age on earth was a difficult time to be alive, but that story *really* illustrates the unbelievable brutality of those times. I can see why neither you nor Thomas ever shared it with me before."

Sabella smiled and said, "Nevertheless, it *is* a true story, and Thomas claimed that it taught him a good lesson about not resisting, at least in that way, the pull of a new and necessary reincarnation. There are other, much better ways to overcome the need to reincarnate in a material universe, as we have been talking about.

"To end the story on a positive note, Thomas lived a productive life, helping his teacher and working together with members of his astral family to create a very successful and influential spiritual community. As predicted by his teacher, he worked out a great deal of karma in the process and made significant spiritual progress through deep meditation and selfless service."

Issoweet spoke up to say, "To finish our session together, Bellina, let me answer your last question, 'How are an astral being's new human parents determined once they are ready to reincarnate on a material planet?'"

"Yes!" Bellina said enthusiastically. "So how *do* we get to choose our parents for the next lifetime, or do they choose us? How does that work?"

"It is a mutually beneficial arrangement," Issoweet explained.

"A soul is vibrationally attracted to its next set of parents, drawn magnetically to the people and situations that will provide needed karmic lessons, both pleasant and unpleasant. In addition, this attraction also emanates from the larger familial and social constellation, including grandparents, brothers, sisters, good friends and life-partners. All of these people help provide needed lessons, guidance, and companionship. It is all seamlessly orchestrated by our souls, in cooperation with the Divine Plan."

Issoweet continued, "Paramhansa Yogananda was once asked the same questions you are asking now. Let me tell you how he responded.

"One of his disciples asked him, 'How do souls come to be reborn on earth?'

"Yogananda replied, 'After passing some time in the astral world, the length of people's stay depending on their stored-up good karma, the material desires residing in their subconscious minds and chakras become reawakened. These souls then are drawn irresistibly back to earth, or to another appropriate planet in the material universe, by the magnetic attraction of their unfulfilled desires or needed karmic lessons.

'At the time of physical conception, there is a flash of light in the ether. Souls in the astral world who are awaiting physical birth rush towards those lights when the vibrations are compatible with their own needs and desires. Sometimes more than one soul enters a womb at the same time, and you have twins, triplets, or other multiple births.'

"The disciple asked Yogananda another related question, 'Are spiritual souls always born into spiritual families?

"He answered, 'Like attracts like—that is the general rule governing reincarnation. Many factors enter in, however, including the right timing or potential availability. For saintly souls, opportunities for reincarnation into highly evolved families are not many, for spiritually inclined people often prefer not to marry or have children.

'For couples desiring spiritual children,' Yogananda continued, 'it is important that they keep their consciousness uplifted when coming together in sexual union. For their vibrations, at the very moment of conception, will determine the quality of the flash of light in the astral world.

'A couple once told me they wanted a spiritual child and asked me to help them to attract such a soul into their family. I showed them a photograph of a child who had died, and who, I felt intuitively, was karmically ready for rebirth. They felt drawn to the photograph.

'I then told them, "Remain sexually abstinent for the next six months, and meditate daily. During meditation, concentrate on this photograph, and invite this soul into your home."

'They did as I had instructed them, and at the end of that time the wife conceived. It turned out that this was the very soul who was born to them."'

Sabella had something to add—this time a story from her own experiences. "I'd like to relate another interesting example of a couple's ability to draw a certain kind of soul into their lives. I re-experienced this past lifetime during my younger years, when, I, also, like Thomas, was traveling through time and exploring other lifetimes and dimensions.

"In the lifetime I was reliving, I had incarnated as a woman named Pauline. She lived in early Ascending Dwapara Yuga in the middle of what was called North America."

Pauline married a fine man named Frank Nichols. They intended to start a family right away. The couple loved each other deeply and both desired children very much. For seven years, they prayed to conceive a child. No pregnancy happened for them. Finally, as a last resort, they were considering adoption. However, at that particular time and place in Ascending Dwapara Yuga, a 37-year-old woman was considered too old to adopt an infant. All adoption agencies where they lived declared her unfit to adopt a baby. She became distraught and began to lose hope.

"One day, in a state of deep discouragement, she went to her church and knelt to pray in a small chapel. Her simple prayer was, 'Lord, you know how much I want to be a mother—to give birth to a child of my own! If it is not your will for this to happen, please take away my desire for a baby. If you remove this desire, I promise to spend the rest of my life working with other people's children, teaching, loving, and helping them in any way I can.'

"She got up off her knees and was astonished at the change of heart. It was a new feeling of joy, lightness, and inner freedom. Her aching heart had healed completely, and she felt free from her intense desire for a child! Within three months, she became pregnant with her first and only child, Mary Jane.

"I later learned more about this inspiring story from Thomas, who had viewed it from a different perspective, during a time when he was exploring an astral loka.

"In that astral world, the soul of Mary Jane, a very old soul at the time, felt the urge to begin preparing for her next incarnation on earth. She was hoping to be born into a good and safe home where her parents would love God; and rooted in God's love, would love her also.

"Her last earth-life had been extremely hard and had ended early. She was born as a Jewish boy who, when he was a teenager, witnessed his parents' brutal murder. After this traumatic event, he was imprisoned in a Nazi death camp!

"His last memory of that lifetime was hearing the screams of hundreds of Jewish children being tortured and brutally murdered. Instinctively he knew that he would soon face the same fate—and so it was."

Bellina asked, "That sounds horrible! Please excuse me for interrupting your story, Gigi, but I must ask a question. What do you mean when you say that '...Mary Jane's soul was an old soul?' What is an *old* soul? I thought that the soul is eternal and has no age."

Issoweet smiled at Sabella and thought privately to her, "Once again I must say that your great-granddaughter is a true treasure. She does not miss a thing, and is absolutely fearless in asking for explanations. Mostly an admirable quality—although, at times, I think it could be balanced with a little more restraint and diplomacy."

"Yes, it's true. Her intense curiosity is one of the many qualities that I admire and love about her. Still, I am concerned that it may get her into trouble someday. I have emphasized the importance of her being more tactful in the way she respects peoples' points of view—and to think carefully, before she speaks. I think she would greatly benefit by toning down her frequent and often emotional outbursts, especially when she is relating to people who deserve deference and respect."

Issoweet mused, "It is better for a person to have strong, albeit misdirected energy, than to have little or no energy at all, Sabella. Energy can be redirected easily into the right channels. I know you can do that with Bellina. She really is a jewel!"

This exchange took place in an instant of telepathic communication between Sabella and Issoweet, which they believed to be private until they noticed Bellina's face turning bright red.

Using her physical voice, Bellina exclaimed loudly, "I heard that! What is wrong with asking so many questions? I thought you *wanted* me to satisfy my curiosity! How else will I understand the grand scope and innumerable details of our investigation?"

"Calm down, dearest," Sabella said. "Issoweet and I apologize for talking about you like that. Personally, I think it is remarkable that you were able to hear our private conversation. We definitely underestimated your ability to read our shielded thoughts! We encourage you to ask all your questions and now is the perfect time. Didn't you hear Issoweet's praise of you, calling you a treasure and a real jewel?"

Even though her eyes were twinkling brightly, Bellina lowered her head sheepishly and nodded her assent.

"Well, then please hear this from one who knows her well. Issoweet's praise of others does not come easily.

"Now, to answer your question. Yes, you are right! It is incorrect to call someone an old soul. The soul is ageless and immortal since all souls are a part of God. Our souls are infinite—we are as old as God!

"The quaint term 'an old soul' is simply meant to imply that a person is getting closer to finishing the seemingly endless rounds of life, death, rebirth, and finally merging back into the Creator, of which the soul has always been a part. Do you understand? And shall I get back to my story?"

"Yes, I understand, Gigi. Sorry for my interruption."

"Not a problem. I think you possess a powerfully inquisitive mind, and I love you for it!" Sabella beamed love at her great-granddaughter.

"I agree!" added Issoweet.

Sabella continued with her story, "Well, where were we? Oh, yes. The soul who would become Mary Jane was looking for a good home in which to reincarnate on earth. The laws of magnetic attraction enabled her to hear Pauline's beautiful and sincere prayer.

"Mary Jane said to herself and to her mentors and guides, 'Pauline is definitely the one I choose for my next mother! She is both dynamic and sweet, plus I really admire her attitudes of non-attachment and selfless service.' And so it happened that a few months later, Mary Jane rested in the womb of her new and loving mother. She was very pleased with her choice of parents."

Bellina asked, "Did her life with Frank and Pauline turn out as well as she had expected?"

"What would you guess, Bellina?" Sabella asked.

"I think she probably *did* enjoy her life in that wonderful home, filled with strong familial love and a sincere love for God. However, I would expect that her life was a mixed bag, enjoyable experiences as well as a few big tests, trials, and challenges. Am I right, Gigi?"

"Yes, you are correct. Nevertheless, the challenges of her youth and young womanhood were perfectly suited to help her move forward in her sincere search for life's eternal verities—a search that eventually lead her to the right teacher and teachings. All the circumstances of that lifetime worked together perfectly to help her make rapid spiritual progress."

Bellina was curious. "What happened to her parents? Did they have other children?"

"No, Mary Jane was their only child. And because she was born relatively late in her parents' lives, both died when she was still a young woman."

"That's sad!" Bellina said.

Sabella replied, "Not really, Bellina. It was their time to go, and their departure gave Mary Jane the freedom to more fully pursue her own spiritual path, for her path was very different from the ways in which her parents chose to worship God. Mary Jane found an Indian guru and followed the path of prayer and meditation. Her parents never could have understood or accepted her spiritual choices.

"Another interesting part of Mary Jane's life story happened when she was with her father Frank, just before his passing at 61. He had been very ill for a number of years with heart disease and emphysema, brought on by his addiction to smoking tobacco.

"As he lay choking and fighting for every breath, he said to his beloved daughter, who was standing by his hospital bed, 'Honey, I know I'm going to heaven soon, because I've already been in hell.' A few hours later, he died.

"We've spoken of people's concepts of heaven and hell before, but surely this kind and wise man had come, in his own way, to realize correctly that he had made his own hell on earth through his addiction to the poison of tobacco."

"Did Frank go to heaven? Or maybe I should restate my

question as, 'To which astral loka did he go after that earthly lifetime?'" Bellina wanted to know.

Sabella answered, "I'm not certain, but it is interesting you should ask that question. Actually, you met this soul recently here on earth in Ascending Treta Yuga and also in Janaloka."

"I did?" Bellina's sharp mind raced back in time. "Gigi, are you saying that Frank eventually became Loralon in one of his future lifetimes?"

"Ah, how interesting are the myriad ways in which our lives are intertwined—don't you agree, Bellina?"

CHAPTER TWENTY-THREE

I watch the roaring, shouting torrent of life force,
Moving through the heart into the body.
I turn backward to the spine.
The beat and roar of the heart are gone.
Like a sacred hidden river,
My life force flows in the gorge of the spine.
I enter a dim corridor,
Through the door of the spiritual eye,
And speed on until at last the river of my life,
Flows into the great Ocean of Life,
And loses itself in bliss.

— Paramhansa Yogananda

Issoweet offered Sabella and Bellina a loving farewell and departed for an undisclosed destination.

After they had rested, meditated, and remained in silence for two days at Sabella's home, Bellina found that she still had what she felt to be important questions to ask Sabella.

When they next saw each other, while out on a stroll by the river, Sabella once again showed Bellina that her thoughts had very few places to hide, by saying to her, "I know of the questions that have come into your mind now. You have heard of people having near-death experiences; and you want to know if they are real and if so, what happens and what we can learn from them.

"You also want to know more about the spiritual eye and the part it plays, both in your meditative life and in the way it functions as the 'passage tunnel' from life to death. Am I right that these are your new questions?"

"Spot on, Gigi! Can we discuss them now?" Bellina asked.

"Yes, I would like that. Will you join me on my deck for a cup of tea, and we can talk about your questions?"

After they were seated comfortably on Sabella's deck, drinking delicious herbal tea and enjoying the fabulous view, Sabella began to speak. "I'll start with your second question, first, if you don't mind. As you know, there are specific instructions for the correct practice of meditation. We are instructed to concentrate at the spiritual eye, at the point between the eyebrows, as a way to enter a superconscious state. The great masters of yoga explain that the point between the eyebrows is the seat of ecstasy in the body.

"Interestingly, evolution shows that the frontal lobes are also the most recently acquired section of our brains.

"Notice the difference between the human forehead and the forehead of most animals. A human being's forehead rises vertically from the eyebrows, whereas the forehead of most animals slopes sharply back. The intellect—the principal faculty that separates human beings from other animals—is centered in the frontal lobes of our brain.

"The intellect, however, is but a limited faculty when compared to direct perception through soul-intuition. The intellect could be described as a halfway station on the soul's long evolutionary climb. As powerful as the intellect may be, it cannot lift us into cosmic consciousness. Soul intuition and Divine grace are needed to take the final steps to perfect freedom in God.

"The spiritual eye, at the point between the eyebrows, is our doorway to the Infinite. In a state of deep meditative concentration, the mind often beholds a round light at this point. This light sometimes is called the third eye. It is a true experience, and not a self-induced vision.

"The spiritual eye is as much a part of every human being as are the body and brain. It is, in fact, *more* of a reality than our body parts, the loss or amputation of which cannot affect our essential being. The light of the spiritual eye can never be separated from our inner reality, for the simple reason that we *are* that reality. Even when we lose our physical bodies at death, we retain this place of inner light, for it is an aspect of our immortal souls.

"Testimony regarding the spiritual eye has been gathered from great numbers of people who experienced temporary, clinical death without fully losing consciousness. Many of these people found themselves floating outside of their bodies, observing accurately what was going on around them at that time. A high percentage of them reported receiving glimpses of a higher world after passing through a tunnel or tunnels of light.

"One fascinating aspect of near-death experiences is that the quality of their experience had little dependence on their belief in God, or if they had any kind of religious affiliation or spiritual practices in their lives. What *did* make a difference, evidently, was the manner in which they had actually lived their lives. Their experiences, it must be added, did not always seem pleasant or uplifting to them.

"These people's testimonies often begin with an exclamation at the surprise they felt at finding themselves no longer inhabiting their physical bodies. As we have said, many of them accurately described events which were later verified, that had taken place nearby—sometimes in the rooms where their body was confined during their out-of-body experiences—sometimes outside the room, in locations close by or even farther away.

"Following the initial shock of finding themselves without a physical body, many said they entered a long tunnel, at the end of which they beheld a brilliant light. Emerging from the tunnel into this light, they realized that the light was actually a conscious entity, whose role, they intuitively understood, was to help them recall and evaluate their actions on earth up to this point in their lives.

"Without fail, everyone who describes this experience reports that there is never a feeling of being judged or of being viewed harshly or unsympathetically. Instead, they describe the being of light as kindly, supportive, extremely loving, and completely accepting of them in every way!

"Most often, at this point in their experience, they were told that it was not their time to die, and that they must return to their lives in the material world. Most of them were convinced that, had they entered further into that light, they would have been unable to re-enter their physical bodies. Many regretted intensely that they could not go further into the radiant light shining before them. Others expressed gratitude for the insights they had been given, into the deeper purpose and meaning of their lives. The rest of their human existences were changed for the better by their near-death experience.

"The great Masters have described these phenomena from their first-hand experiences in deep meditation, when the soul sees and then merges into the tunnels and lights of the spiritual eye. The long tunnel, they explain, is actually the astral spine, through which the energy and consciousness must pass before one can leave the body through the doorway of the spiritual eye—whether temporarily in ecstasy, or at the time of physical death.

"The deepest states of meditation resemble the actual death experience, with this one important exception: *One can always return from meditation at will.*

"In deep meditation, as in death, the energy and consciousness rise through the tunnels of the spine, and become centered in the sixth chakra: the medulla and spiritual eye.

"As we've discussed before, an unenlightened human being, after death, most often sinks into a temporary sleep-state, leaving the body by the little-known doorway through which it first entered physical consciousness. That doorway is the medulla oblongata, which is located in the brainstem and is the receptive pole of the sixth chakra.

"The medulla oblongata, as you know, Bellina, is also the seat of the ego. After the sperm and ovum unite at the moment of conception, they begin the creation of the physical body starting with the medulla.

"A sincere spiritual seeker, who meditates regularly and concentrates deeply on the spiritual eye as much as possible, is able, at the time of death, to exit the body through the spiritual eye—the positive pole of the sixth chakra—rather than through the ego-saturated and more negative pole of the medulla.

"Those who, at death, are able to keep their minds focused on the spiritual eye can soar through it and out into high astral or causal realms or even into conscious freedom in the Infinite. In meditative ecstasy also, one's consciousness passes through this doorway and the three tunnels of light, into blissful union with God.

"Worldly, ego-absorbed humans, who prefer to remain firmly bound to the material world, sink passively backward into that medullary light at death, as if in sleep, instead of soaring out of the physical body and material universe through the spiritual eye. Retaining their ego-identity, they subsequently experience only as much of the astral world as their own inner clarity of consciousness permits. The after-death states, to which they attain, are not the same as superconscious freedom in God. These souls inhabit rather, and without conscious will on their part, a level of the astral regions merited by their deeds in the material universe.

"Materially attached beings must reincarnate on the physical plane to continue their soul-evolution, once again inhabiting new bodies. Here they gradually refine their ego-awareness, and in the process, shift the polarity of self-identity from ego-identification to soul-consciousness, from the medulla to the spiritual eye. Thus, you can easily see why it is important to focus on the spiritual eye in meditation, throughout the day, and most especially *at the time of one's death!*

"Of course, it makes sense to have a steady practice of keeping our focus at the spiritual eye, which will make it much easier to do all this, at the moment of death. You can see how this would be much more effective than thinking something like, 'Excellent! Now I know where to focus my attention, when the time comes for me to die. Why bother to do it beforehand?'

"A practice like this must become second nature to us, bringing us the ease we will need to have to concentrate where we need to concentrate, at the time we most need to do it.

"Those who want to know and merge into God must humbly ask for help and guidance and then strive to follow in the footsteps of the great Masters, who have already completed this inner journey!

"In ecstatic inner communion, we find our gaze drawn upwards automatically, and our attention absorbed in concentration at the point between the eyebrows. From the beginning, all sincere spiritual aspirants should focus their gaze and concentrate their attention at the spiritual eye while meditating. Thus, we will hasten the coming of ecstasy's dawn. This practice enables us to cooperate much more easily with the natural flow of divine grace. It is also a perfect practice to help us prepare ourselves for death.

"Gradually, but eventually for all, and with a steady increase of devotional magnetism, God's grace is attracted more and more into human consciousness. Eventually, the soul, soaring upward on rays of heavenly grace, passes through all the tunnels of the spiritual eye and out into the infinite freedom of Spirit."

Bellina asked, "Sabella, do you recall how we went through a tunnel of golden light, when we followed Loralon through his death experience? What exactly *were* we experiencing then?"

"Bellina, I'm sure you know the answer if you will think about what you studied in your spiritual anatomy classes in the Halls of Wisdom. I know this is true, because I wrote the outlines for most of those classes, myself!"

Bellina answered, "I remember most of what I learned then, though it's been a while. In contrast, the first-hand experience of speedily traveling through the golden tunnel of light and then emerging in the astral world called Janaloka—that was another thing entirely! It had a much deeper impact on me than merely studying this information intellectually!"

Sabella replied, "Yes, I very much agree with you about that concept! It is the primary reason why I insisted we must actually *experience* Loralon's death, in the intimate and very personal way we did, by closely following him through his complete process of dying. By the way, Bellina, I commend you on your bravery. Many metaphysical explorers would have had second thoughts before plunging into such unknown territory!"

"I admit that I had a few reservations and trepidations at the moment, Gigi. But in trusting you completely, I found my fears were unable to hold me back!"

"Let's continue, and please pay close attention! This is very subtle and important information for you to know," Sabella intoned seriously.

"The spiritual eye can be seen in deep meditation, as well as at the time of death, as a golden halo around a blue field, in the center of which is a five-pointed star, representing the Christ Consciousness.

"First, our consciousness must penetrate the outer golden ring or halo of the spiritual eye, which represents the astral body and the astral world. As we concentrate deeply on the golden aureole, it becomes an elongated tunnel of golden light, taking us to the astral universe.

"If we do not pause on our journey in the astral realms (as we did in Janaloka), we then can pass into the deep blue-violet field. This field can become an elongated tunnel of bright indigo light; as we travel through it, we become aware of our causal body and the causal universe. You remember that we traveled through that blue-violet tunnel from Janaloka to the causal loka that we briefly visited with Thomas.

"When we are able to pass beyond our causal body and the causal universe into the final silvery-white, star-shaped tunnel, we then enter a state of Cosmic Consciousness, or superconscious union with God, from which the three universes of creation originate."

"That seems like a fairly straightforward explanation, Gigi," Bellina said, with a solemn face, but lost control almost immediately, bursting into laughter. Her laughter was contagious, and Sabella let herself be carried along on a wave of mirth.

CHAPTER TWENTY-FOUR

Well, it ain't that I don't know what grief is,
This old heart has had its full share!
But grief's one thing,
And complaining's another,
Why multiply grief with despair?©

— Swami Kriyananda, "The Non-Blues," from *Songs of Divine Joy*

A few days later, Sabella gave Bellina the long-anticipated news that they must finalize preparations for their formal report to the High Council—an event only seven days hence.

"Seven days!" Bellina mentally cringed. "Will we be ready?"

"Absolutely, Bellina. I reviewed everything recorded in your reports of our explorations, adventures, and conversations, and all seems to be in good order.

"In the next few days we need to work on proposals outlining methods to disseminate this information to those with an immediate need for the healing effects of this sanctifying wisdom.

"It would be most helpful for older folks and those approaching death to understand the imminent changes. We will need clinics to aid and support souls in transition, and develop training programs for those serving in these clinics."

"That sounds like more than we can accomplish in a week, Gigi!"

"Not really. We will need only some short outlines for our first presentation—seed thoughts and basic ideas. The details can be filled in as the project progresses. I spearheaded a project much like this years ago, when I founded the Intergalactic Chakra Healing Clinics. I will help you in every way I can, but you should know that this will primarily be your project to complete, and will take much of your time for many years."

"And why is that, Gigi?" Bellina's thoughts quavered with dread. "Are you going somewhere soon?"

"I certainly hope so, Bellina! I am sure you can understand that I will be joining Thomas in Hiranyaloka in the not too distant future, but please do not concern yourself with that now. We will have plenty of time to bring this important project to fruition. You do see this as an inspiring life-track to be embarking on now, don't you, dear one?"

Bellina's eyes were shining. "I do, Sabella. I really do! Who could not be moved to the core of their being, changed forever by experiences such as we have had recently? I want as many beings as possible, from all over the material universe, to know and deeply embrace the true meaning of life, death, rebirth, and immortality, thereby dispelling all fear of leaving the material plane, when the time is right. I can think of no better life mission to embrace!"

"That's the spirit!" Sabella was gratified to feel Bellina's sincere enthusiasm for what was to come.

"As I see it, Bellina, we still have two topics to clarify before we meet with the High Council. One is, 'Helping those who are grieving for a departed loved one,' and the other is, 'Explaining the concept of *immortality* to all.' Which would you like to tackle first?

"Good grief!" Bellina chuckled at her intended pun. "Let's *do* discuss the subject of grief first. However, before we begin, I would like your advice about something that is troubling me."

"Of course, Bellina. What is it?"

Bellina began, "Ever since we returned from our visit to the astral and causal lokas, I've had a nagging sense of what feels very much like homesickness. I find my heart being drawn back to Janaloka, with a desire to live a harmonious life with the good friends I have there. Is it wrong to harbor a desire for heaven?"

Sabella smiled at her great-granddaughter's serious face and said, "I was a little concerned that you would experience this kind of 'homesickness', Bellina. It's good that you are self-aware and honest enough to admit what you are feeling!

"Although Janaloka is indeed a heavenly place, you must remember that a better and higher goal awaits you."

"Please explain more about this higher goal, Gigi. Are you referring to places like Hiranyaloka or other high realms that I haven't visited yet?"

"No, dearest Bellina. Let me tell you a story to illustrate what I mean. Yogananda often told this story, and his students loved to hear it. I know you will, too.

> There once was a saint who lived in India. He was very noble, gracious, and generous in every way. When anyone treated him badly or made outrageous demands of him, the saint very humbly and innocently served that person. To the saint, it did not matter at all if he was scorned or misunderstood, because he realized it was God who was coming to him in that form. If God wanted to insult him or treat him rudely, well, that was God's business. He would take it as a good test and an excellent lesson in how to remain even-minded and cheerful under all circumstances.
>
> Eventually, an angel, who had been testing him all this time by bringing these negative people into his presence, visited him. The angel wanted to determine the true mettle of the saint.
>
> The angel said to the saint, "You have passed all my tests perfectly and have thus earned the merit to let you ascend directly into heaven, without the loss of your bodily form."
>
> Well, of course, one cannot enter an astral heaven in a physical body, but what was meant here is that the saint would be able to leave his body without any loss of consciousness.

Immediately another shining angel appeared before them, driving a flaming chariot that stood ready to carry him to heaven.

The saint said to the angel, "It is very nice of you to come here and offer to take me to heaven in this way like this, but before I accept your offer, I want to know more about the heavenly place, to which you are offering to transport me. What can it give me that I truly want?"

You see, the saint had been striving for God-realization; he had not been looking for heaven.

The angel answered, "Well, this is a very unusual question! Never do people consider whether they want to go to heaven, and they *never* ask what it is like before they agree to go there. However, since you have asked, I suppose I must answer.

"Heaven is a place of amazing beauty, with no death, and you'll mix with the shining angels, devas, and the gods. You will have a life of great happiness and experience the delight of being with joyful and peace-filled companions—saints, like yourself!"

The angel continued for some time, describing heaven and lavishing praise on its ethereal delights. Finally, the saint had a question, "I think everything about the heaven that you describe is marvelous! However, I have never found anything to be completely advantageous. Everything seems to have some disadvantages, as well. Would you please tell me the disadvantages of heaven?"

The angel was extremely surprised, and said, "Certainly no one has ever asked me that question, but since you have asked, again I must answer. You can only stay in heaven as long as your good karma will allow. After that, you must return to this world. Toward the end of your stay in heaven, you begin to realize that all your good karma will soon be exhausted, and you will have no choice but to return to earth. At that point, your happiness quickly begins to fade away. You begin to feel sad that you must return to this world. That is the reason human babies cry when they are born; they are extremely upset about having to contend with physical bodies and the material world, yet again.

"Another disadvantage is that while you can enjoy the fruits of your good karma in heaven, you cannot make rapid spiritual progress there—to be able to do that, you need a physical body."

The saint thought this over for a moment, and then said, "Well, thank you very much, but the disadvantages of heaven, as you've outlined them, are so colossal, that I cannot imagine anybody in his right mind wanting to go there. Isn't there anything better?"

The angel replied, "Well, yes, you can go into the lightless light and the darkless dark. You can merge into God, as all the great masters and sages have done; but for that to happen, you have to stay here on earth and meditate more deeply."

Hearing these words, the saint sent the angels and the fiery chariot back to heaven and sat down to meditate. This he continued to do for many years to come. When it was finally time for him to leave his body, he merged his being into the Infinite One."

Bellina sat spellbound, listening to this wonder-filled story.

"Why do you think I just told you this story, my dear?" Sabella queried.

"To help me not lose sight of the ultimate goal of all life, and to not get caught up in the wonders of a temporary restful, rejuvenating, between-lifetimes location like Janaloka."

Sabella replied, "Yes, I do see that you fully understand this important principle, and that it is critical that all of us remind ourselves regularly of life's ultimate realities.

"Now, let us move forward into our topic of how to deal most effectively with grief. Please define grief for me, Bellina."

Bellina thought carefully for a few moments, and then replied, "Hm-m-m, grief is an emotion associated with the sense of pain you feel in your heart at the loss of a loved one. You may feel distraught, disoriented, and unable to function normally. You look for the loved one out of habit. Not finding him or her, you feel confused, wondering where he or she is now. This deep and searing loss brings great sadness and seems to rob us of any future possibility of happiness. If you indulge your grief, you could even feel that your life really may not be worth living, without your loved one. You could be angry at God or even at the one who died, for leaving you and making you feel so much pain.'

"Thank you, Bellina. You have described clearly some of the *symptoms* of grief, but what is the root cause of it? Where does it come from?"

Bellina thought a little longer. She soon recalled what she had learned about grief and other harmful emotions, when she was visiting the great Heart Chakra Pyramid of King Bhima.

"Yes, of course. Now I know what you are *really* asking me. Grief is one of the numerous negative or harmful emotions that reside in the heart chakra—harmful, because they impede the inner life force or prana in its beneficial upward flow through the astral spine. The life force becomes temporarily immovable in its upward journey, and may even reverse its flow, dissipating itself in downward and outward directions. That is one reason excessive grief can feel so exhausting!

"I remember Bhima showing us what causes grief. There are cords or cables of energy that go out from the heart chakra, wrapping themselves around many objects, situations, people, or anything else to which we might become attached. Thus, instead of living in our central beings, we live primarily in more outward ways, absorbed in all the things and events *outside* of ourselves.

"Then, when someone or something outside of ourselves, to whom or to which we are firmly attached, departs or is damaged, injured, hurt, or destroyed, the cord of attached energy violently jerks on the heart chakra, causing a pain to which we often react with a negative emotion, like grief, rage, or deep sadness. Essentially all harmful emotions, including grief, are caused by attachments and thwarted desires.

"The solution is to live more in our Higher Selves, in God, and at our superconscious center within. If we feel ourselves being caught up in grief, we must strive to detach from whomever or whatever we think is causing the grief and return to our inner, higher Selves—the place of pure inner peace."

Bellina continued, "I also remember that Yogananda said, 'Ordinary souls who are attached to their bodies and families find it very difficult to maintain mental balance, when they are confronted by seemingly cruel death, which seems to come like a horrible tyrant or villain, to mar the harmony and peace of life.

'There are some persons who are so habitually and strongly attached to their possessions, that when they have to discard something like a worn out but much loved garment, they grieve over it. Likewise, ordinary mortals, no matter how much truth is offered to them, grieve when they have to give up their much loved but worn out bodies.'"

Sabella praised her great-granddaughter, "You have explained clearly the root cause of grief. However, the next question is: Should you carefully explain all of the things you have just said to me to someone who has just lost a loved one? Or demand that they immediately rise to a higher level by saying something like, 'Get over it! Detach from your feelings for your newly dead wife. That's sure to make you feel better right away!"

Bellina was startled to hear Sabella's harsh words. "Well, I certainly know that's not the best way, but why is that, Gigi, because it would be the *truth*, wouldn't it?"

"Ah, yes, the *truth*! It may be factually true, but is it beneficially truthful, if you were to say things like that to a grieving person? Remember it is always best to speak the *beneficial* truth. Even if what you have to say may be a fact, it's unwise to say it, if it would be hurtful or misunderstood by the one you are addressing. In most cases, it may be best not to say anything at all."

"Yes, I see what you mean, Gigi. So what can you do to help a grieving person? Jump right in there and grieve with them? Surely, that would not be a help to anyone. It would be like jumping into deep water to save a drowning person, when you yourself cannot swim well enough to save him. I think neither person would benefit from that course of action!

"I'm sure you've contemplated this question before. What do you think would be most helpful?"

Bellina mused, "How best to help a grieving friend? I suppose that depends on how you define help. It seems to me that most folk wisdom falls under the category of helping people avoid the pain of loss. Finding ways to distract the grieving person is a common suggestion; things like helping them to clean their home, suggesting they take a tranquilizer and get some rest, going shopping, getting a massage, taking a walk in nature, or even going to a movie. You might also support them in their trials by offering to help with funeral arrangements, bringing them home-cooked comfort food, helping with housecleaning, or just creating a soothing environment.

"While all these suggestions might be helpful for one who is grieving, the only suggestion that rang true for me at the highest level was to offer love, light and continuous healing prayers, both for the grieving friend and for their dear departed one.

"You are correct in your assessment. Except for your suggestion of offering prayers, the rest of these ideas would only be superficially or temporarily helpful, at least at the level upon which we are discussing this issue," Sabella said.

"This is a lot to absorb. I think you and I need a break right about now, complete with a long swim to lift our spirits."

The nature break *did* lift their spirits. Soaking their bodies and cooling their brains in the clear blue-green waters of the shining Joyuba River always helped them to become more centered and grounded.

Sitting on the warm sandy beach, letting the sunshine dry their bodies, Sabella said to Bellina, "I just remembered something important that Swami Kriyananda said on the subject of grief: 'The wise never grieve for a soul who has departed from one body residence to enter another. It is attachment and selfish love that make one grieve for departed loved ones and friends. If we really love them, we will continue to love them after they are taken away from us by death. We will understand that this is a part of their advancement on their paths through life, death, and reincarnation.

'In the sorrow of separation from their loved ones through death, fools cry for awhile and then forget, but those who are wise find the strength within themselves to seek their lost love in the heart of the Divine. Death can teach us to be in love with the Divine only, and not to be attached to the mere temples of flesh, in which the Divine temporarily resides.'"

"That seems very clear," Bellina smiled at her great-grandmother. "It reminds me of another quotation about grief by Swami Kriyananda. It appears in one of his small books called *Secrets of Friendship*: 'The secret of friendship is giving your friends strength and understanding during their sorrows, and not sharing their grief so deeply that you intensify it.'"

Bellina was curious, "I think his beautiful words go right to the heart of how we can instruct people in the best ways to deal with their feelings of grief and loss. But exactly *how* do we give people '...strength and understanding during their sorrows?'"

"By first acquiring sufficient inner strength and self-understanding ourselves!" Sabella said quietly. "It's hard to give what you don't already possess."

"And how do we do *that*?" Bellina grinned. "Wait, don't tell me. I know the answer! By deeper, longer, thirsty, Guru-given meditation, right?"

"Yes!" Sabella smiled radiantly. "And through the perfect and divinely inspired intuitive guidance that persistence in deep meditation can offer us, we are shown the most sensitive and appropriate ways to help a grieving person move from sorrow to everlasting joy. Shall we meditate now?"

And so they did.

Sabella closed their meditation by gently transmitting these wise words of Yogananda's to Bellina's mind, "There cannot be room for the dark disturbing emotion of grief in wise beings, who are absolutely certain that they and everyone are made in the image of God. A person of wisdom does not indulge in grief for anything or anyone, through the certain knowledge that, although everything is constantly changing, our souls always continue to be unchangeable in life or in death, because we are a part of the infinite and immortal Divine Spirit."

Sabella continued, "However, please be aware that even fully realizing this wisdom does not spare us from the pain of separation. Even Yogananda exhibited grief, when his mother passed, and when his guru, Sri Yukteswar departed this earthly plane. The important point here is not indulge in too much grief, or think that death causes nothing but sadness. All is in Divine order! Realizing the ancient wisdom of the immortality of the soul can soothe the pain and grief, and allow us to move on with our lives, but we do not get to escape the pain inherent in life."

Bellina asked, "Gigi, is there anything which is *not* changeable in life or in death?"

"Remember this, dear one! All things must change! All things *will* change and pass away! Only God and the soul, that part of us that is a part of God, do not and cannot change! That is the immutable strength we must find within ourselves through meditation, and once found, share it with those who do not understand these eternal verities and therefore sadly grieve their losses."

Sabella fully agreed with Bellina, and then added, "Saint Teresa of Avila said it beautifully in this way:

Let nothing disturb you,
Nothing affright you,
All things will pass,
But God changes not!©

The two women sat together on the riverbank for a long time, blissfully chanting together "Saint Teresa of Avila's Admonition," that ancient and always stirring chant.

The birds, frogs, and crickets, and even the gurgling river, added their voices to the music. For a little while, Bellina thought she heard Sofieli's angelic voice chanting along with them. Joy, joy, joy, and more joy!

CHAPTER TWENTY-FIVE

*The fundamental instinct of life may be summed up
in this way:
It is an unquenchable desire for immortality,
And more specifically, a desire for eternal existence
in a state of perpetual enjoyment.
To overcome your fear of death,
Deepen your awareness of the central part
in your being, which never changes,
But weaves itself like a thread through life's tapestry,
Of seemingly unrelated circumstances.
The consciousness of change is allied to the fear of death.
Seeing changelessness at the heart of change,
Is the secret of immortality!*

— Swami Kriyananda

That same evening, sitting beside a crackling fire in the fireplace of her cozy pyramid home, Sabella took Bellina's hand and squeezed it affectionately. "I think that now would be as good a time as any to talk about the inspiring subject of immortality. After our final discussion, we should be well-prepared enough to present a complete report about our mission to the High Council, and we can close with our recommendations for new, related projects.

"Bellina, my dearest one, I want you to still your mind and open your heart to the great mystery that is life! Its origins are in the unknown, and into the unknown it returns—what stupendous mysteries the contemplation of death brings forth!

"We mortals have many misconceptions about death, to the degree that the idea of death has grown exceedingly strong in false importance and has fixed within us ideas of pain and annihilation. Instead, death must be seen as a phenomenon necessary in the successive steps that the soul must follow, in order to return from change to changelessness. It is necessary for the change of death to come, so that the soul may finish beholding the motion picture of its many lives and be released to go back to its true home: immortality!

"God made humans to remain alive forever as immortal beings. We were created to behold the drama of change, with our changeless, immortal minds. After enjoying watching change dancing on the stage of changelessness, we were meant to return to the state of eternal blessedness. Then the power of delusion crept in, causing us to concentrate only on the changes of life and on life's outward appearances, rather than on our underlying immortality. Thus were born the ideas that make us fixate on our false conceptions of what death really is.

"Death seems to swallow up the good, hard-working people as well as the bad, lazy folks, all alike, releasing their form into elements and the ether. Is it not odd that death is universally feared, and yet often death brings peace and relief, when one's life feels overwhelmed with pain, grief, ill health, or seemingly unending troubles?

"What a waste of energy and wisdom it is pursuing the goal of making this impermanent, frail body comfortable. We must wake up! Never can we coax the harvest of imperishable immortality and unending, ever-new bliss from the barren soil of our frail bodies.

"We can *never* find lasting comfort from our slowly disintegrating physical forms. We can *never* squeeze the honey of divine happiness from the rocks of sense pleasures.

"However, comfort and joy can ceaselessly flow into the pails of our lives, when we squeeze the honeycomb of meditation with the eager, strong hands of will power and ever-deepening concentration.

"Why would anyone want to remain intoxicated with material desires when they trap people in the death-like sleep of ignorance?

"At the level at which most people engage in material activities, they are walking and working in a dream of delusion, during a sleep of ignorance.

"Why do most people have such confidence in devoting all their time and energy to amassing a material fortune, which they must immediately abandon when death calls? As we know, nothing material can make the transition of death to the astral realms and through our journey to the great beyond.

"Why not prepare *now* for our last day on earth? Thus, when, inevitably, we have to leave behind everything to which we have become attached, it will be a much easier journey for us to make.

"Please don't misunderstand me, Bellina. I do not mean that anyone should be ungrateful and not enjoy all the good things that life has to offer. What I am saying is that we should not allow ourselves to become attached so firmly to people and things that we will feel intense mental agony when we are separated from them.

"If we do not grieve for earthly enjoyments, when our physical bodies are cast aside in death, then we can be more present and able to move about freely in the astral realms, offering us a much better experience of the hereafter. All the things we cherished in our lives and were sure we had lost, will be returned to us, by the hand of God.

"Every material thing is taken from us in death, so that we will not remain matter-bound and forgetful of our immortality.

"Everything in creation must move through the long tunnel of spiritual evolution—the tunnel is unfathomably long! We do not escape the limitations of human life after one human lifetime only. Indeed, the soul's eternity of existence is not only from the time of its birth in human form, but from the beginning of time itself—indeed, from even before time's beginning. The soul is eternal, as God is eternal. As an ancient Hermetic teaching states it, 'Thou art from old, O son of man, yea, thou art from everlasting.'

"By cultivating the great power of deep, daily meditation, we will reap the treasures of intuitional perceptions and eternal, ever-new peace and joy—these things, and *these things alone*, will be of use to us at the time of physical death.

"We must make ready for our deaths by renewing our acquaintance with God every day. In this way, at the end of the trail, when we pass through the portals of this lifetime's last day, we may be allowed to enter the everlasting kingdom of God and remain there for all eternity as immortal souls!"

Bellina was stunned into complete silence by the tremendous power of Sabella's speech. Her great-grandmother's eyes blazed with direct realization of the truth of her words. Her skin seemed to glow with a beautiful, astral light.

"Good heavens!" Bellina wondered quietly and with great awe. "Who *are* you really?"

"Just Sabella, your same old Gigi. However, speaking about immortality is deeply important to me. As you have seen, I can easily become carried away with this inspiring subject. I hope my energy and enthusiasm were not overwhelming for you.

"No problem, Gigi. I loved it all. In fact, I could listen to your inspired discourse all over again!"

"I don't think so, Bellina. Once was enough." Sabella sat quietly, gazing into the fire, with a great sense of peace and accomplishment on her dear face.

They sat in silence for a while longer, and then Bellina asked, "Sabella, please help me to understand more clearly why the vast majority of people are so afraid of death?"

Sabella said, "Good question! There are three major reasons:

"First, people do not realize that everyone is immortal! They cannot ever die! At death, they just change bodies and circumstances.

"Second, people labor under the delusion that no one has ever died and then come back to report what dying is like, and what transpires after death. This is not true at all, as we have discovered for ourselves. The Wise Ones have always taught this truth to those willing to listen and learn from them.

"Finally, many people are so deeply afraid of death, that they refuse even to think or talk about the subject at all! They will even avoid being around the dying. This is complete psychological denial and a self-defeating attitude, indeed! Who really cannot see that death is inevitable for everyone, including themselves?

"This angst is rooted in a strong fear of the unknown. Although they have died and been reborn millions of times, they remember little, if anything, about the process of dying and their sojourn between lifetimes. People are unaware of the importance of 'dying daily.' As quoted in the ancient Judeo-Christian Bible, Saint Paul says, 'I protest by our rejoicing, which I have in Christ, I die daily.' (First Corinthians, 15:31).

"Yogananda explained that through deep meditation, such as was practiced by Saint Paul, we learn to stop the heart and breath and consciously leave and return to our bodies at will. Without a doubt, this experience shows us that *the body is not all there is*! Familiarity with the experience of this 'little death' removes all our fears of bodily death. How could it not be so?

"Here's another relevant story that Yogananda often told, and which was included in his famous *Autobiography of a Yogi*:

"In 1915, when World War I was raging in Europe, I had a vision. The vision descended on me as I sat meditating one morning in my little attic room at 4 Garpar Road in Calcutta.

"My consciousness was suddenly transferred into the body of the captain of a battle ship. I ordered my sailors to shoot our ship's cannons toward the shore, but soon, a huge shell was fired at us and hit our ship's powder magazine. The giant explosion of ammunition tore my ship apart. I jumped into the water, together with a few sailors who had survived the explosion.

"I reached the shore safely, but one of the enemy soldiers

leveled his gun at my heart and shot me! I fell groaning to the ground, and I felt the blood and life-force leaving my body."

Sabella interrupted her story by saying, "Bellina, I know you've heard this story before, but I want you to pay close attention to the way Yogananda describes his reaction to this part of the vision of his death.

"Instead of going into a state of fear and panic, he said to himself, *'Well, I know how to stop my heart and breath and go into a state of cosmic consciousness and eternal joy. I have practiced death many times, so I know what it is like!'*"

Sabella commented, "Nevertheless, even with this important realization, Yogananda's vision did not end there."

"The body-dream of my death seemed so real to me, that as I was still moaning about having to leave my body, suddenly I began to breathe deeply again.

"I found myself mysteriously transported back to my home in Calcutta. I joyfully pinched this body, which was free from all injury. I inhaled and exhaled deeply to assure myself that I was alive. What a great relief it was for me then, to realize that I was alive!

'However, my sense of safety and well-being was short-lived. Again, I found my consciousness transferred to the captain's body lying dead on the gory shore. I became utterly confused!

'I prayed, "Lord, tell me! Am I dead or am I alive?" I did not know if I was sitting at 4 Garpar Road in Calcutta meditating, or whether I was dead on the battlefield.

'The Light said, "Neither! Behold, your form is nothing but the light of the Cosmic Dream!"'

Sabella said, "The story continues with Yogananda's explanation of the mechanics of the great cosmic movie of our lives, but I will stop here, because the main point I want to make is that Yogananda had little, if any fear of dying. He said that he did not panic (though he did say he moaned a little—great dramatist that he was!) because he had practiced dying ahead of time, on a daily basis.

"By using the techniques of Kriya Yoga, he had learned to stop his breath and heartbeat.

"Yogananda also said, 'You do not have to die alone, in the dark! Instead, you can be guided through the luminous spiritual eye, into the infinite light of God. If you practice the scientific meditation techniques I have taught, you can easily learn to go into periods of breathlessness and blissful stillness of mind, at will. Thus, when death comes to you, you can say, "Ah, I see that death is here for me now, but I do not need to focus on the feeling that I am choking or struggling to breathe. Death is offering me the ability to live in greatest joy, in my breathless Spirit."

'Thus, at the time of your death, you will be able to say inwardly, "Oh, I see that dying is just like going into the breathless state in meditation. This is not painful or frightening at all—not in the bad, cold, and dreary way death has been depicted in the past." Instead of forced or involuntary relaxation, you will be able to control your body's energy patterns and not live confined to the body like others, who possess only a limited lease on the body, only to be ejected forcibly at the end of their life-term.'"

Bellina commented, "This story of Yogananda's vision and the amazing example of his life clearly show us the best of all ways to overcome any lingering fears of death."

Sabella heartily agreed, and said, "In closing, I want to impart a bit more information on the subject of immortality. In a way, death is a test of love."

"Love?" Bellina asked. "What kind of love? Whose love? I don't understand!"

"Let me explain," Sabella said. "As we have been discussing lately, an ordinary person does not perceive the pre-natal and post-natal continuity of existence; hence they are afraid of death. However, wise truth-seekers, using powerful meditation techniques, shift the focus of their consciousness from the changes of birth and death to the changeless Divine.

"A meditator who has opened the spiritual eye, who perceives and communes with it daily in meditation, beholds all change as dancing on the bosom of changelessness. That mystical third eye becomes the tunnel or portal from life to death and then to life again. We can learn to leave our finite physical bodies consciously, whenever we wish, through the spiritual eye.

"The ordinary person, at the time of death, finds his soul moving through the spiritual eye more or less unconsciously. However, one who practices daily, deep meditation during his mortal existence and concentrates on seeing the pathway of the spiritual eye, connecting matter and infinity, is able *consciously* to follow this path during his transition from changeable matter into the unchangeable Infinite.

"Then we begin to see, much more easily, how the change called death is only a connecting link in the long chain of immortality, previously hidden from our view. We, too, become able to live in the world without attachment and with a loving happiness that nothing can destroy—not even death itself!

"Let me emphasize something I said earlier, for it is very important! A wise person does not overly grieve for a loved one who has departed the body. It is attachment and selfish love that causes us to indulge in too much grief.

"When we are able to love people unconditionally, only then can we truly perceive the essence of the Divine within them, their immortal souls! Now do you see how death can be a test of love and of whether or not we have learned to love unconditionally?"

"Yes, Gigi, I can see that now." Bellina said softly.

Sabella said, "In our immortal souls we live in eternity, but trapped in our personalities, we lose the consciousness of immortality. We must get rid of our human imperfections—like chipping and polishing away the extraneous stone on a statue, until the image hidden within is revealed in all its perfection.

"Bellina, now do you understand why I chose to close our

investigation into the secrets of life and death with the deep and all-encompassing subject of immortality?"

"Yes, I do, Gigi. By embracing and living in the constant awareness of our immortality, we find ourselves transformed into greatly expanded beings of light—deathless souls, who are able to live continuously immersed in a state of ever-new joy! I am so grateful that I am beginning to realize this truth more fully!"

She knelt and placed her forehead on her great-grandmother's divine lotus feet, shedding tears of joy.

"Sit up, Bellina. It is time for meditation and then sleep. We will need inspiration and rest for what faces us tomorrow. We must be at our best, when we meet with the High Council. My dear great-granddaughter, please know that I love you now and always!"

CHAPTER TWENTY-SIX

The secret of winning people is to be deeply convinced,
Of the truth of your proposal,
And to have enthusiasm for the truth as you perceive it.
Remember, enthusiasm is not excitement.
It is deep conviction.

— Swami Kriyananda, from *Secrets of Winning People*

Bellina and Sabella transported themselves to the majestic courtyard of the High Council's main chamber.

"Let's sit here and meditate, Bellina. They will let us know when they are ready for us to enter the chamber. I doubt we will be waiting long."

Sabella was right; they were soon standing before the noble assembly of some of the wisest souls on earth. Gathered here were those responsible for carefully guiding the planet's inhabitants toward living their lives in a state of perfect peace, joy, and faith in God.

To Bellina's surprise, Sabella told her to stay where she was, standing before the Council Members, while she went and took her place in what was obviously the chair reserved for the High Council's Supreme Guide.

Bellina sent Sabella an anxious mental query, "What is going on, Gigi? Why am I standing alone here before the High Council? Why are you sitting there instead of standing beside me and helping me to present this report?"

"While we were away, Bellina, the High Council's Supreme Guide, Lauwknor Laughingwater, stepped down from his long-held position. His predecessor was your great-grandfather Thomas Timetraveler, and before him, Simeon, my first and most cherished spiritual teacher.

"You may remember Lauwknor from our first visit here. He was a great leader and a dear soul, too!

"Anyway, while we were exploring other universes on our mission, he left his body in a conscious, glorious transition to the highly advanced astral planet, Satyaloka. As soon as we returned, I was informed that the High Council unanimously elected me to the office of the High Council's Supreme Guide. I gladly and gratefully accepted the position.

"I was honored and had no thought but to accept the position. I wanted to surprise you, but did not want to distract you unnecessarily during our debriefing. I asked that the ceremony, marking my formal inauguration to this position, be held later.

"It is now time to present our report. I will assist you if needed, but I am sure that you will be able to make this presentation on your own, fully and clearly."

Bellina felt a distressing flutter in the pit of her stomach upon learning of her status as sole presenter before the Council. She quickly minimized her trepidations, squared her shoulders, straightened her spine, took a deep breath, and launched into presenting their carefully constructed report.

She alternated between mentally reporting the details of her investigation, and the conclusions they had drawn from them, with several transmissions of the mind-movies that she and Sabella had carefully created for this presentation. There was a wealth of information to share.

Although they had been asked to present only a bare outline of what they had learned, Bellina found that it took her almost a full day, including several rest breaks, to complete what she felt should be said. The High Council members did not seem to mind at all—they obviously were enthralled and interested in all that she had to offer.

When Bellina had finished her presentation, she asked for questions.

Indeed, they had many questions, and Bellina spent another

hour fielding them all. For this part of the session, Sabella left her chair to stand beside Bellina and help her answer questions. She wanted to support Bellina, to offer energy and and information, and to ease the possible stress of this Q&A session.

Bellina projected calm confidence. She was never flustered or mistaken in her concise and clear answers—a fact which pleased and impressed Sabella greatly. As was to be expected, there were some *very* subtle questions asked by the High Council members, for these were some of the most spiritually advanced souls on the earth at that time. Bellina glowed with enthusiasm, as she capably and satisfactorily answered them all.

Finally, a friendly young Council member, Nicholas Notea, addressed Bellina, "Your report was excellent, Bellina! It was thorough and clearly explained.

"Now, we would like to know how you plan to use this inspiring information to help the residents of our planet at this time?"

Sabella returned to her chair, sensing that Bellina was enthusiastic and ready to describe their plans to the Council. Her eyes were shining as she said, "Sabella and I have thought about and meditated on this matter at great length.

"We can best summarize our proposals with two simple questions: First, how do we educate seekers—both students in the Halls of Wisdom and anyone else interested in these often unpopular and widely misunderstood topics of death, dying, and life after death? And second, how can we help them to integrate these teachings into their lives so that the fear of death recedes from the hearts and minds of all people?

"I think we can all agree that the time has come to bring these exceedingly important teachings to the residents of earth in a dynamic way!

"Yes, indeed!" and "Hear, hear!" rang through the great hall.

Encouraged, Bellina continued, "During one of our many discussions, Sabella and I talked about the program that Sabella created many years ago, and how it could be used to help create this project. Her curriculum for the CP/AECS, that is, the "Chakras Paradigm/Advanced and Experiential Course of Study" graduate studies programs in the Halls of Wisdom—has more than proven its value and success over the ensuing years and would serve as an excellent model for this program.

"We feel that we can successfully transfer most of these tried and true methods of teaching and training graduate students to this new subject.

"Our plan is to train graduate students in the Halls of Wisdom in all the broader aspects of this information. Those who chose to continue into an advanced study program will become thoroughly trained teachers and administrators who can establish new clinics around the world. We plan to call them 'Immortality Realization Clinics'. We would provide support and resources from the Halls of Wisdom to those who chose to embrace this endeavor as their life's work.

"These Immortality Realization Clinics will have two primary goals: "The first is to educate anyone who is interested in learning more about death and dying, life after death, and supporting subjects, such as the laws of karma and reincarnation. Our goal is to create an educational process attractive enough to make these challenging subjects more than palatable, even appealing, so that this critical information reaches all, or at least a very large portion of the population.

"Second, the IR Clinics will have adjacent 'Heavenly Transition Gardens.' These facilities will provide beautiful, comfortable, and spiritually nourishing accommodations for those approaching death.

"People who chose to come to this garden-like facility to die will be supported on all levels by our highly-trained staff. These helpers will have conducted their own personal investigation into death and dying, beginning with our training in the Halls of Wisdom, and continuing in their own lives and meditation practices and studies. By the time they are ready to begin assisting the dying, they will have the understanding, compassion, and skills to aid these souls at the highest levels. Their care and wisdom will support the dying in dispelling any lingering fear of death and smooth every aspect of their transitions.

"We will also offer training in the Heavenly Transition Gardens, for those who wish to assist their loved ones to die comfortably and in their own homes, if that is their wish. This training will be open to all who wish to learn these skills: men, women, old and young, even children and animals, who show both the desire and talent for giving such a service to those who need it."

"Animals?" One older High Council member raised an aristocratic eyebrow.

"Oh yes!" Bellina enthused. "Remember how I told you about my experience in Janaloka with the great astral eagle, Garudina? I contacted her recently, and we discussed a unique plan for the education of those especially intelligent and compassionate animals, who often are the *best* possible companions and guides for those approaching death."

The High Council Members were extremely impressed as Bellina, expertly and confidently, presented plans for the Immortality Realization Training Courses for students in the Halls of Wisdom. The new Public Immortality Realization Clinics and Heavenly Transition Gardens were to be established somewhat later, as students became trained well enough to start and run them effectively and smoothly.

Bellina continued to address the Council. "The ten precepts which Sabella and I offer as guidelines for the Immortality Realization Clinics and Heavenly Transition Gardens are based on principles offered centuries ago in Ascending Dwapara Yuga, by Swami Kriyananda. He proposed the creation of establishments that he called Evening Hospice Centers. The precepts are as follows:

"We will strive to assist all participants in:

1) Facing and letting go of the past, with no guilt or judgment, accepting all our past errors as simple facts, while striving to realize that it was God, regardless of our imperfect understanding, who did it all.

2) Relinquishing attachments to all things, positions, situations, and people, by releasing, one by one, every desire and attachment, large or small, into the Supreme Bliss of God's presence within us.

3) Releasing the grip of the ego, in order to embrace our higher soul nature more perfectly.

4) Offering every regret into God's love and infinite compassion.

5) Forgiving all past hurts and betrayals.

6) Continuously sending out universal love to all souls, everywhere, especially including any so-called enemies.

7) Fully understanding that all souls are motivated, however much they have been misguided temporarily, by the same soul craving for Sat-chit-ananda, or ever-existing, ever-conscious, ever-new bliss.

8) Concentrating more and more on infinity and immortality, while gradually letting go of all that binds us to anyone or anything in the material world.

9) Developing and practicing ever-deepening devotion to God and Gurus.

10) Learning to embrace immortality and to overcome all fears, most especially the fear of death, by fully realizing that we are not this body. We are so much more!

Sabella was thrilled to watch her dynamic great-granddaughter in action. She realized how right she had been in asking for Bellina's assistance on this vital mission. She had to keep reminding herself that it was not wise to exhibit excessive pride in a family member's success, especially in a situation like this—thus she suppressed her desire to stand up and cheer, as the session moved toward its close.

Nevertheless, she felt great waves of inner joy from observing Bellina's triumphant moments before the High Council.

Bellina could see Sabella's broad smile and twinkling eyes. She knew that she had done well with the presentation and was grateful for Divine guidance, as well as for the superb help and encouragement she had received from Sabella and others.

It definitely was time to close, and she was about to ask if there were any final questions or comments from the Council members, when Sabella rose and once again stood beside Bellina. She grasped Bellina's hands in her own, and stood facing her.

"There are two gifts I would like to give you now Bellina, as we stand before the High Council. These gifts are being given to you in commendation for your courageous accomplishments during our mission and in anticipation of what you undoubtedly will achieve in the years to come."

Sabella released her great-granddaughter's hands and reached up to take a pendant from around her own neck. Bellina had not noticed it before, because it had been hanging on a simple golden chain, mostly hidden under the collar of Sabella's formal royal blue robe of office.

The pendant was small and delicate. Handcrafted by a skilled jeweler, it was simple, but exquisite! It was made of brightly shining pink-gold, studded with many small pink and silver pearls. The pearls were set into the gold in the image of a partially open gateway.

As Sabella placed it around Bellina's neck, she said in formal tones, "Sabellina, you found your way through the gates of death and beyond and returned to share many inspiring tales of your travels. You have dedicated your life to helping others overcome the fear of death and embrace what comes after death. I commend you for your courage and for all that you have already accomplished during the time of this mission."

Sabella slipped the beautiful pendant over Bellina's head, and it settled near her heart chakra. Bellina placed her right hand over the pendant for a short moment, and then lifted it up, touching the pendant to her spiritual eye, absorbing its great blessings even more deeply. She then lowered it and opened her eyes to gaze deeply into Sabella's, conveying loving gratitude for her support and for this inspiring gift.

The path of Bellina's life was laid out before her clearly now. Her mission would continue for many years, until her own transition, when her life on earth would end and the next phase of her journey would begin in some heavenly astral realm. Immortality was truly hers now, never to be lost. What greater gift could anyone ever receive?

However, a bit dazed by the powerful blessings flooding her, Bellina forgot that Sabella had mentioned that there were two gifts that she wanted to present to her today.

Sabella reminded her, leaning over to whisper in her ear, "Don't you want your second gift, O child of my child's child?"

Even during this solemn occasion, Bellina simply could not stifle a little giggle. Sabella had never called her *that* before. She answered, "Yes, of course, dearest mother of my mother's mother. What else will you give me today?"

Now it was Sabella's turn to strive to remain poised and not laugh at Bellina's give-as-good-as-she-got humor.

"Please kneel before me, Bellina and close your eyes."

Bellina composed herself and did as she was instructed, all the while wondering what was going to happen *now*. In a gesture of blessing, Sabella placed her warm hands, palms downward, on the top of Bellina's head. Those dear hands softly caressed the rainbow-raven locks of her beautiful, intelligent, and beloved great-granddaughter.

After a few moments of silent blessing and sweet, wordless inner communion between them, Sabella transmitted to all present, in loud, ringing thought-tones, "Bellina, henceforth you shall be called Sabellina Clearlight, for within you clearly burns the clear light of God!"

CHAPTER TWENTY-SEVEN

The true yogi always knows in advance the hour of his death.

— Paramhansa Yogananda

The years passed quickly as Sabellina Clearlight, always aided and supported by Sabella, introduced and established the new Immortality Realization training curricula into the Halls of Wisdom Graduate program.

The first year the new courses were presented, Sabella Lovingheart and Sabellina Clearlight taught all of the introductory seminars and courses to the graduate students, fortunate enough to attend.

The first seminars had only ten students. Sabella was clear that the initial seminar group must be small, teaching their carefully thought out ideas to only the brightest and most receptive graduate students. While a large number of students had applied for admission into the course, only a few were chosen. Sabella's fame as a teacher and her position as the present High Council Leader always made her courses popular, but with this groundbreaking program, the demand was overwhelming.

The chosen few were the Halls of Wisdom's finest students, both intellectually and spiritually—the best of the best! They were hungry to receive this training from such a great soul and accomplished teacher as Sabella Lovingheart. Bellina had an inspiring time being her graduate assistant and occasionally leading some of the workshops herself. These seminars continued for an entire academic year.

At the close of the year, Sabella and Bellina met to find ways to improve the next group of seminars. They also finalized plans for which supplementary seminars, classes, and workshops would be offered and in what order, completing the whole Immortality Realization graduate program.

They also founded the prototype of an Immortality Realization Clinic and its associated Heavenly Transition Garden Retreat. They received invaluable help from several of the first graduates of the program.

After a time, they delegated leadership of this facility to a pair of the brightest and best of their students, a husband and wife team. As directors of the first clinic and retreat, this extremely energetic couple spearheaded a movement that blossomed into hundreds of facilities on earth, and eventually on other planets as well.

The graduate program Sabella and Bellina began was so inspiringly successful that almost all of the graduates became either founders or directors of clinics, or instructors in the program at the Halls of Wisdom.

Sabella gradually and confidently turned over the reins of the project to Bellina, who fulfilled Sabella's expectations by rising to the challenge energetically and skillfully.

In the early years of their project, Sabella learned through the always-active academic rumor grapevine, that Bellina was being courted by Nicholas Notea of the High Council.

Sabella could not have been more pleased for Bellina. She knew Nicholas to be a fine, intelligent, and honorable young man, from her years of shared service with him, on the Council.

Sabella was also a long-time friend of his family. She first met his grandfather Notea Nightingale and his great-aunt, Nila Nightingale, on her very first visit to the High Council, many years ago. They had been members of the High Council, even as small children—much to Sabella's surprise and delight.

Nevertheless, she was taken aback when she learned of their budding romance through the grapevine, instead of from her great-granddaughter herself.

A few weeks later, they found themselves together in a private place, which was a rare occurrence in those busy times. Sabella told Bellina that she knew about her romance with Nicholas, quickly adding how pleased she was to hear of their relationship and how much she admired him.

She also asked Bellina why she had not felt comfortable in sharing this good news with her.

Bellina blushed a bright shade of pink and stammered a bit, saying, "Gigi, I am relieved that my secret is out and thrilled that you approve. I am not really sure *why* I tried to keep the news quiet. I guess I always knew that the news would get back to you sooner or later.

"When our mutual attraction became obvious to us both, I became inexplicably confused. Things were moving along so fast for us, perhaps too fast. I found myself deeply in love with him, and just kept putting off telling you about it, because I did not want it to seem like I was withdrawing any of my energy from the deep and loving relationship that you and I have.

"Forgive me, dearest Sabella—it's obvious that falling in love clouded my logical mind much more than I realized. Nicholas is my first romantic relationship, and I was shy and reticent about sharing my feelings for him with anyone, including you. I feared that public knowledge of our new love would somehow crush its tender beginnings. Does this make any sense to you? It *does* all sound a bit silly or immature to me, trying to explain my feelings to you now."

Sabella smiled at her flustered great-granddaughter and gave her a big hug. "Please don't worry another minute about it, Bellina! I understand completely. I kept my earliest feelings for Thomas a secret from *everyone*, including him, for a very long time—no doubt, longer than I should have.

"Take comfort in the understanding that your love for Nicholas has my deepest blessings. Rest assured that it could never diminish our love for each other. That is the nature of love. As you grow older, you will realize that its capacity to expand is limitless."

Shortly after this conversation, Nicholas and Bellina visited Sabella, asking for her formal blessings on their union. They also requested that she perform their life-linking ceremony, which they wanted to happen within the next year. Sabella joyfully blessed them and their union and agreed to perform the ceremony.

Just a few months later, a large gathering of friends and relatives celebrated with them at an inspiring ceremony. It was an exceedingly joyful occasion for Nicholas and Bellina, and it was enjoyed thoroughly by all in attendance.

The night before the ceremony, Bellina was drifting off to sleep when she heard a soft voice singing nearby—a celestially beautiful song. Opening her eyes, she perceived the dazzling presence of Sofieli, floating in the air just above the foot of her bed.

"Sabellina Clearlight, I have come to offer you my blessings for your union with Nicholas. Angels do not life-link in the way humans do, but we certainly feel the joy of a union between well-matched humans. I will attend the event tomorrow for a little while, but I will be invisible, for I do not wish to startle anyone there. Nevertheless, you and Nicholas will feel my presence with you, as I rejoice in your good fortune!"

"Oh, Sofieli, it is so blissful to be with you again. Thank you for your blessings and for joining us tomorrow."

Sofieli gently swooped down to plant a soft angel kiss on Bellina's cheek. Then, with an unexpected splash of glistening stardust, she disappeared.

****

Ten busy and productive years sped by. One bright spring day, at the close of her morning meditation, Bellina felt strongly guided to set aside her busy schedule and spend a few hours relaxing at her favorite small beach on the Joyuba River.

Bellina had not seen much of her great-grandmother lately. Sabella was spending a large portion of her time alone and in silence, as was natural for someone in her stage of life—especially considering the extremely busy and productive life she had lived thus far.

Bellina missed seeing her Gigi as often as she had in the past, but she knew her great-grandmother was living her final years inspired by divine guidance.

Bellina sat on a small boulder in a shallow part of the river, letting her first-born dangle his tiny feet in the river. He giggled and kicked in delight at the coolness and beauty of the sparkling water. Little Thomas was just over a year old, and while he was completely engrossed by this new river experience, his mother was enjoying it even more.

"Wah-Wah!" he said loudly, and kicked at the water vigorously, squirming in her firm grasp, as though he wanted to dive headfirst into the water. She held him tightly under his little arms, and slowly lowered him a bit further into the river. She moved off the boulder to sit on the sandy, shallow river-bottom, letting little Thomas sit safely between her outstretched legs.

He was shrieking and laughing with delight now, splashing water with his chubby little hands and feet. No doubt, he would become another member of a long line of ardent river-lovers. Bellina knew she would need to teach him to swim very soon.

"What a dear soul he is," Sabella transmitted her soft and loving words to Bellina.

"Gigi!" Bellina turned to look at her great-grandmother who was sitting close by, at her preferred spot on the beach, drinking in the sunshine and leaning against her favorite sun-warmed boulder. "I didn't hear you arrive. Excuse us. Little Thomas is making quite a racket!"

Thomas then turned to look at Sabella. With a huge smile, he extended his arms toward her irresistibly, saying, "Gella!"

What else could she do? She waded into the river and lifted the wet little boy into her arms, not minding one bit that he was dripping all over her clothes. He put his arms around her neck and nuzzled his head under her chin.

"What a charming fellow you are, just like your namesake!" Sabella said, covering her great-great-grandson with sweet kisses.

Bellina came out of the water, and they all sat together on the sand, little Thomas playing and cooing his delight at everything around him. A small blue butterfly landed on his downy head, and then flew to his outstretched hand, where he watched it with complete fascination.

"I'm glad to find you here, my darling," Sabella said, "for I have something important to tell you. It will soon be time for me to join my sweet Thomas in Hiranyaloka, and I wanted to tell you now, to give you time to adjust to the idea. I also want you present with me, just as Thomas asked me to be with him, as he 'kicked the frame.' Will you be there for me, Sabellina Clearlight?"

Bellina had sensed the approach of this event, being so inwardly close to her great-grandmother. She had resolved to be strong, so that she could be of service in any way that was needed, when this time inevitably came. Despite all her planning, tears poured down her cheeks. Little Thomas saw this and began to cry, too.

"Sorry, Gigi! I know this is a momentous event in your life, and I am honored you have asked me to be present during your transition. I promise to have myself completely under control by then. I am honored that you are making this request of me! Do you know when you will be leaving us?" Bellina was carefully drying her tears and those of her son.

"Yes, Thomas and I spoke about it last night. Please meet me right here, one week from today, just before sunset. Thank you, dearest one, for agreeing to be with me and to support me with your loving presence, on this most joyful occasion. I sincerely hope that you will rejoice with me, for I have waited patiently for a very long time to be reunited with your great-grandfather."

One week later, just before sunset, Sabella Lovingheart and Sabellina Clearlight sat on the warm beach sands of the Joyuba River. Both were adorned in their finest robes. Bellina wore her cherished Immortality Pendant and her silver and white ceremonial robe. Sabella was dressed in her formal blue Robe of Office. On her head was the magnificent pearl and ruby crown that Lord Krishna had given her, when she visited his sixth chakra pyramid, many years ago. Bellina had seen it on display in Sabella's home, but had never known her to wear it, for *any* occasion.

Bellina was calm as she hungrily gazed into the human eyes of her beloved Gigi, one last time. Sabella was already inwardly focused, eyes looking upward, toward her spiritual eye. No final words or thoughts were exchanged, nor were they needed.

"Bellina, by the power of the higher Kriya technique, I consciously kick the frame!" Sabella's words rang within Bellina's mind with inconceivable power.

Bellina watched carefully and listened in wonder as the cosmic sound of rolling thunder filled the air around them. Sabella's body began to disappear gradually, like a scroll being rolled upward. She slowly became invisible, starting from her lower body and progressing up to the crown of her head. Her magnificent pearl and ruby crown winked out of sight, and the thundering, oceanic sound of AUM reverberated loudly, to such a degree that it carried Bellina along with it, until she had no choice but to close her eyes and merge her own consciousness into the great oceanic sound of AUM.

When she next opened her eyes, it was dawn. There was no sign of Sabella's ever having sat on the spot in front of her. The sand was smooth and pure white, with a shaft of early morning sunshine illuminating the place where Sabella Lovingheart meditated on this earth, for the very last time. All nature felt the joy of this bliss-filled parting into freedom. Dozens of colorful birds sang joyfully, and seven bright, blue butterflies were flitting about Bellina's head. The Joyuba River whispered its soft morning songs. Sabellina Clearlight's heart was filled with absolute, unwavering bliss.

Inwardly Bellina said, "Dearest Gigi, I am yours and you are mine always. Thank you for all your loving blessings, which have so greatly shaped and guided this lifetime. May I be worthy to carry your legacy forward, for as long as I live on earth and even beyond. I realize you are with me now and forever. I thank you for your unconditional love; and for every moment we spent together; and I thank our Divine Mother, who dwells within you and within us all, and who loves us beyond our comprehension...." Sabella Clearlight could say or think no more.

It was done, and it was enough!

Slowly she stood up and left the beautiful river-beach with a full and grateful heart. It was time to prepare herself to tell her family and Sabella's many friends and admirers about her exalted departure from this world.

As she slowly walked away, she sensed an angelic presence beside her. "Sofieli!" she cried out in joy. "I'm so glad you are with me now."

Sofieli replied in angelic musical tones, "I always keep my promises. Did I not tell you that I would always be with you in times of sorrow or need, to soothe your aching heart, and uplift you into the Divine Light?"

Her dear angel friend enfolded Bellina in her massive, glittering golden angel wings, with which she had adorned herself especially for this occasion, and sang a sweet angelic lullaby of divine love to her.

EPILOGUE

In disease or in health, in success or in failure, in poverty or in prosperity, in joy or in sorrow, in disaster or in safety, <u>in life or in death</u>, I stand immutably, unalterably, unshakably loyal, devoted, and firmly loving Thee, my Heavenly Father, forever, forever, and forever!

— Paramhansa Yogananda, *Whispers from Eternity*

As we reflect on this story, we may rightfully ask, "Was Bellina sad? Was she tempted to sink into grief or cry and mourn the loss of her dear Gigi?"

No, she was not. Not at all! For she had come to realize through personal experience, from the depths to the heights of her being, the truth about all of life's greatest mysteries—the secrets of life, death, and life after death.

Bellina also understood and embraced her own immortality, as we must all do, sooner or later—helping us to avoid suffering by embracing these truths!

Until the day she left the material plane to rejoin her dear friends in Janaloka—the angels, astral animals, and other ethereal beings—Sabellina Clearlight never stopped creating imaginative ways to help the people of earth dispel any lingering fears of death.

Bellina did this through intense educational programs, primarily the Immortality Realization graduate courses in the Halls of Wisdom. Graduates of her training courses founded thousands of well-staffed public Immortality Realization Clinics and their auxiliary Heavenly Transition Garden-Retreats.

Through these programs and facilities, participants were offered their own personal experiences of life after death, by means of powerful meditation techniques, and other spiritual tools that she and her staff developed.

Bellina also created a dynamic and extremely successful program for children, knowing that many children bring the fear of death with them, from previous lifetimes.

She also realized that young children are still inwardly close to their recent visits to the astral lokas. She found that the memories of these worlds could be awakened easily within them by means of this program, especially adapted for children. Once a child was able to reconnect with their memories of their life-after-death experiences, every fear of death was dissolved away, effortlessly and permanently.

For this is what happens as Treta Yuga progresses toward Satya Yuga: The fear of death will be eradicated from the hearts and minds of all human beings. Everyone can realize fully the absolute truth of their immortality.

> *When the corruptible shall put on incorruption,*
> *And mortals shall put on immortality,*
> *Then shall be brought to pass the saying that is written:*
> *Death is swallowed up in victory!*
>
> — Saint Paul, *Holy Bible*, First Corinthians, 15:54

I WILL HOP FROM ETERNITY TO ETERNITY

From *Whispers from Eternity,* by Paramhansa Yogananda

My gold-gossamer astral body, shining with the spark of immortality,
Hopped, cricket-like, from one blade of existence to another.

Thou hast clothed the barren soil of eternity,
With grass-blades of many cycles of time,
I will hop to them one by one, from one blade of pleasure to another,
Until I can leap to the safety of Thy reassuring hands.

With living threads of Thy joy I was formed.
I am happy to have danced my part in this cosmic show.

But I have done, now, with restless hopping.
I would find rest, at last, in cosmic changelessness.

Human lives, again, like slowly moving camels,
Plod ponderously over broad, sandy deserts,
Toward the oasis of self-awareness.

As developed beings, their astral bodies pass also,
From planet to planet.

Only in Thee, at last, do they find,
What they were seeking always.
Lord, give me again the perfection of fulfillment,
In Thy Love of Infinity.

WHAT IS A YUGA?

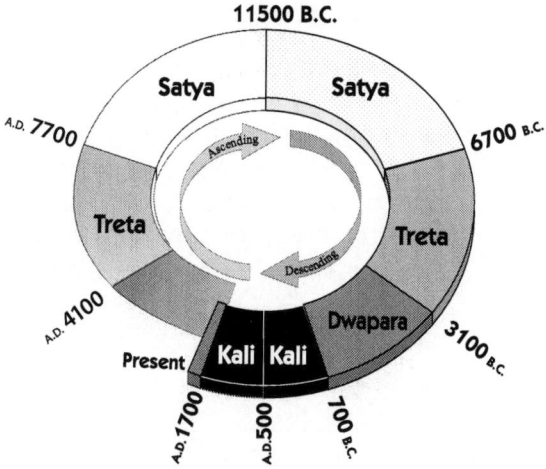

Through the Gates of Death—And Beyond: Adventures in the Lokas of Immortality takes place in Ascending Treta Yuga. It is the third novel in "The Treta Yuga Trilogy."

Yuga is a Sanskrit word, which means an eon or extremely long period of time.

A *loka* simply means a location; it is also a term used to describe vast cosmic or inter-dimensional realms of existence.

In India, and particularly in the teachings of yoga, time and history are described as moving through repetitive cycles rather than in a linear fashion. The yuga model of time explains that there have been in the past, and will be in the future, both higher and lower ages.

Just as our planet moves through summer, autumn, winter, and spring each year, it also moves through a much longer cycle of yugas, accompanied by progressive or regressive changes in the consciousness of humanity.

Toward the end of the 19th century, a man with exceptional abilities as a sage wrote a book called *The Holy Science*. Swami Sri Yukteswar (1855-1936) of Serampore, Bengal, was a master of great wisdom, deeply learned in the ancient wisdom of India. In his book, he described an age-old system of celestial chronology, expounded by ancient astronomers, describing how our planet moves through great cycles of time called *yugas*.

The Holy Science was published 1894. In it, Sri Yukteswar described this celestial model in detail, and corrected certain errors, which had crept in over recent centuries. He announced that the earth had actually left the lowest age of Kali Yuga and had entered the next and higher age of *Dwapara Yuga*. This is contrary to a current belief that our planet still has more than 400,000 years of Kali Yuga (the darkest of the four ages) left—a daunting concept, indeed!

The ages described in the yuga theory also are four: *Satya Yuga*, the spiritual age; *Treta Yuga*, the mental age; *Dwapara Yuga*, the energy age; and K*ali Yuga*, the dark or materially-oriented age of spiritual ignorance.

According to Sri Yukteswar, a full yuga cycle takes 24,000 years to complete—12,000 years of ascending consciousness and 12,000 years of descending consciousness.

Our solar system moves closer to the center of our galaxy during the ascending cycle of the yugas and is closest at the junction of ascending and descending Satya Yuga.

The explanation Sri Yukteswar gave for the existence of the yugas is that our sun has a dual star, and that these two stars revolve around each other. Because of the nature of this celestial motion, our solar system moves in a great elliptical orbit toward, then away from the tremendous vortex of energy at the center of our galaxy.

The ancient yogic wisdom says that the galactic center emits rays of spiritual energy, and that the closer our solar system comes to this center, the more of its powerful energy floods and uplifts the earth. As the energy increases, human consciousness becomes correspondingly more enlightened and aware.

As our solar system moves away from the source of these beneficial rays, human consciousness becomes duller and we are less able to understand things as they truly are. Spiritual progress becomes much more difficult.

Our solar system reached the farthest point from the galactic center about 500 AD, at the heart of the Dark Age, which occurs at the bottom of the cycle, the junction of descending and ascending Kali Yuga.

We are once more moving toward the galactic center, and consequently, people are gradually becoming better able to understand the subtle truths of life. For example, we recognize that matter is not essentially solid, but is made of slowed down or condensed energy. In fact, it is only because we have moved into the more enlightened age of Ascending Dwapara Yuga that we are even able to understand the concept of the yuga cycles.

The two lower yugas are Dwapara Yuga, "The Age of Energy," and Kali Yuga, "The Material Age."

In 1900 AD, our planet moved into Ascending Dwapara Yuga, and we find, amazingly, just in one century, how much we have advanced. Everything we know of modern times—airplanes, cars, electronics, radios, television, computers— came into being after 1900, and we are just at the beginning of this new "Age of Energy." The discoveries that lie ahead of us are enormous, and all will be based on an awareness of energy as the underlying reality of matter.

A very different kind of world will unfold as we advance into this new era. Before the end of Ascending Dwapara Yuga in 4100 AD, we will bypass the limitations of the speed of light and conquer the delusion of space and distance. We will be able to visit the most distant galaxy as easily as we are now able to visit anywhere on earth.

The two higher ages are Treta Yuga, "The Mental Age," and Satya Yuga, "The Spiritual Age."

After 4100 AD, the beginning of Ascending Treta Yuga, people will understand that consciousness engenders energy and that with their own minds they can direct energy to accomplish their goals. As people's mental control, intuition, and knowledge of the universe evolves, mental telepathy will arise naturally. This kind of growing mental power is one of the hallmarks of Treta Yuga.

Treta Yuga will also be an age marked by humanity's ability to overcome the limitations of time. In Treta Yuga, most people will realize that time, like space, is a delusion, and that the most ancient civilizations exist, not in the distant past, but right now, in the eternal present.

This novel takes place in Ascending Treta Yuga about 3,900 years from now.

Actually, it does not matter in which yuga we find ourselves, or on which planet we reside—Paramhansa Yogananda said there are many inhabited planets! For as we reincarnate through many lives, we learn that the best way to advance spiritually is to tune in to the highest octave of the yuga in which we find ourselves, and to use it selflessly for the highest possible good for ourselves and others.

The yogic sciences teach that the goal of life is self-realization and oneness with all that is. That goal is possible for us during any lifetime, in any yuga.

If you would like more information about the yuga theory and its explanation of the history of our planet, including interesting ways of predicting the future, we highly recommend *The Yugas*, by David Steinmetz and Joseph Selbie, published by Crystal Clarity Publishers, www.crystalclarity.com. This is, in my opinion, the best book ever written on the subject.

Nayaswami Savitri Simpson
Ananda Village, California, USA

Printed in Great Britain
by Amazon